Cumberland Isle

Bryan Rendzio

Published by Bryan Rendzio, 2023.

CUMBERLAND ISLE

First edition. June 23, 2023.

Written by Bryan Rendzio.

Table of Contents

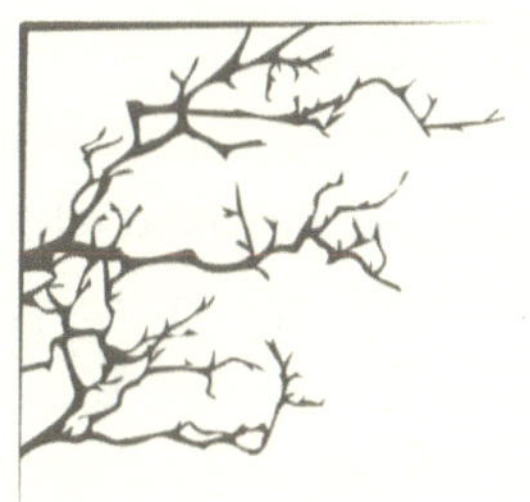

Preface

I want to take this opportunity to thank you for embarking upon this adventure with me. *Cumberland Isle* came about after my many years of traveling to the St. Marys, Georgia area. There is an aura about the secluded island that entices and engrosses even the most skeptical and logical of minds. It is a living creature that defies you to accept the unknown. This novel tracks the struggles of the protagonist Emily Duval. This story, however, not only encompasses a historical mystery on its face, it also forces the reader to envisage the first key stroke through the last. The five-year process of creating this work has enabled me to grow as an author, as well as an individual.

In her worst nightmares, Emily Duval could never have imagined that her honeymoon would find her stranded on a remote Georgia island surrounded by nothing but death. This young lawyer has a resilience about her, which has been forged through an existence of battling emotional demons. Emily has mentally planned every aspect of how she and her new husband would be relaxing on their romantic vacation. She would soon learn, however, that control and predictions of perfection are fallacies beyond anyone's control. While shopping at a local antique store in St. Augustine, Florida, Emily becomes drawn to the diary of a young woman who lived during the 1940s. As it turns out, this mysterious person had a connection to Cumberland Island. Emily cannot believe that she has uncovered such a treasure about the very place that she is about to explore in the following days. Cumberland Island's splendor comes with a balance of darkness and treachery, which will draw Emily toward the ill-fated souls who remain trapped on the island. Through her journey, Emily will learn that some things cannot stay buried. This novel will in fact trap you, the reader, on the island with Emily. Neither this novel nor the island will let the inhabitants leave alive.

Acknowledgments

The pages of this novel have come to fruition through the sacrifices of many. First and foremost, I want to thank my beautiful and loving wife, Stacy. Without her support, none of this would have been possible. She truly completes me. I also want to thank my two boys for inspiring me with their energy and pure love of life. This novel is about family, and my family has helped me get my inspiration to each and every reader of this story.

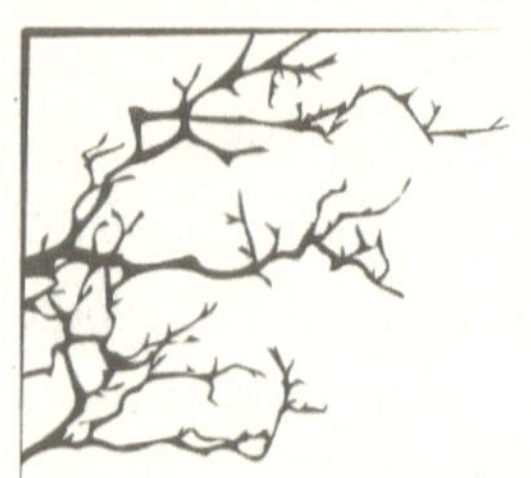

Chapter 1

As Emily brushed her blistered fingers across her forehead to wipe away the night mist and her sweat, she came to the disquieting revelation that it was blood. She tried to scream, but there was no sound. Emily had succumbed to exhaustion and fear. She felt imprisoned in her own body. The darkness of the night provided little comfort, and the air around her was bitter and stagnant with death. With each labored breath, Emily was coming to the realization that this island was going to be her tomb.

"How can this be my end?" Emily said to herself, as she tried to keep her wearied mind from betraying her. There was a desperation in her mind as she tried to keep focused on anything other than her present circumstances.

"One deep breath, followed by another," she told herself. Emily continued this cadence for a few minutes and watched, almost hypnotically, as the cinereous-colored smoke from the cold air left her chapped mouth. Eventually, the pain began to fade as she let her mind transport her back in time to her wedding a week earlier. Eventually, she stopped hearing the sounds of her breaths, and she could imagine the perfection of her wedding day. The sounds of the ocean no longer came from the shores of this desolate island. Instead, her mind was envisioning the sounds of the water lapping on the shores of St. Augustine, Florida as she prepared to be wed.

This was Emily Duval's day. As a young girl, she shared the dreams of most of her contemporaries—a perfect late autumn southern wedding with family, friends, and the man she loved by her side. She was a free spirit by nature but admittedly a perfectionist when it came to her work and the things that mattered the most to her.

This young, twenty-eight-year-old woman was striking with a slender build, and auburn hair that was accented by soft touches of red highlights. Emily had hazel eyes and subtle olive skin that was complemented with faint freckles. She had a personality that met no stranger. As a child she was often teased for being so skinny with knobby knees. This changed as she reached high school, where the once awkward-looking girl with glasses found herself the envy of her classmates. She was a three-year starting forward on the varsity soccer team, as well as co-captain of the debate team.

There was nothing that at first glance would show any blemishes on Emily, except for a small scar under her chin from where she took a head-first fall onto a table as a small child. She once asked her parents how she got it, and she heard everything from fighting pirates in the Caribbean to a battle with a ten-foot grizzly bear. Eventually, she discovered the not-so-exciting truth. The slight imperfection would not even be noticeable but for the times that she rubbed it with her right thumb when nervous or in deep thought. If she were a poker player, this would be her poker tell.

Emily's fellow lawyers knew that Ms. Duval, as she was known in the professional world, was a force to be reckoned with inside the resplendent, ivory-colored halls of the St. Johns County Courthouse. As a prosecutor, she had made a name for herself in her five short years of practice. While completing her law degree, Emily received offers from several large corporate firms from Tampa all the way up the I-95 corridor to Washington D.C., each one promising her riches that most young, legal newbies would take without any hesitation at all. Just the thought of one day being on that long, egotistical list of mostly dead partners in a firm name made most soon-to-be attorneys drool. After all, what person in their right mind would not give their soul to be memorialized even after death, forever embossed on the top of some legal letterhead that traveled the world threatening lawsuits and sanctions? This, however, was not for Emily. At least not for now.

It was not that she was troubled by the challenges of a large law firm. Quite to the contrary. This young woman knew in her heart that she could handle the pressures and complexities of anything. The stress of researching through some firm's dusty, time-honored law library for some last-minute case law did not scare her. Emily knew that the role of young associates in large firms was to be the low-level grunts who always got a frantic call from some senior associate or partner who needed something in ten minutes for a hearing. She could handle this rite of passage and would indubitably break through any rookie treatment that the senior associates would throw her way. Emily was, after all, the Managing Editor of *Law Review*, and had served two years as the lead brief writer on her school's moot court team as well.

She had been in the trenches at various law firms during her summer internships. The most interesting one was a white-collar defense firm in Philadelphia where she spent countless nights buried in old books in the firm's basement. The work was exciting enough, but she really enjoyed being surrounded by all of the rows upon rows of actual historical documents. The firm she worked at was one streetlight and small coffee café away from Independence Hall, no more than a two-minute walk. In her spare time, she would search for old archives in the firm's library, and once she found a book that dated back to 1789. The binding was so brittle that parts of it crumbled to the touch. It was not so much the book's words that captured her attention. To Emily it wasn't just a bound document with words. Instead, it was the simple fact that she was holding a piece of history within her palms. This was a time capsule, in a sense. Her mind wandered with the sheer thought that one of the founding fathers could have actually been holding this same book in this very same building while determining how to mold and shape the very framework of this nation.

Emily's intelligence was only matched by her values and her unyielding conviction. She wanted to serve the public, and more importantly, it was her ultimate goal to stay close to the very people who had influenced her and had kept her rooted for so many years. Emily had a piece of paper with a tattered, handwritten note on it that she always kept in her pocket. It read *roots and wings.* She wrote it in college after one regretful night of drinking, and it was her reminder that no matter what she accomplished or where she went in life, she would always remember the people who helped get her there. It would be doubtful that a new private jet, a solid marble palace in the Alps, or some other unimaginable wish could break the ties and tenets that were, in fact, Emily Duval. She was just fine with making her public servant's wage in the small city of St. Augustine.

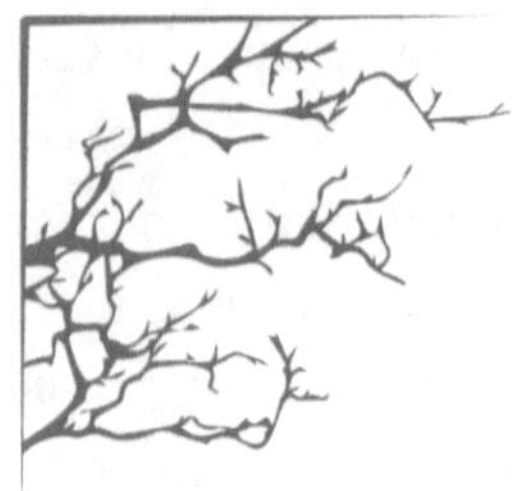

Chapter 2

"Where's my girl?" a loud, hearty voice yelled out.

"In here, Dad. I'm getting in some last-minute prep time for my vows."

"Hell, darling, I'm sure that you've had those words memorized for a month," Judge Duval stated with a smile.

Emily raised her left eyebrow and gave her dad a scolding but lighthearted look like a parent might give to a child. "Dad, you're in a church. You can't use that kind of language."

"I know, I know," he replied with a self-assured smile as he hugged her.

Emily's father's full name was William Augustus Duval, III, but everyone in Northeast Florida knew of him simply as "Judge," and rightfully so. He had been a sitting judge for nearly twenty years in Jacksonville—the city just a stone's throw to the north of St. Augustine. Besides, he carried the last name of the county where Jacksonville sat. He was a large man, standing around six feet four inches and weighing anywhere from three-hundred-twenty to three-hundred-forty pounds, give or take during the holiday seasons. He had a full, pepper-colored beard that he always grew around November, and impeccable gray, slicked-back hair like the head of a New York brokerage firm. From head to toe, he was polished and poised. Due to his weight, Judge always took nasally, labored pauses between talking.

Judge Duval was a direct descendant of William Pope Duval, the governor of the Florida Territory from 1822 to 1834. For those unfamiliar with the area, Duval County often seemed to go unnoticed. It was just a necessary pit stop or bathroom break on the way to Ft. Lauderdale or Miami. Jacksonville was by no means a bustling metropolis like Boston, New York, or even Charlotte, for that matter. However, it didn't matter. Judge loved the area and never left an ear wanting more when people asked if he was somehow related to the famous "Duval." This man felt that the entire area from Jacksonville to St. Augustine was a treasure that many overlooked, like a ship buried off of the coast somewhere that explorers always narrowly missed. To Judge, this area just south of the Georgia border was a slice of Florida that still maintained southern charm, with just a splash of northeastern flare in various pockets to keep it lively and relevant.

"So, Em, this guy must be special since you're making me get dressed to the nines and dig up all of that cash in the backyard that I've been hiding away from your mother for all of these years."

Emily knew that her father was joking. Ever since she was old enough to crawl up onto his lap, he had called her "Em." She was the middle child of three, and Judge always made a special place in his heart for her. Some would say this was because she was the middle child who sometimes had a tendency to get lost in the shuffle of siblings. In reality, however, it was probably because Judge could relate more to her than his other kids. Judge and Emily each shared the same drive and temperament. For better or for worse, Emily was her father, which she embraced for all of its advantages and shortcomings.

Emily hugged her dad and gave him a smile that made his heart melt no matter whether this time marked the hundredth or the nine-hundred-ninety-ninth time that she had done this in her life. At this moment, Emily allowed herself to embrace the warmth of being daddy's little girl. This was especially true since she knew that her father adored her soon-to-be husband. Emily's beau had made a special point to take Judge out and properly ask for his daughter's hand in marriage. Even though Emily and her fiancé had been dating for three years before he popped the question, the poor man still nearly suffered a panic attack with the thought of approaching Judge to ask for the blessing to marry Emily.

Judge was always one for dramatics. When Emily's fiancé asked Judge to meet at a small bistro near the St. Johns River, Judge gladly agreed. Judge, however, knew exactly what was about to go down. It was for this reason that Judge showed up to the bistro still wearing his judicial robe. To this day, he laughingly told everyone that he simply forgot to take it off after court, but no one believed him.

"You know he's the right guy for me, Dad, otherwise why would I have booked this wedding on such a sacred day?" Emily laughed because she knew that the only thing that her father loved to talk about more than being a judge or his famous last name was the fact that he played college football as a second-string tight end for Florida State University. Judge had a display in his home office that would make a cable network antique picker lick his chops. The walls were ensconced with pictures of Judge with other famous alumni. Everyone from actors, evangelists, and athletes to Congressmen. If you looked closely, you could find a law degree or some relic achievement from his law school days. However, his passion was himself and showing off his likeness in every picture from his former playing portrait to the time he was at the White House meeting the president after FSU won its first national championship. Judge was a huge booster and never missed a chance to celebrate with his old team, even if his playing days were behind him. His desk and bookshelf contained every sort of FSU knickknack from bobble heads to customized beer steins.

The one item that always stole Em's attention as a girl, however, was Judge's mahogany case where he housed his many football rings. She still remembers sneaking into her father's office and immediately being welcomed with the inviting scent of authentic Swiss chocolate perfectly combined with the faint suggestion of a day-old cigar. She always made a beeline for the case, where there had to be at least eight rings perfectly fitted into their cushioned holder. The top of the case had a crystal-clear glass cover to showcase his football legacy. Each ring was a unique piece of art, some with diamonds and others with brilliant rubies. It was a shrine that, to this day, remained unmatched in her mind.

Some days, as a small girl, Emily would spend hours sitting in her dad's brown leather chair just enjoying every sense that the room seemed to bring to life. That old chair was perfect with its cracks and faded armrests. There was an indention in each armrest from where Judge's large arms had pressed into the leather and created a permanent imprint. It always made her feel close to her father, since there was a modest scent of his cologne that seemed to stick to the area where he would rest his head while reviewing legal briefs or reading the Sunday paper.

Emily also loved to run her fingers across the grains of his cherry-stained, oak desk, as if the imperfections in the wood were maps to let her fingers find some adventure. Judge almost always knew that Emily was in there since something was inevitably out of place. This never bothered him though. One of his fondest memories was coming home from an especially arduous day during a two-week trial and finding Emily passed out in his chair. He smiled and gently carried her upstairs. As far as Emily recalled, she snuck out of the office and crept up to bed without anyone ever knowing her secret adventure.

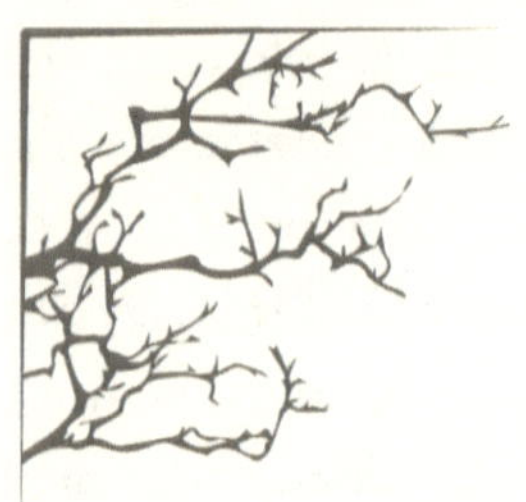

Chapter 3

For a moment, Emily allowed her mind to find that place in time back in her father's office. Her brief daydream, however, was broken with her father's boisterous voice, and she found herself once again at the church for her wedding day.

"Yeah, sweetheart, thanks for booking this thing on rivalry weekend."

Emily knew that her father loved his football. Maybe just a small part of her reason for setting the wedding when her dad's alma mater was playing its rival team was to test his love. But in her heart, she really wanted a November wedding. The weather in North Florida would dip into the low forties during this time of year, and the typical drenching humidity was pleasantly almost non-existent. Whenever anyone asked her about Florida, the inevitable question was, "Don't you wear shorts and bathing suits all year round?" People always seemed astonished to know that there could be even one mile of the Sunshine State that saw actual changes in the seasons, including leaves that changed colors. It seemed that anyone she ran into while on travels around the country just assumed that all of Florida was covered with palm trees and fluorescent-lit art deco buildings.

"Did I hear you from down the hall saying that you're hiding money from me, you old fool?" Emily and her mother, Marjorie, shared many physical characteristics, and their personality to boot. Marjorie gave Judge a hug with a loving pat on his lower back.

Emily had one older sister and a younger brother. Of the three children, Emily physically most resembled her mother.

"Me? Never dear," Judge chuckled.

"All right, quit telling stories and let me get our little girl ready for her big day."

Marjorie loved to plan events. She was a former businesswoman who grew up in D.C. and had spent the last ten years working with charities to help support her husband's efforts. In the socialite and philanthropist circles she was even more famous than her husband. This self-confident woman, with dyed caramel blonde hair and chestnut brown, horned-rimmed glasses, knew what it took to make people relieve themselves of the burden of those heavy wallets and pocketbooks during charitable events. Judge would always tease Marjorie because her face always found its way to the local newspaper's front page more than his trials.

She prided herself with making strides to help abused women and their children as her primary charitable focus. Marjorie's closest friends even joked with her that it was her sweet, Magnolia-scented perfume that lulled people into giving her charities money. She always wore this perfume, even when gardening. It had a subtle scent that was not overpowering to the passerby.

This day was Marjorie's championship game. She was perhaps living her memories vicariously through her daughter, but she knew that this was Emily's day. The wedding was taking place at Palms Presbyterian of St. Augustine. Her family worshiped there, and Emily would not get married anywhere else.

Before she knew what was happening, Emily found herself engulfed in the center of a flawless circle made up of her bridesmaids, one of which was her older sister, with her mother at the helm. The women of all ages were focused to get the bride's makeup, hair, and dress just perfect. Arms were flying in the air, and elbows were making near-misses in what almost appeared to be controlled chaos. The wedding was set for six o'clock sharp, and everyone in this room was making sure that this day met with everything that made up childhood fairytales.

The church could not have been more perfect. It had an ambience that even non-spiritual attendees had to respect. It was not ornate. It was not donned with gold trimmings or haughty statues glaring down at the souls who sought refuge, answers, and new beginnings within its halls. Instead, it was a modest place of worship with an old but beautiful organ. The silver of the organ pipes played in harmony off of the dark cherry wood of the building's frame that covered the main area from floor to ceiling. The ascents of natural light were brought in by a few large stained-glass windows. The pews were covered in a soft red felt that made the entire room seem inviting. Today would be a proud day for this church as it prepared itself for a wedding with nearly two hundred people.

At the other end of the church stood a slender man with short, dark brown hair who was pacing back and forth in a small room that was no larger than a broom closet. He narrowly missed his father each time he made his way to the other end of the room that was ten feet by ten feet at best. It sounded as if the two men were in a slow tap dance each time their rented, perfectly polished shoes clapped the cedar floor. Heal to toe. Tip, tap, tip, tap, tip, tap.

"Dad, is it normal to be this nervous for a wedding?"

"Trent, let me tell you, son, when I married your mother, I almost passed out before I ever made it to the altar. I thought someone was going to have to use a wheelbarrow to get me there."

"Glad to know this runs in the family," Trent replied with a nervous smile.

Trent Decker IV had a powerful name that would insist on some lineage of royalty or at least a few senators somewhere down the family line. However, Trent came from a modest family and had no physical features that would set him apart from anyone else in a shopping mall or at a ballgame. He had a thin face and a fairly pale complexion. Trent almost always wore his Ray-Ban wire eyeglasses. On a typical day, Trent liked to keep a five o'clock shadow that he kept close to his face with a cheap, corner store trimmer each morning. He felt that it gave him a sophisticated, yet tough look that Emily loved and would never let him shave off. Emily actually hated the stubble but gladly humored Trent since she knew that it somehow boosted his manhood. Today, it was shaved clean for the wedding. Hours earlier, Trent enjoyed an old- fashioned straight razor shave with a warm towel dry. There was a little two-man barber shop that he sometimes liked to go to since they always offered him a cold beer while getting a trim. It was a great way to calm his nerves.

Trent's father was a child psychologist who devoted his time to helping underprivileged children in struggling school districts. He stood about four inches shorter than Trent at five feet, seven inches tall. Despite his passion to right the evils and limitations that society placed on less privileged youth, Trent's father was a math genius who actually helped pay his way through Duke by tutoring student athletes in everything from basic college algebra to calculus.

In addition to his father's "nervous" gene, Trent also inherited his math skills. Trent was a young aerospace engineer who specialized in military aircrafts. He had a modest but challenging job as a civil contractor for the Navy. If it had to do with design or performance of any aircraft, Trent could tackle the task. Like his bride-to-be, he was considered an up-and-comer in his field. In addition to the mental perks of the job, Trent enjoyed the fact that he was actually placed in a facility at the St. Augustine airport. This was a unique, quaint little airfield. It was mostly used by wealthy businesspeople who wanted to get in and out of the area with little hassle, especially during local golf events. The airport, which was in a spot between the Atlantic Ocean and a small strip of quasi-coastal highway U.S. 1, was quiet and efficient. Maybe this was why the Navy chose this spot to base its E2-D advanced Hawkeye airborne early warning aircraft. This was Trent's pride and mission.

"Trent, you know your mother would have been so proud of you, and she would have loved Emily as her own daughter."

"I know, Dad," Trent said as his eyes began to gloss over with what were unmistakably tears.

Trent had spent more years of his life without his mother than with her. She passed away from breast cancer when Trent was only twelve years old. There was not one single day where he did not think of her or look at the picture that he kept in his apartment. Trent had a small shoebox of items that had photos of him with his mom as well as a note that she wrote to him when she knew that she was going to die. It was about forty pages and tried to cover every milestone that she would miss. His mother knew that she would be gone before Trent's first date, his graduation, and his wedding day. Trent read the note a few weeks before the wedding, as he did before each life-changing event in his life. He always cried when he heard his mother's voice through the words of the letter.

"You know, I can't remember a day where you and mom did not seem to be the pinnacle that couples strived for, like some Norman Rockwell scene."

"Like everybody, we had our bad days, but you know she was my soul mate, and I thank God every day for each second that he gave me with her, and for giving me you."

The two men rarely hugged. They loved each other but typically chose to express it with an inside joke or two followed by a handshake. However, almost in unison, Trent and his father hugged and cried. It was cathartic. These two left-brained men had found their way to a sensitive place, and that rarely occurred.

"You're going to make my makeup run," Trent said with a manly sniffle and a smile to break the moment. Even though this day was yet another reminder that his mother was gone, Trent knew that she wanted him to live each day with vigor. He also knew that she was looking down with a tearful smile on her only baby boy this day. With another hug and pat on the back, Trent's father left the room and took his place with the other family members.

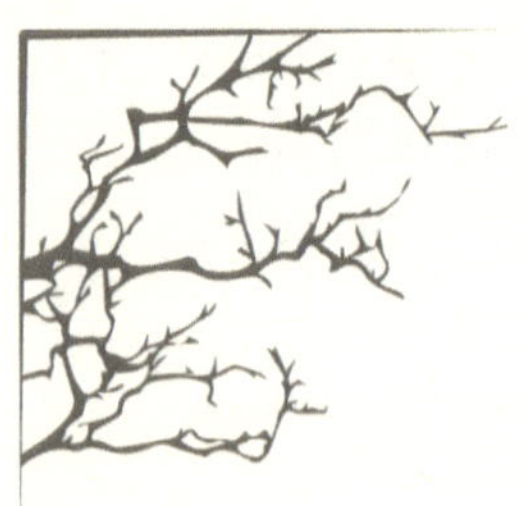

Chapter 4

Evening was approaching, and all of the last-minute preparations were in place. Like every wedding, there were a few odds and ends that required attention, but no one told Emily. There was no need to worry her with little details like the distant relatives who were running late or a few bridal party members who were less than fully prepared for their roles. The sun was setting over the Atlantic Ocean in the distance, and the last remaining rays of God's light were softly making their way through the church's stained glass. It was almost as if the universe was giving its final blessing before the big event. The ushers walked the last few people from the entrance into the chapel and to their seats.

Emily looked stunning in her stylish but conservative wedding dress. She hated the flashy dresses that she saw all over the contemporary fashion magazines that professed what every woman who wanted to be anybody should wear. Emily wanted to keep it simple, just as she did in every aspect of her life. She was donning an A-Line, strapless dress with a full skirt that flared out at her feet into a five-foot train. She was ready for her moment in the spotlight, except for a few final touches to her hair.

Emily's mother finished putting a final barrette in Emily's hair to keep it in place, and Emily's sister gave one final hug for good luck.

"Where's my Em?" Judge stated as he cracked open the door to the dressing room. Judge was never known for being subtle.

"I'm ready, Dad."

"Are you sure? I've got a car waiting out back if you want to make a break for it," Judge said, laughing.

Emily just snickered and hugged the man that she had looked up to her whole life.

Emily and her father made their way to the chapel's doors. There was a moment of silence. Then the doors opened and the music began to play. Emily's parents had hired a harpist to play the processional. Between Judge and Emily, it was hard to tell which one was gripping the other's hand harder. As Emily walked past all of the people who in some way shaped her life, she smiled. At the end of her vision, she saw Trent. Immediately, her smile got bigger as she focused her loving eyes on his gaze like a tractor beam. On the outside Trent looked like a poised tux model. However, Emily knew that he was a wreck. Trent hated being in front of a group of people, even if they were family and friends. She was right. Trent's knees were shaking inside of his pants like they were made of spaghetti.

As Emily made it to the front of the church, she leaned her head around her father and whispered to Trent, "I love you." Trent replied by placing his hand on his heart and saying, "I love you too," without any words coming from his mouth.

Pastor Crowly asked Judge, "Who gives this woman away?"

"Her mother and myself," Judge replied without missing a beat. Judge prided himself on his humor, but he also knew when to keep the campy comments to himself.

Judge kissed Em and walked to his seat next to his wife. He gave Marjorie a kiss and placed his hand on her knee.

Pastor Crowly went through all of the standard questions for the couple, as well as the group who were there to witness and approve this bond of love. In his own quirky way, the pastor went into some speech about love and whether these two were ready for such a momentous step in life. It was almost as if Pastor Crowley were going to pull the plug on this wedding without any warning. Emily and Trent were facing each other and holding hands by this time in the ceremony. Each looked at the other with slight concern.

Just then, the pastor moved on to the conclusion and the "kiss the bride" part. Emily and Trent were relieved, and before Trent could kiss his new bride, Emily took both of her hands and grabbed Trent's head. She pulled him toward her and planted one on him. His friends would later laugh and say that Trent blushed. Everyone suspected that Emily would wear the pants in this relationship, but if there was any doubt, this ended it.

"That boy doesn't know what he's got into," Judge whispered to Emily's mother, smiling.

Marjorie just chuckled under her breath and tried to keep from laughing out loud. Every once in a while, she even had to acknowledge that her husband was pretty funny.

The wedding goers moved from the church to a historic eighteenth-century hotel. The trip was quick since it was only a few miles due east of downtown. As typically occurs, the wedding party was whisked away and had to take a few pictures before arriving at the reception. Everyone piled into the three limos that were waiting outside the church. Emily and Trent had their closest friends in their limo. And at Emily's insistence, all of the limos were stocked to the brim with beer and wine. Everything from ice-cold beers in coolers to Chablis were being passed around in everything from champagne flutes to clear plastic Solo cups.

"So, how does it feel to be Mr. Duval, my dear?" Emily said to Trent with a playful tone.

"You know we're not naming our kids with some hyphenated last names, right?" Trent responded with a kiss to his new wife.

"Of course we're not you fool," Emily responded. "They'll take my last name!" She would never do that, but she was always one to get the last word even when joking.

The couple engaged in a few moments of public displays of affection in front of their friends, who were so busy slamming beers that they were not disgusted by any means. Emily was not one for any over-the-top displays of PDA, but she was hoping to get a rise from one of her girlfriends who might say, “Get a room!”

The party arrived at the hotel—The Royal St. Augustine. It was a majestic place that carried with it the ambience of historical value. It was the oldest known hotel still in existence in the United States. The charm of this place was that it was first established as a boarding house for the Spanish soldiers who colonized the area. It had changed hands several times since its inception back in 1723. After the British took control of St. Augustine sometime around the 1740s, they kept it alive as a bed and breakfast stop with a pub to keep the occasional passerby quenched from thirst. In the 1920s it became a full-service hotel due to generous financial support from the railroad mogul Henry Flagler. There were a few features that various owners and community benefactors added through the centuries to modernize this historical treasure for comfort. However, the core hotel remained in its original condition, as evidenced by the scars on its south wall from a cannon attack that took place during an early British siege on the city.

The night was as perfect as a nineteen sixties Florida postcard. There was a slight ocean breeze, and the temperatures were maintaining around fifty-five degrees. There was not even a slight touch of humidity in the ocean air. The wedding guests were randomly making their way through the hotel’s entrance into the beachfront ballroom and courtyard. As each wave of people entered the distressed mahogany doors of the hotel, they were welcomed with views reminiscent of a European castle. There was beige, notched crown molding running with the walls that had flecks of gold from the original construction. The main ballroom was showcased with a magnificent silver- and crystal-donned chandelier. The walls in several rooms had a deep, rich burgundy color and an almost hypnotic glare from the fire light that danced on the imperfections in the walls. There was a sweet smell in the air from the holiday, apple-spice candles that burned throughout the different rooms.

A few of the wedding guests paused as they entered the hotel to admire the authentic Spanish-era artifacts enshrined in an etched glass display case along the wall. Everything from swords to helmets were on display. There was even a picture of Teddy Roosevelt at the hotel during a brief hiatus before he united with his Rough Riders in Tampa during the Spanish American War. The courtyard, which had a harmonious blend of Crema Valencia colored marble, provided an unobstructed view of the vast Atlantic, while also offering a glimpse of the Castillo de San Marcos, which was the oldest masonry fort in the continental United States. The fort nestled itself along the Matanzas Bay on the edge of St. Augustine and was the pride of the city.

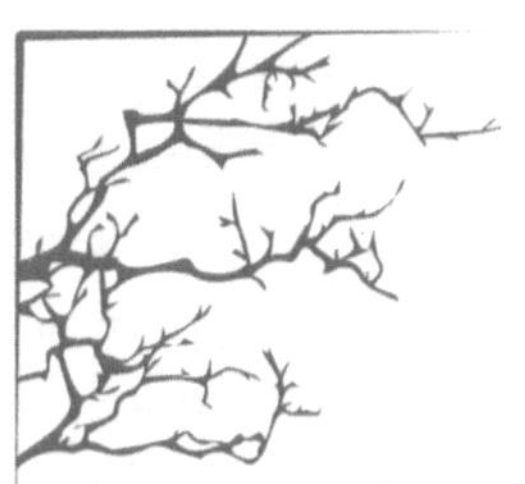

Chapter 5

Toward the end of the reception, Judge had gathered a small following of gentlemen, including Trent. About fifteen minutes earlier, Trent's dad gave his son a big hug and went to pass out in his room. Judge and Trent stared at the ocean as they smoked what Judge said were Dominican cigars and drank a twelve-year-old single malt Scotch. Trent knew better since Emily boasted a week earlier that her dad was breaking out a reserve of authentic Cuban cigars that he received years earlier from an unnamed political buddy in Washington, D.C.

"Look at that view, son," Judge said to Trent as he placed his huge hand on Trent's shoulder. Trent appreciated that Judge was calling him son.

"It's amazing," Trent replied. The men stared at the orange-colored moon reflecting over the Atlantic Ocean. The orange tint reminded Trent of a Creamsicle that he loved as a child. His mother used to buy them from the ice cream truck during summer vacation. For a moment, Trent's mom was with him again on this night.

"Look at the blanket of light sitting on the water like an endless road going into the dark abyss. Doesn't it look like a path that could take you anywhere?" Judge was profound in his own mind after a few scotches.

"Sure does," Trent replied. "It makes you appreciate that life is an adventure."

Trent was not a Scotch drinker, but his father-in-law promised him that he would like this one. He was right. It was so smooth that you could drink it on the rocks. Judge always preferred his Scotch neat with no ice. The conversation included everything from Judge's college football days to a recent trial that Judge oversaw. The conversation did not matter to Trent. He was soaking in every minute of this—the waves of the ocean in symphony, the taste and smell of a good "Dominican" cigar, and the fraternity of gentlemen who were sharing in this moment together as other statesmen and industrialists had previously done at this very spot. There was a manly blend of salt air mixed with various scents of cologne from the men, as if they were discussing the future of the country or making some inside, high-power stock deal within an exclusive fraternity.

As the night faded, the guests thinned out, and only the closest family and a few drunk friends remained. "All right hubby, it's time for us to make our grand escape from this thing," Emily said as she kissed her new husband. She had spent the evening dancing and going from table-to-table making sure that she acknowledged and thanked each and every person for attending this occasion.

Trent, with the help of a few drinks replied without missing a beat, "You just lead the way, sexy, and I'll follow you anywhere."

Emily blushed a bit since Trent was not known for being a romantic. She appreciated the fact that he was making such a vulnerable gesture. It reminded her of why she fell in love with Trent in the first place.

Their initial meeting was nothing short of the sort of romantic mini movies that seemed to take over television networks on the weekends. Emily had just moved into her quaint apartment, just big enough for a law student. No frills or any elegant crown molding on the walls. It was just a plain, cookie-cutter, two-bedroom place. This suited her just fine. She knew that she wouldn't be entertaining any large dinner crowds and only needed her own place of serenity to crash her head at night after attending classes and studying all day.

Probably about a month after moving in, she saw Trent in the distance walking his two Labrador Retrievers. One was black and the other one was yellow with a hint of strawberry blond. He seemed so awkward as he struggled to keep from getting tangled up as the dogs turned and shifted on every step, almost like a game to see who could trip him first. Emily started to smile and was entranced by his goofy charm. There was something about Trent that she instantly liked, and she knew that she needed to meet this man.

Over the next few weeks, she seemed to just narrowly miss him, seeing him as he was just entering his apartment. Emily had two dogs of her own. She was the proud owner of a Golden Retriever and a smaller yellow Lab mix. Emily had a plan. She studied Trent's habits and knew the approximate times that he started walking his dogs each day. One day, she happened upon Trent just as he was leaving his apartment. Trent stood there and smiled with a bashful but entrancing smile. After a minute of pause, Emily started the conversation.

"Hi, I'm Emily."

"I'm Trent. It's nice to meet you." Emily could tell that Trent was nervous by the cracking in his voice.

Beyond that, Trent was not putting forth much for Emily to respond to. Luckily for him, Emily was never at a loss for words. Her parents claimed she was chattering almost from the day she was born. Emily knew that she had to take the bull by the horns.

"So, how long have you lived here?"

"About a year. I'm in engineering school. How about you?"

From there the conversation flowed, and before they knew it, they were standing there talking for twenty minutes. Trent knew that he had to find a way to see Emily again. As fate would have it, it was a Thursday night, and the local Jacksonville minor league baseball team had a tradition of dollar beers and fifty cent hotdogs for each Thursday home game.

Emily, thinking that she wanted to get to know more about this guy, looked at Trent and asked "What are you doing tonight?"

"A friend of mine and I are going to the baseball game. It's at 7:30. You should go."

"That sounds like fun. I think I just might," Emily said with a confused grin.

As she walked back to her apartment, Emily could not help but wonder whether that was actually Trent asking her out on a date. Emily had been asked on many dates in her life, and this was by far the strangest proposition. There was a challenge about Trent, however, that kept her fascinated by the young man.

"Man, that was smooth," Trent thought as he prepared to feed his dogs. Even Trent could not believe that this gorgeous woman approached him, almost begging for a date, and all he could muster was, "There's a baseball game, you should go."

"I must be the biggest idiot in the world, or at least Jacksonville," he said out loud. He smacked his forehead with his open palm. No number, no official date, and he didn't even know what apartment she lived in.

Trent and Jay Williams went to the baseball game, and Trent kept a keen eye on the crowd in the off chance that Emily did show up. About thirty minutes went by when Trent felt a warm quick touch to his left shoulder. He turned, and sure enough, Emily showed up for the game. She was with two of her girlfriends, one of whom had an off-and-on boyfriend in tow. Trent, Emily, Jay, and Emily's friends spent the next few hours socializing while double-fisting dollar keg beers. Every once in a while, they even looked at the field when something noteworthy occurred.

As the game wound down, Jay paired up with one of Emily's friends. As Trent, Emily, Jay, and his new date were preparing to leave the ballpark, Emily's other friends quickly took her aside to be sure she was ok with going home with Trent since Emily did not drive to the game. They all agreed that Trent seemed to be harmless and not some creepy made-for-movie stalker. Even Emily's friend's quasi-boyfriend agreed. However, his approval was more for show to let everyone know that he was still relevant in the circle of friends.

The two couples made their way to a nearby pub and enjoyed more conversation and some late-night appetizers. Finally, Trent shined as he donned just enough attention on Emily without appearing to be needy or desperate. Trent was a gentleman to the core as he opened every door for Emily. As she slid into the car seat, Trent could not help but be taken aback by the beauty that was so close. Even Jay approved via a text message that simply read "Dude, you scored on that one!"

Trent and Emily finally made it back to their apartment complex and agreed to go get their dogs for a quick walk together. The couple enjoyed the cool night air, and the dogs enjoyed the impromptu outing. As Emily and Trent were preparing to part ways, two of their dogs tangled the couple up as if by some master plan. Trent was within inches of Emily's face, and they shared a long embrace and kiss right outside for the whole apartment complex to see. Then, just to add some more sexual ambience, the sprinkler system went on and doused the pair until they were soaking from head to toe. There was one sprinkler that was broken, shooting straight into the air like a fountain. It wasn't that romantic in any other situation, but here and now, it added a nice touch.

Trent wanted nothing more than to scoop Emily up and take her back to his apartment and make love to her at that very moment. However, Trent was not the type to do the things that get some guys laid and others slapped. Besides, Emily was special, and Trent wanted to explore where this relationship could go. Trent gave Emily a firm kiss, and formally asked her out on a date the following week. The formal date turned into another, followed by months of dating exclusively. They were both smitten and knew that they were meant to be with each other for a lifetime.

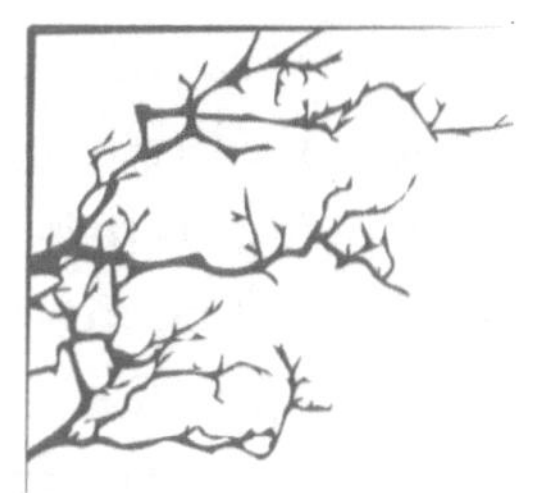

Chapter 6

Trent and Emily retired to their ocean-view honeymoon suite in the Royal St. Augustine. Their room had a balcony that looked straight out over the Atlantic. The night was clear and cold, and the crisp air made it perfect for the windows to remain open. The couple lay on the floor on a blanket in front of a fireplace. And this was the real thing, not some faux gas fire place. The hotel had actual fire places dating back from when the first brick was laid. There was something about an actual wood-burning fireplace that Emily loved. The smell of oak logs burning and the sound of crackling embers. They sipped some real French champagne, and then proceeded to consummate their marriage in most of the rooms of their suite.

At one point, Emily with her perverted sense of humor said, "We need to be sure we do it at least eight times tonight, just to be sure that this contract of marriage is binding."

Trent, somewhat out of breath, just laughed and then commenced to tackle her to the ground like a predator going for its prey. Emily had rarely seen this side of Trent, and she loved it. Emily was definitely the stronger of the two in the relationship, so she savored the few moments when he would show her that he was the alpha.

The next morning the two awoke under just the sheets. Emily leaned over to kiss her new husband, and Trent began to embrace Emily's naked body.

"Again? I thought you would be whipped after the all-night session?"

"Are you kidding me? I could do this all day." Emily rolled on top of Trent and pressed her warm body against his. She pinned Trent to the bed and began to kiss every inch of his body. Trent just lay there, letting her press and thrust against him. There was something erotic with having this beautiful woman dictate every move and motion in this sexual experience. She was meticulous in every moan and every breath.

When the two finished they showered up. Both were sweaty and smelled of sex. Emily's naked body and wet, sweaty hair were an aphrodisiac for Trent that almost made him beg for more. He held back since he knew that they had a busy day of drinking wine and antique shopping in the Old City—what the locals called the historic downtown area of St. Augustine. Emily loved every brick and corner of St. Augustine. It was a quaint little city that hosted tourists year round. The attraction came from its Spanish-era charm. After all, the city had a full-size Spanish fort and even still had remnants of the original wall that surrounded the city when founded. On top of its historical value, the streets were lined with antique stores and small pubs.

Emily loved the history and warmness that flowed like an inviting mist down St. George Street. You could not go more than a step or two without encountering the inviting smell of fresh peanut butter fudge or authentic Colombian coffee. Emily had the perfect honeymoon planned. A romantic local hotel, a couple of days of antique shopping coupled with the occasional stop for a bite and a local drink. After that, the two were off to Cumberland Island for five days of camping. This time of year was perfect for this adventure since the mosquitoes and snakes were not a factor.

Emily and Trent made their way down to café in the hotel for a quick pre-day snack and mimosa. After that, the pair made their way to downtown St. Augustine.

"There's St. George Street," Emily said, as if she were the general leading a charge.

Trent softly held Emily's hand as they started down the street. First stop was an old antique store that Emily had probably been in a dozen times. Today was different though. She was not window shopping and was looking for items that she and Trent could use in their new lives together.

"So how are we planning to lug all of this stuff you want to buy back to the car that's a mile away?"

"That's why I have you, my dear husband," Emily replied without missing a beat. "Besides, we're looking for the small stuff like coffee table conversation starters, not imported China hutches."

Emily and Trent made their way through a few shops, and then decided it was time to relax with a Café Con Leche. They enjoyed the sunshine and cool coastal breeze that made its way through the outdoor courtyard where they rested their feet. There were tropical palms and purple, Wisteria-covered walls on three sides to provide a small piece of private conversation for the patrons. Emily had managed to find a few small items in the shops that would surely speak to any guest that arrived in the Decker home. She found an iron Spanish cross to place in a small art niche at their apartment that neither Trent nor Emily could ever seem to fill. She also nabbed a couple of carved, wooden candle holders.

Trent could not help but to be entranced by Emily's smile and her inviting eyes. He knew at that moment that he was the luckiest man he had ever known. Emily had been speaking for minutes about the items that they bought. Trent heard nothing and just nodded as he simply enjoyed being in Emily's presence. She might as well have been talking about ancient Greek history. He did not care as long as she was talking to him.

"What are you looking at, you crazy fool?" Emily asked with a laugh.

Trent quickly responded, "That ugly Clemson sweater you're wearing, of course."

This was always a running feud between the pair since Emily had ventured out of Florida to attend Clemson for her undergrad degree before returning to Jacksonville for law school. Before attending graduate school in Jacksonville, Trent enjoyed four years at Florida State University. Love brought them together, but football would always leave that teasing spark of a rivalry that the two playfully fostered.

Emily and Trent watched several banana trees sway in the breeze as people walked by their café almost as if for their people-watching enjoyment alone. There were the older couples still holding hands as if newlyweds, followed by the occasional young couple with screaming kids in tow. It was a spectrum of time and life that connected Trent and Emily to the universe, given that they had yet to experience all of the ups and downs of marriage and life. On top of all of views, the sounds were equally as relaxing. There was the sound of water lapping from the novelty waterwheel of a local tavern coupled with the horse-drawn carriages galloping across the brick streets. Emily closed her eyes as she had done as a child. She swore that without her eyes to deceive her, she was smack in the eighteen hundreds. Clip, clop, clip, clop, clip, clop.

Then as quick as she closed them, they opened.

"On to the next place, hubby," she said.

Trent just smiled in response and grabbed Emily's hand. The pair came to an inconspicuous corner shop that had a small wooden sign that had clearly been beaten up by years of harsh Florida storms. As the wind caught the sign, you could hear the creaking of its two rusted metal hinges while it swung on two weathered brass hooks above the door. The shop, which was named *Coastal Treasures* had two pirate flags that were intended to bait any nearby children who would undoubtedly beg their parents to stop in and buy a toy sword or a cheap, plastic pirate hat. Once inside, however, the store offered much more than the quaint novelty mecca that its street face displayed.

As soon as Emily stepped inside the shop, her senses were captured by an appealing smell of vanilla-orange incense. It was quiet except for the continuous creaking from an old, oscillating fan that was slowly moving from left to right providing a brief breeze. She immediately noticed a glass case to her right containing brilliant gold and silver Spanish coins that were recovered from a couple of wrecks about forty miles south of the St. Augustine area.

Within a few minutes of Emily and Trent perusing, an older gentleman came up from the back office. He walked with a slight limp and appeared to be about seventy years old, with a perfectly trimmed beard and small wire-framed glasses. He was donning the typical Florida attire—colorful Key-West-style, button-up shirt, cargo shorts, and beige boat shoes of some sort.

"How are you young folks doing today?"

"These coins are beautiful," Emily said to the owner.

"Thank you. I was fortunate enough to be a part of a salvage operation about twenty years back and managed to take home my share of treasures."

Trent, being the self-professed cheapskate, was drawn to the prices.

"These things don't come too cheap, huh?"

"Nope. Unfortunately, they are quite rare so the lowest price I have is nine hundred dollars."

"What's the most expensive one that you have ever sold?" Trent asked.

"Three thousand dollars. That one came from that famous ship the *Atocha*. It was a magnificent gold coin that had some rare markings. I kept one and sold the other."

Emily loved the look of the jewelry, but her passion drew her to the bookshelf in the back of store. There was something magical about this little store that had hidden treasures of literature tucked behind the aisles of novelty junk for kids.

She had found her heaven.

"So, you like the old ones, huh?" the owner said.

Emily's smile could not be held back.

"Yes, I am an addict for old novels and journals."

"Here's one you that I know you'll like."

Emily took a look at the torn, tattered cover and fell in love before even opening the first page. The book was nothing special to look at, but it definitely had a story. At this moment, it was not even the story inside that seduced Emily. Rather, it was the life of the owners who read it along its journey and the story of how it somehow found its way to this shop.

"Where did you get it?

"I don't recall specifically, but I remember finding it at a yard sale about ten years ago."

Emily started carefully flipping the pages and realized that it was a diary or journal of some sort. No dates that she could make out from flipping through it. No name either, but a wealth of personal thoughts and a tale of how someone lived and loved.

"How much for it?" Emily asked.

"I typically don't let these go for anything less than a hundred dollars, but you both seem like a couple who could give this book a new era of life. How does thirty bucks sound?"

Emily grasped the book, and said in one fast breath, "Sold!" She did not want him changing his mind.

Trent and Emily continued looking over other items at the store, and they mainly just kept learning of the adventures of the owner. The gentleman was a fantastic story teller and kept Emily entranced with the soft, raspy sound of his voice. He sounded like an old folk singer or some sixties beat poet. After all, the point of the shopping in St. Augustine was to experience life and not simply shop. The pair were sponges, soaking in every detail of the owner's stories about where he acquired the various pieces. The owner was happy to share the stories since this was the reason why he kept the store open. The money he got typically kept the lights on but did not make him rich. This was the owner's wealth, moments shared with strangers over a cup of coffee or tea.

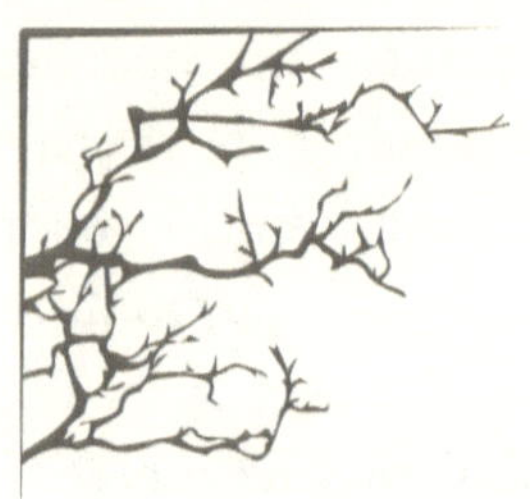

Chapter 7

As they left the shop, Emily clenched the craggy, brown paper wrapper that covered the book. Trent did not even make a playful pull at the book. Even he knew when to not cross the line. Emily had found a new fixation that she was not letting out of her sight. She was reminiscent of a girl wandering the aisles of a Walmart in search of the perfect toy, not knowing what she really wanted until she saw it in front of her eyes. Emily and Trent made their way back to the hotel for some poolside relaxation and sunset cocktails.

"So, you're not going to read that book tonight, are you?"

"Why? You afraid it will cut into our private time?" Emily smirked.

Trent laughed and said, "I guess you're right. I only need five minutes of your time anyway."

Emily laughed so hard she nearly spit out the sip of her soft drink that she just took. Trent laughed as well and held Emily in his arms as the two watched the sun set over the water. The next day, they made their way to the beach for some reading and paddle ball. They had managed to get a spot near the cabana bar. They sipped some iced tea and enjoyed the local music, which should have just been labeled "Tourist Mix." It contained every song that you would expect to hear on a cruise. Either way, they soaked up every minute of it. The water was as smooth as a sheet of ice. Trent managed to drown out the sounds of people around him. At one point, he caught himself becoming hypnotized by the sound of the ice in his drink clanking against the side of the worn glass. Emily was listening to the sounds of the seagulls off in the distance. There was a sort of beach calypso vibe happening for both Emily and Trent.

Trent started to read his "trash mags." At least that's what Emily called the magazines that Trent always seemed to find as they checked out of the grocery store. He was such a chick. He loved to read about the celebrity gossip, and he didn't even care if most of it wasn't true. It relaxed him, and that was all that mattered. It made him feel better knowing that even the richest and most famous of people had the same problems as the average folks who actually worked to survive.

Emily, on the other hand, carefully opened her new book. She made sure that there was no sand near the pages.

"Whose book are you?" she asked softly under her breath.

She examined the first few pages to see if there were any names of a possible owner, but there was nothing. It was unquestionably a journal or diary since it had handwritten pages. It was the most beautiful handwriting that she had ever seen. Emily was already jealous of whoever created this work. Emily's world was all about text messages, laptops, tablets, and other electronic gadgets that seemed to slowly erase the brilliance and intellectual sexiness that came from pen and ink.

Before Emily knew it, she had spent an hour and a half in the magical world that the author had created. All that Emily knew for sure was that the journal was created by a young girl or young woman with a youthful soul who kept her free spirit alive into her wild young-adult years. Emily knew one thing for sure. This was the story of a life. A girl who was probably about seventeen and lived somewhere in Georgia. Emily surmised this from the fact that the locations the girl described sounded just like a few just north of Florida. The girl described a few weekend trips to Savannah with her family. She also captured a few seashore trips to some seasonal beach house near Jekyll Island. There were no descriptions of the girl, but

Emily imagined her to be a petite, medium-height brunette with soft eyes as blue as a summer afternoon.

Emily flipped through the pages, as if to let fate or chance find the lucky entry that she would read. She did this for a few minutes. She found one entry that she thought was particularly moving. The way that this girl wrote was as if she were simply transcending a summer picture or feeling into words with no difficulty whatsoever.

7 September 1943 - Today, my mother, sister, and I traveled to the seashore for a much-needed weekend retreat. The weather has been unseasonably warm for this time of year, so we are taking full advantage of Mother Nature's gift of extended summer. As of recent, my life has seemed to be consumed with thoughts that betray my sanity. It's like a whirlwind blowing off of a cliff. There's nothing that I can pinpoint, just the overwhelming pressures that poke at my soul. My pleasure comes from the times that I am in the arms of Jackson. I love him with all of my heart and would die if he ever ceased being mine. We went to a movie last week, and I truly enjoyed every moment of his presence. At one point, I leaned in to rest my head against his shoulder. As I brushed across his face, I could feel the prickles from the roughness of his beard. He smelled of a musk aftershave. Jackson is the half that completes who I am. I cannot wait another day to see him. For now, I will treasure the scent of the ocean and the innocent blue sky above.

Trent softly nudged Emily's shoulder. "I'm going up to the bar for a beer. You want one, beautiful?"

"Sure. Thanks."

Trent brushed some sand off of his purple, flower-patterned board shorts, and Emily could not help but catch a glimpse. She absolutely loved the fact that she was married to this man. There was no denying the affection and chemistry that bonded this couple. It was beyond friendship and sex. It went to the core of their beings, as if they could not exist without each other.

He soon returned with a couple of cold beers with a cut lime in them. The beers were in clear plastic cups with the hotel's logo etched on the side. It was perfect advertising, and Trent swore that this cup somehow made the beer taste better.

"You know the bartender told me that there's a tropical depression forming, headed toward Miami this week."

Emily winked at Trent. "Those things rarely make it to land, and if they do, they always hit North Carolina. Something about the Gulf Stream or jet stream or something."

"You're probably right. Not even God himself would dare ruin Emily Duval's honeymoon."

"You mean Emily Duval Decker don't you, silly?"

Trent smiled and puckered his lips to give Emily a playful air kiss as he took a swig of his beer. He had to get used to calling her that, but he had a lifetime. Trent wiped the foam from his upper lip, and stared at the distance to the horizon. He was just enjoying every bit of this mind-freeing vacation. No worries, and no work.

Emily read a bit more and figured that she had absorbed a good one-eighth of this mysterious girl's life, from what she read. She had no doubt that this was an amazing person. Nothing special in particular, but the manner in which she described things portrayed a woman who loved life, loved her family, and apparently loved a young man. Emily let her imagination wander through the life of this mystery woman as she read entry after entry. She learned that this woman was in true love, the kind that would make you die for the other person. Apparently, from the entries the woman met her beau, Jackson, as he tripped over her at a general store.

5 January 1943 – Today I met the most magical, awkward young man. As I was sweeping up a pile of white, dry grain rice that a customer accidentally spilled, this man came stumbling around the corner. He was looking down at some can of soup in a cute, clumsy fashion. Before I could say a word, he knocked me right off of my feet. He looked up and was as bright as a beet from embarrassment. As I sat there on the floor, I couldn't help but laugh uncontrollably. He began to laugh as well, after he apologized at least ten times. We ended up talking outside the store for hours about nothing. He was such a delight to speak with and was so sweet in his innocent, quirky way. There was something secure and comforting about him that made me feel as if I had known him my whole life. It took him every ounce of courage that he had to ask me if he could take me out on a date. I played coy, but inside I was shouting with delight, like a child with a new doll.

Emily finished reading the entry, and she smiled because it reminded her of her relationship with Trent. It was as if the romance in the pages of this old book was just a mirror of her modern-day love with Trent. She put down the book. For now, it was time to dance the last night away in St. Augustine before heading to Cumberland Island for the remainder of the honeymoon.

Trent surprised Emily with a romantic dinner at a local Colombian-themed restaurant. This place was renowned for its authentic Spanish food and atmosphere. It was like walking into a South American country with lush live trees and ornate fountains right in the middle of the dining area. The sound of tricking water could be heard all over the restaurant as the water from the fountains found its way down decorative rocks. The smell was amazing as well. From the moment that she entered, Emily could smell fresh guacamole and steamed vegetables. It made her think of walking down the streets of Chile with the scent of Chancho en Piedra emanating from the local outdoor restaurants.

Mr. and Mrs. Decker, as the maître d' called them, ate steaks and drank wine until the better part of eleven o'clock. Emily enjoyed a plate of enchiladas verdes, and Trent shoveled down a carnitas plate of some sort. They listened to the sound of authentic music being played by a couple of older gentlemen who would walk by every twenty minutes or so.

After dinner, they walked hand in hand to a nearby English pub to do karaoke and dance. As they opened the heavy wooden door to enter, it was as if they pair had hopped a red-eye flight to London. The place seemed no bigger than a large garage. The walls were covered with rugby and soccer flags of all teams and nations. It would have been no surprise if a group of soccer hooligans crashed through the door screaming about Manchester United.

A raspy voice came across the bar. “Okay, mates, what’ll it be?”

The bartender definitely had an authentic British appeal to him. He looked like a stocky, former soccer player who had lived life in the fast-lane for the better part of his forty to fifty years.

“What do you recommend for a newly married couple?” Trent asked.

“A good pre-nup! My last wife took me for almost everything I had. We worked it out. She got the kids, and I got this bar.

Emily chimed in, “Unfortunately for him he married a lawyer!”

“God help you, mate. Actually, I’m only joshing you, mate. Been married to my second wife for nearly twenty-five years. She is the brains of this operation.”

“I need to meet this fine woman,” said Emily.

“First round is on me. Congrats to you both.”

The first round happened to be a shot that was dropped in a cold glass of some dark Irish beer.

“You know what this means, don’t you?” Emily said to Trent.

“It’s not that time is it?”

“Yes it is! Karaoke time.”

Emily had never been one to shy away from a good country karaoke song. And luckily for the audience, she could actually carry a tune. Now Trent, he was a different story. He could barely lift the slightest semblance of a melodic sound. To put it bluntly, neighborhood dogs would run and cover their ears when he occasionally sang in the apartment to a song that he liked. Emily always teased him by telling him, "Dear, there are a lot of things that I love about you, but your singing is not one of them."

Emily belted away at a few songs, and Trent loved to watch her sing. Trent left for the "blokes" room to relieve himself of a few beers. As he was leaving he noticed that Emily had found herself surrounded by the local sharks looking to impress this pretty prospect. Trent was not the jealous type. He was confident in what he had, and besides, he knew that Emily could handle herself. As he approached, he found two beers on the table.

"Look babe. These nice guys just bought us a round."

Now Trent knew full well that the guys were not the nice-guy types who just wanted to buy the newlyweds a drink to toast. The sharks swam back to their booth and took the defeat, at least until the next prey walked in. After a full night of drinking a variety of traditional British ales, they retired back at their hotel before the journey to Cumberland Island.

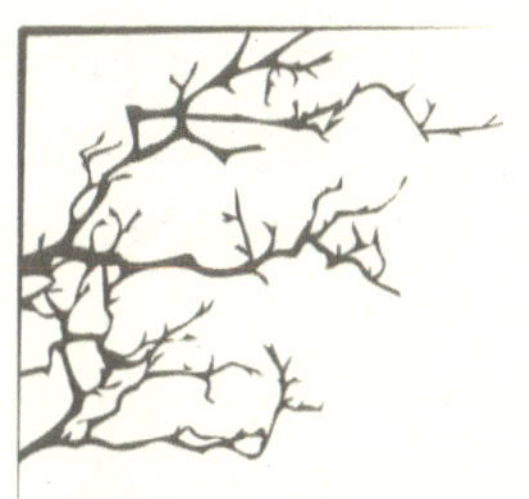

Chapter 8

The next morning, they packed up their suitcases and stuffed everything that they had into Trent's old Nissan Pathfinder. It was earlier than either liked to get up.

"Tell me again why we're leaving at six in the morning?"

"There are only two ferries that leave St. Marys to Cumberland Island each day, and the second leaves just before noon. I don't want to miss it because of some accident on the interstate or because of construction delays."

Trent was extremely diligent with keeping on track and being early to everything. He even had his watch set ten minutes early. If you asked Emily, she would wink and say that he was a precisionist, her polite way of saying *anal retentive*. However, her friends had a running joke that any time Emily was invited to an event they would have to tell her that the event was thirty minutes earlier than it actually was just so she would only be five minutes late. Emily knew that punctuality was not her strong suit, but she didn't care. After all, anyone who wanted to see her could wait, right? This is what she always lightheartedly thought to herself.

Luckily, Emily's parents took all of the wedding gifts, so the only items that they had to worry about was their camping gear and the few trinkets that they scored from their shopping adventures in St. Augustine. The day had promise. The temperature was lingering around sixty degrees, but the sun was shining.

Emily had her quick-time outfit on for the trip, which consisted of an old college tee shirt, jeans, sneakers, and her hair tucked under her favorite ball cap.

"So, do you have the ferry location for Cumberland Island locked into your phone?" Trent asked.

"Of course I do, what kind of navigator do you take me for, honey?" Emily replied. "We check into the Cumberland Island National Seashore, which is just over the Florida-Georgia border in St. Marys, Georgia. From there we take the ferry to Cumberland."

The two-and-a-half-hour trip from St. Augustine to St. Marys did not offer much to see, except for pine trees and the occasional truck stop or fast-food joint. They seemed to pass every shop, each of which boasted to be the last true place where tourists could buy Florida oranges, pecans, and other assorted novelty gifts before hitting the Georgia border. It became a running joke between them as they drove. They passed the first hour by playing a word game that they always played on long trips where they would try to find words that started with each letter of the alphabet. The goal was to go from "a" to "z" in the alphabet by picking out a word that started with "a" and then moving to one that started with "b" and so on. Emily always won because she remembered where most of the words were on the various billboards. Besides, she had the obvious advantage on this trip since she was not focused on driving.

She finished off Trent within the first forty minutes. She softly punched Trent's right arm. *Zack's Southern-Fried Chicken Shack*! That's z-end of the game. I win!" After basking in her victory, she leaned over the middle console and dug through her day-bag to find her new book.

"Keep your eyes on the road and off of my rear assets."

Trent chuckled. "How'd you know I was checking you out?"

"You're a guy. Besides, let's face it, I'm gorgeous," Emily said with a smile as she puckered her lips into a cute pouty face.

Truth was Emily enjoyed every bit of attention that Trent gave her. She found the book pretty quickly but purposely pretended to dig in her bag to give him a sexy show. Emily secured herself back in her seat and buckled her seatbelt. Trent began to stare at the road while all the time fantasizing about his life with Emily.

Emily nuzzled her head into a pillow that she had wedged between the seat and the door. She held the book in her left hand and let it rest on her leg. For Emily, the anticipation of opening another chapter in this world of faded words was just as exhilarating for her as the act of reading it was going to be for her. Every sense in her body tingled as she stared out the window. Her eyes followed the rows of pine trees as they passed, as if someone were rolling them across her view on a piece of paper like a movie set. She was completely relaxed at this very moment.

She took a deep slow breath and opened the journal on her exhale. She was now in a mental place to do justice to whatever account this young woman had in store for Emily. Every word was prophetic, as if the writer didn't even know how to put in needless transition words. The more that Emily read, the more that she realized that her life and the world of this unknown woman were parallel in many ways. Each was a free spirit. However, this take-on-the-world attitude was born of deep depression that apparently plagued the woman's life.

This was a path that Emily knew all too well. For she, too, had faced her own emotive demons, and luckily for her she scraped and fought her way back to her faith and family. For each entry of love and hope, there was another page consumed with purging thoughts of suicide and despair. Emily could not believe that this person had the same issues that Emily had once faced. Even more intriguing to Emily was the fact that this poor girl was facing these issues back in the nineteen forties. Presumptuously, Emily just figured that depression was something born of the cocaine cowboys and tech wave of the nineteen eighties. She always naïvely just figured that depression was something that could not have been a plague to society throughout history.

Emily pretended to keep reading, but her mind kept taking her back to her sophomore year of college. It was just after the fall midterms. Emily and her friends were out celebrating the fact that they had survived, or at least taken, their exams. Before Emily knew it, she and group of about seven others were on their way to a music festival in Atlanta. The weekend was a complete blur. Emily and her friends frequented every beer tent that they could find. Luckily for her, a couple of the girls had just turned twenty-one and were able to put their wrist bands to use for all of the partygoers in the group. After about six hours of the alcohol-induced music experience, Emily's friend Jennifer went searching for Emily since she had been missing for about an hour. As luck would have it, Jennifer just about tripped over Emily as she was getting ready to search the group's party van. What she discovered was Emily had thrown up all over herself and passed out cold right next to the car.

When Emily awoke on Sunday, she felt more than just a hangover. Her mind kept flashing images of her making out with a random guy from the festival. Obviously, this was not Emily's style, but she did not beat herself up for this one since she was not in any relationship, and this was college, after all. She was more disappointed in herself for getting so drunk that she passed out. God forbid that some other drunks had found her before her friend. The situation could have been much worse. But she could not shake this uneasy feeling. She knew that this experience would not define her, but even still, this moment in Atlanta sparked something that she had not let come to the surface before that time. It was like a precise explosion of emotion that was waiting idle for someone to ignite it.

The entire ride back to South Carolina, Emily could not help but feel as though she were below the surface of her own sanity trying desperately to swim to the top to breathe. Her friends would never know this, since Emily always put on a front of content happiness. She just presumed that the alcohol-induced weekend made her feel low. The feeling, however, did not go away. Months passed, and Emily put on her fun face around friends. On the inside, however, she was miserable and was slipping further into her dark mental dwelling. There was nothing that she could pinpoint to justify her feelings. After all, she seemed to have it all. She was on track to graduate Magna Cum Laude on her worst day. She had good, supportive friends. No matter how good the day was, Emily's mind always kept her up at night with thoughts of anxiety. It was like her mind was in a battle with itself, with one lobe struggling to find emotion while the other lobe was on a mission to make her feel crazy. She thought about how she was not good enough and how she could never amount to what her parents wanted from her. Could she be a better person? Could she have done more to study for a recent test?

After months of this, Emily knew for sure that this was not just the typical college worrying that her friends were facing. She was smart enough to know that there was something wrong, whether it was a chemical imbalance or something else. She was tired of waking up in cold sweats and not knowing why. It took every ounce of pride to finally call her parents to let them know. She feared that if she didn't bring them in to help that her mind would win the ultimate betrayal—death. She was shocked at how supportive and receptive both of her parents were when she called them. Emily could never forget the call. She was crying uncontrollably. In her mind, she was letting down the family name, and God forbid that anyone found out that Judge's daughter was crazy.

Both of her parents dropped what they were doing. This included Judge having a senior judge finish his trial docket during a two-week jury trial. Emily knew that she had a stalwart family, but not even she could have imagined the strength that it must have taken for her parents to be by their little girl's side to overcome this disease. With her parents' help, Emily immediately went into therapy sessions. She tried several anti-depressant drugs, but they clouded her mind. She hated taking them and often avoided taking any medications despite her doctor's orders.

It took Emily six months, nine days, and three hours of therapy in order for her to have the mental tools to work each day to fight the depression. Her saving grace, in her opinion, was the fact that she did not shy away from the condition. As with everything, Emily hit this head-on. She would be damned if she let depression beat her. Each day, she woke and vowed to fight the feelings that her body was mixing like a chemical cocktail inside her. Through therapy, Emily was able to realize that she had been afflicted by depression her whole life. As she opened up with her therapist, she remembered feeling anxious even as a young child. This continued into her early teenage years, where even the most miniscule of things would seem insurmountable. She just always buried her feelings deep inside, presuming that everyone had the same thoughts.

Emily chose to not let her depression define her. Instead, she defined it by giving it the most infinitesimal space in her body to occupy. She did not ignore it. Instead, Emily awoke each day with the full comprehension that she was going to beat it today. That is how Emily chose to live each day, and that is exactly what Emily accomplished. Emily's carefree spirit and willingness to try almost any adventure was a pure reflection of the defiance that she placed in the face of depression.

Emily finding this journal had to be fate since it portrayed a young woman who could have easily been Emily, had each swapped moments in time. Emily knew nothing in the world happened by pure chance, and somehow this journal offered a purpose and a connection. After about twenty minutes of letting her imagination roam within the four corners of this journal and her own psyche, Emily looked up at Trent.

"This journal is amazing. It's killing me that I can't figure out the name of the girl who wrote all of this. I did find the initials 'AES,' which I figure were her initials."

"I wonder what that stands for?"

"Probably 'Amanda Emily Stevens,' or could be some fifth-generation traditional southern name that I'd be able to figure out. One thing is for sure, she has a great gift for capturing her perfect moments in time. She keeps mentioning her fiancé, Jackson. Listen to this."

Emily began to read a passage from the book.

11 June 1944 – Today was the best day of my life. Jackson finally proposed to me. He asked me to go with him to Tybee Island for the weekend. I had no idea that he was going to propose. I had always figured that he would ask me the question, but I presumed that it would be next year, maybe around Christmas or just after the New Year. He picked me up and was a gentleman, as always. He opened every door for me and made sure that my needs came first. Earlier this evening we had a beautiful dinner on the beach. Jackson must have saved for three months for this trip. We shared a medium-rare filet, which given the war rationing in effect was a scarce treat. I could tell that he was nervous since this was not his typical meal. He always felt uncomfortable when people were watching him, like he was not supposed to be eating fancy meals. After we ate he took a large sip of his cabernet and reached down. Before I knew it he was on one knee. His hands were shaking. He was so nervous. He could barely get the words out. He read the most beautiful poem to me and then asked for my hand. I grabbed the ring as quick as I could before I awoke from what seemed like a dream. Later, as we walked back to the hotel, I realized that my family was standing by the pool. It was a complete surprise. Jackson had arranged for all of them to share in this experience with us. Jackson had asked my dad for permission a week before. He made this the most special day of my whole life.

Emily thumbed through the journal reading a few more passages to herself. She then found an entry that caught her attention. She read it aloud to Trent.

21 August 1944 - Today, Jackson and I are going to Dungeness for a party. This is such a delight to be invited to a party at the Carnegie mansion. I am told that it does not get used much, as the family has all but abandoned it except for special occasions. Jackson and I are in knots since this is the most magnificent event that either of us has been to. I had to borrow my mother's Sunday dress. Jackson's boss from the mill has graciously invited us to this art charity auction and gala. Jackson has been working on a new idea, and his boss is helping him meet the people who can finance his vision. Hopefully, there will be a Carnegie or a Rockefeller descendant in attendance or someone of that sort there who will see the vision as well. I am so nervous. I just hope that I do not fall over my feet if Jackson gets up the nerve to ask me to dance.

"Emily, you know where Dungeness is don't you?"

"Where?"

"Cumberland Island."

"It was originally owned by General William George MacKay, who was the cousin of Confederate President Jefferson Davis. Thomas Carnegie, the brother of the steel tycoon Andrew Carnegie bought it from MacKay after MacKay's son and grandson died on the property. I think Thomas Carnegie had like eight or more kids. Carnegie would have died well before 1944, but his family probably held on to the mansion."

"How in the world do you know that? Forget it . . . I don't want to know."

This sent her head spinning. The sleuth inside Emily was taking over the controls in her brain. She grabbed her phone and began to methodically search Cumberland Island. Several months ago, she had checked the place out for the camping information but did not focus on the historical facts. Now she was on a mission. Her fingers were moving across the phone like an artist painting a picture. She looked at every website she could find. Finally, she found a site that gave her the revelation that she was searching to find.

"Holy shite!" This was Emily's go-to word that she always used to get her point across with the shock of profanity without having to let her beautiful lips slip into that dirty place. "What?" Trent was sitting on the edge of his seat waiting to hear what Emily had found.

"Listen to this. On August 21, 1944, a man named Jackson Mitchell Jones disappeared on the island. He was last seen at the Carnegie charity event with his fiancé, Addison Smith. That's the girl from my book. 'AES' must be Addison Smith. His body was never found after he and Addison left the party to catch the ferry back to St. Marys. The police scoured the island and held Addison as the prime suspect. After several months of on-and-off questioning, she was eventually cleared because the police could never recover a body to convict her."

Intrigued by this mystery, Emily kept searching other sites. "Here's some more. Addison swore to everyone that she and Jackson were walking down the river trail on their way to the ferry. She told police she could see the lights of the ferry. It was just the two of them on the trail, and it was almost pitch black out except for the light of the moon and the sporadic trail lanterns. They heard a noise like someone was following them. They picked up their pace, but the sounds kept getting closer. Jackson told her to hide behind an old oak log that had fallen about ten feet from the trail. Jackson backtracked on the trail until his silhouette disappeared, as if the island swallowed him up. She waited there for two hours. Finally, she took a few steps toward where she and Jackson had come from on the trail. She was so scared that she turned toward the ferry landing and ran as fast as she could. The last ferry was gone for the night since it was about midnight. She kept hidden by the landing, occasionally closing her eyes for five to ten minutes at a time. She never saw or heard from Jackson ever again. Apparently, there were the conspiracy theories that he had some plan to steal money from the Carnegies and ditch Addison on the island. Other theories hypothesized that someone had him killed to steal his new invention. None of the theories ever panned out, and his disappearance might as well have happened in the Bermuda Triangle. It's as if the island just swallowed him with not even the courtesy of justification or reason. Addison eventually moved to Savannah from her home near St. Marys. She never got married, and she refused to believe that Jackson had some sinister plot to leave her stranded on that island. She died ten years later in 1954. To this day there are some who claim to see Jackson walking aimlessly on the beaches at night or by the ferry landing looking for Addison."

"Oh my God," Trent said. The hairs on his arms were standing straight up. "What's the last entry in her journal?"

"Just her date at Dungeness. It has to be her."

Now both of their minds were spinning. "So, do you still want to go to Cumberland even if it's haunted?"

"Of course. Emily Duval Decker will not be known as the coward. God help any ghost who gets in the way of my honeymoon!"

"That's my girl."

"Is there anything else on the web about this mystery?"

"Nope. That's all that I could find. There's probably not much that was archived since it was so long ago. With the lack of technology, Jackson's story was doomed to fall into a paper media black hole."

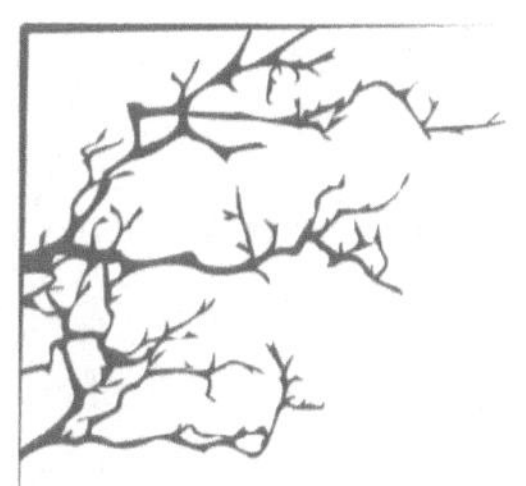

Chapter 9

Before they knew it, their exit was within a few hundred feet. Trent had slowed his speed once he hit the Florida-Georgia state line. For some reason, he was a magnet for the Georgia State Troopers who patrolled Interstate 95 from Brunswick to St. Marys. In one year while traveling for work he managed to get four tickets in a seven-month span. It was so bad that he received a letter from the Department of Motor Vehicles advising him that if he got one more ticket he would lose his license for a year. Needless to say, he was not a fan of driving this stretch of road.

Almost with a sense of relief, Trent said, "Exit three, Kingsland and St. Marys. This is our exit."

Emily brushed the back of Trent's head and replied, "Another ticketless day, my dear."

Emily could not help but be mesmerized by the sheer, overwhelming, gaudy stores. As soon as any car rounded the left exit ramp and reached the stoplight at the bottom, they were bombarded with what could be described as nothing short of a commercialized amusement park of gas, sex, and every cheap novelty known to man. Every fast-food chain that Emily had every known was right in front of her like a cholesterol almanac, each offering some special that professed to be better than the others without actually calling them out by name. There had to be at least nine gas stations lined up within a mile of each other. They each had the same saying on their signs, saying *Lowest Price for Gas in Georgia*. This made Emily laugh out loud since they all had the same price. She thought for sure that the last store on the line would at least undercut the others by one hundredth of a penny or some ridiculous amount, just to prove that it was truly the lowest price.

As they made the left turn from the light toward the coast, Emily saw an adult novelty store. She nudged Trent and asked him if he wanted to make a pit stop. Why not? she figured. They could fuel the car, eat, and satisfy their adult appetites as well. She was kidding of course, which Trent knew as he laughed. The thought of going into an adult toy store with Emily still made him uncomfortable, even though he had seen every inch of her body and had undoubtedly covered at least one or two chapters in the books that the store offered.

They made great time and could not believe that the car ride had passed so quickly. They finished the trek by making their way the final eight miles down the back roads off I-95. The faded asphalt road slowly narrowed down a lane the farther east that they drove. They started to feel the noticeable dips and potholes in the road. They felt like they were being transported into another time, when life moved slower and meant much more to people. As they approached the coast, a sign appeared.

"Welcome to St. Marys. Founded 1842." It was a charming sign that had a soft blue background accented by gold lettering. Trent reached over and gently placed his hand over Emily's hand in her lap. Her skin felt soft and warm, and she smelled of a vanilla body lotion that she liked to use on days when she knew that she would be wearing shorts or skirts. She placed her right hand over his hand and rubbed his thumb with her thumb. There wasn't a cloud in the sky. It was a deep healthy blue that almost made the air feel rejuvenating and fresh. However, the old, worn road made sure that it did not reveal all of the sky's charm. On each side of road there were huge palm trees mixed with the occasional pine, which created a sense of natural southern elegance. It was almost as if they were the ancient, majestic guards of the city. Each tree had their own stories from their hundreds of years of life. Some had branches torn by storms, many had scars from black bears brushing away the bark, and a few even proudly displayed bullet pits from the various battle skirmishes that they experienced front-and-center. As the old Pathfinder arrived in the town, the trees opened up like a sword line at a royal wedding. To Emily, it felt like arriving in Charleston for the first time. There was a tacit tenderness that surrounded this place, with an equal mix of well-deserved natural haughtiness.

Emily could hardly wait to stretch her arms and feet from the trip. She placed her flip flops on and shot out of the Pathfinder like a cannon. She stretched her arms like she'd been stuck in a prison cell for weeks. The first thing that she noticed in St. Marys was the salt air that crept up on her senses like an old friend. It immediately took her back to childhood trips with her family to Ocean City, Maryland. It reminded her of the boardwalk and saltwater taffy. She always picked through the rectangular box of taffy to get right to the strawberry and vanilla flavored ones. From untwisting the thick, off-white wax paper to savoring each bite, it was a perfect moment in time. She loved the experience of letting the sweet treat melt in her mouth. But more than anything, she cherished the atmosphere. The weeks she spent fighting and playing with her family on the beach was something that she knew she could never get back. She had a snapshot in time that no one could ever take away from her. Even the sunburns didn't bother her all that much.

She took in a long breath and then asked Trent, "How much time do we have?"

"About two hours." Trent knew that they actually had over three hours, but he wasn't about to let Emily know that. She would no doubt find a way to make them late despite the fact that they had so much time to check in for the ferry. "Let's check in and get our ferry ticket. Then we can check out the town."

"Sounds like a plan."

They made their way to the Cumberland Island Visitor Center to get their tickets. In front of them there was a family of five. Two twin boys and a girl who appeared to be a few years younger than her brothers. The parents looked like they actually wanted to get the kids a one-way ticket to the island and sneak back to the minivan. Two of the three were always fighting over something trivial and ridiculous. If it wasn't the boys fighting with each other, it was them teaming up on the girl. At one point, the girl kicked one of the boys so hard that he started to cry. The mother scolded the girl, and of course, the girl cried. Emily wondered if this whole family was going to start crying from the stress of their vacation.

Emily raised one of her eyebrows, and she whispered to Trent. "I never want kids." She then kissed his cheek and grinned. Trent knew that she actually wanted a house full of kids no matter how crazy, chaotic, or down-right nutty that idea sounded.

"Welcome to the Cumberland Island Visitor Center, folks." The park ranger was a tall gentleman of at least six feet, five inches tall. He had a gray close-trimmed beard. He smelled of some cheap cologne that he probably used to mask any odor after a long day of being outside. "Are you looking for a day pass or a multi-day package?"

"We would like a five-day pass for the Sea Camp Beach area. That's the one that has the restrooms and showers near it, right?" Emily was impressed with Trent's research and his take-charge approach. It turned her on.

"Yes, sir. That is the site that is just off of the beach area. It's four dollars per person for each night. The ferry cost is twenty dollars per person."

"That sounds good. We'll take that package."

"Let's see, the total damage is eighty dollars." Trent reached in his pocket and pulled out four twenty-dollar bills that looked like they came straight from the mint. They were crisp and without sign of wear. The ranger took out a piece of paper and added everything up for a receipt. "Sorry, computers are down. I'll have to give you a handwritten receipt." The ranger handed Trent the receipt, as well as the ferry tickets for each of them. "Don't forget, the last ferry leaves Cumberland each day at four forty-five. If you miss that one, you'll be stuck until the next day."

"Got it. Thanks."

"You folks have a good time, and thank you for visiting Cumberland."

The ranger started to turn away, but quickly stopped himself. "I almost forgot to mention . . . take this piece of paper as well." He handed Trent a bright orange index card with some emergency information. "They're tracking Tropical Storm Xavier out in the Atlantic just North of Miami. All of the hurricane models are projecting that the storm will make a northeastern turn back out to sea. Worst case, it may skirt past us about a hundred miles out. I wouldn't expect it to strengthen to a Cat One Hurricane."

Emily chimed in. "Do you think there's a chance that it could hit near Cumberland?"

"Probably not. Most of these storms hit near the Outer Banks in North Carolina. But just to be safe, we're giving everyone this cheat sheet with all of the emergency numbers that you need to get ahold of a ranger while on the island."

Trent analyzed the sheet. It had a map of the island on the back that identified all of the ranger stations, and on the front, it had every number except for the direct line to the President of the United States.

"Do we need anything else for the week, Emily?"

"Nope." Emily was always prepared. "Actually, to be safe, we may want to stop at a store and get some extra matches, as well as some extra hotdogs and water."

They made their way to a store at the corner of the street to get the last-minute rations. The store was a small local general store that seemed to cater mostly to the visitors going to Cumberland. The exterior of the store had an old-timey look, like it could have come straight from an eighteenth-century Carolina coastal city. The shelves were covered with everything from canned beans to camping lanterns. The smell of fresh boiled peanuts enveloped every inch of the store. Trent loved to try the local eats when he went to new towns. He looked down at the peanut pots, and his nose enjoyed every sensation from the traditional southern salt-and-water recipe to the Cajun flavored.

Needless to say, there was one extra ration that left the store with Trent. He could not resist the Cajun flavored peanuts, so he got a cup full. The store clerk took an old metal slotted spoon and scooped a cup's worth into a piece of newspaper that was folded into a cone shape. This was what Trent loved. The food was impressive, but the classic presentation made the event. He thought that this was probably the same way that peanuts had been boiled and given to locals for centuries.

Aside from picking up another pack of hotdogs, as well as three cans of camping beans that were simply labeled "beans" on a white label, Emily and Trent were already covered with plenty of food and camping gear. Emily went to an outdoor-sports store months ago and purchased each of them a trail backpack that had all of the essentials, such as a sleeping bag, blankets, extra canteens, lantern holders, flashlights, and first-aid kits. She also bought a new tent that the salesperson assured her was so easy that a seven-year-old could set it up. Trent had been camping his whole life with his father and friends, so he also had a sturdy survival knife, a small hatchet for firewood, and extra ropes to secure a tent. They calculated how much food and drink that they would need for the five days and gave themselves a few extra days' worth of food to be safe. Emily found a cooler that they could stuff everything in, which somehow did not seem to be all that heavy. It had large wheels good for pulling along a beach.

"Let's soak in some local flavor."

Trent snickered. "You mean aside from the peanuts that I just inhaled?"

"Yes, you pig! I want a good local meal before we live off of beanie weenies."

There was a small restaurant just across from the ferry landing. Tent liked this because he wanted to be sure that they could see the boat when it arrived. He had a constant fear of being left behind or being late for anything. The restaurant was not much to look at. It was a simple place. It had plain white curtains covering the windows, and everywhere there were simple paper placemats that donned a blue trim to somehow make them seem ornate. The floor had the indistinct smell of bleach and looked like a nineteen fifties diner, with black and white checkered tiles. The walls told a story, however, with pictures of ships and locals that had to date back to the mid-to-early nineteen hundreds. There was a smell of local honey and cinnamon coming from the kitchen. There was a shelf near the door that had mason jars with homemade jam and jellies. Each one had red cloth wrapped over the cap, which was held on by brown butcher string.

"How y'all doing today?" The waitress was a skinny woman with peppered hair and a smile that could warm anyone within miles. She made this place with her presence.

"Great. Any specials today?" Trent asked.

"Yep. We have eggs benedict with a side of hash. We also have a five-stack of pancakes with bacon. How bout I start you with a couple coffees and orange juice while you look over the menus?"

"That would be great. Thank you." Emily was taking pleasure in this place.

The waitress came back with two small plastic glasses of juice. She also poured some coffee for each of them in small white cups. Nothing special, but if they sold traditional diner coffee mugs, these would be them. They were so basic that they almost seemed to be unique. Emily's cup had a small chip on the rim, probably from a fall during a busy day.

"I'll leave the pot here for ya, so you can get some more if you like. Have you decided on breakfast?"

The orders were placed, and then the conversation about the island began again. Emily went with the special. She was not sure whether she even liked eggs benedict, but it sounded delicious just because of the way waitress offered it with her deep Georgia accent. Trent went with his staple, fallback meal of two eggs over easy, white toast, and waffles. He always ordered an extra piece of toast since he liked soaking up any extra egg yolk with buttered toast.

"So, do you think that Addison's guy was murdered?"

Trent took his hand, and with his thumb and forefinger began slowly rubbing his chin. "Hard to say, but if he made it off of the island, I would think that the police would have found him. The currents around here are pretty predictable." Trent was somewhat preoccupied with the triangular peg game that he seemed to gravitate to at each diner he stumbled across. As smart as he was, this game always seemed to frustrate his ego. He would jump one peg and take out the peg that he jumped, but he never seemed to get to the last one.

Emily punched him in the shoulder. "Focus on me, and not that silly game. Ya think it was some sort of love triangle or something?"

"A what?"

"A love triangle. Do you think Addison and Jackson were swingers or got caught up in some twisted love triangle?"

"Seriously . . . you've been watching too many Lifetime movies."

The waitress came by periodically to check on the couple. After about five rounds to the table, and three "ya'll folks okay?" later she finally placed the small, handwritten receipt on the table. "I'm not trying to kick y'all out or anything. Take your time, honey. If you need me just holler. You can pay at the front, or if you just want to leave the cash here on the table that works just fine as well."

Emily and Trent both said, "Thanks," in unison.

Emily followed up with, "Very good meal and a charming place."

"Thanks, darlin'." The waitress gave Emily a soft pat on the shoulder as if she reminded her of her own child and then walked away.

Trent took another sip of his coffee. After savoring the dark-Colombian flavor, he took the last piece of his waffle. He dragged it across his plate to gather the last remnants of egg clinging to the plate. Trent was never one to leave any food on his plate.

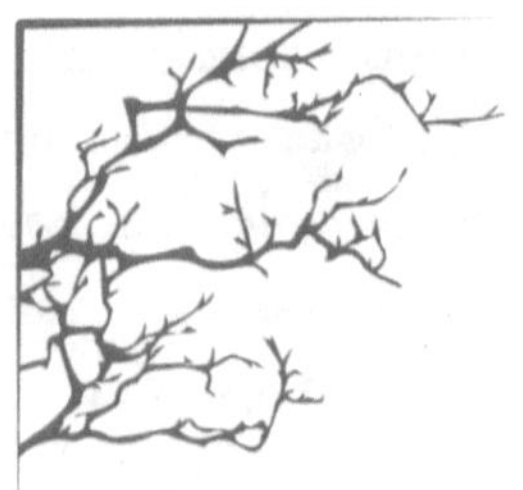

Chapter 10

Just then a loud whistle blared in the distance. It was the ferry. Trent placed some cash on the table to square up on the breakfast and tip. He made sure to tip the waitress well since it was not just about the food but the whole experience. She made it an exceptional dining experience. Trent took Emily's hand and guided her up from the table.

"That's us, beautiful! Let's get the show on the road."

The ferry was just pulling in as they approached the docks. The *Cumberland Queen* boasted two stories, and it looked like most ferries that they had seen other places—the Nantucket Ferry in Cape Cod or the one that they took to visit Prince Edward Island in Canada one summer. It was a bright white vessel with an orange stripe across the side. The campers began to disembark one by one. For the most part they appeared to be worn down and hung over from long days of hiking and nights with nightly cocktails. Every once and a while, there was that one person who appeared as though she could turn right back around and do it all again.

The ferry was finally cleared of the folks returning from Cumberland. The crew consisted of one captain and two helpers. They all cleaned the tiny ship to make it ready for the new visitors. Finally, it was time. A man's voice, probably the captain, came over the vessel's loudspeaker.

"This is the eleven forty-five ferry to Cumberland Island. All aboard if you have a ticket for this ferry."

There were about forty people gathered, give or take five. Emily and Trent were near the front of the line. They had their camping gear tightly packed on each of their hiking-style backpacks. Everything was either rolled and attached or hung by a clip. Trent also had their cooler full of food and drinks for the week. The rolling of the wheels up the metal ramp sounded like a horse trotting across an uneven brick street. Clip clop, clip clop, clip clop. It was almost melodic, with each split-second pause as each wheel tried to find its way over the open groves in the ramp.

"If you like, you can place your cooler and gear over here." The ferry's first mates were extremely friendly and took everyone's gear and coolers as they embarked. They were young locals who could not have been more than twenty years old. Clean cut guys who seemed to enjoy their jobs.

"Let's get to the second level and head for the front of the boat." Emily knew that she needed to be outside and at the front of the ferry since she had an aptness to get sea sick, even on short excursions. There was no argument from Trent, since the trip was supposed to take forty-five minutes from dock-to-dock, and he did not want to start off the day with Emily sending back the food she had just eaten. They found a nice spot on one of the attached benches. Not much for comfort. They were fiberglass and had no cushions or padding. Trent leaned in to Emily and gave her a kiss.

"Hey, beautiful."

"Back at ya, handsome."

They snuggled into each other for warmth, but mostly to connect with each other. Emily placed her head on Trent's shoulder and held his hand. He had his arm around her back. The weather was pleasant with a cool breeze, but temperatures remained in the high sixties to low seventies. All week was supposed to be this way, barring any unforeseen weather events from Xavier. The water looked angry with some choppy waves. The water in the river was dark blue with brown patches toward the shoreline. St. Marys was tucked away at least six miles from Cumberland and the Atlantic Ocean, so Emily knew that this ride would be a bumpy one if the water here was this rough.

After about ten minutes, the ferry was about as full as it was going to get that day. Probably about half capacity. Even though they had not even left the dock, Emily was almost lulled to sleep by the rocking of the boat together with gentle sea breeze against her face. Just then a shadow appeared and caught the eye of Trent. A sweet, subtle smell of peaches was present in the air.

"Do you all mind if I sit here? I have a tendency to not do well on these things, so I like to get up front." The shadow and voice came from a petite blonde woman about their age. She wore a light blue sundress that covered her two-piece bathing suit. Trent tried to keep from ogling her, but she was stunning to say the least. She had a perfect milky-white complexion. Her blonde hair that seemed to get blonder with each passing ray from the sun. Her beauty did not get past Emily either. She was not the jealous type, but she stared at Trent from the corner of her eye to be sure that he was not mentally undressing this new acquaintance. Emily sat up and stretched her arms.

"No problem at all. Sit, sit." Emily could not help but to notice the silver necklace hanging closely on the woman's neck. It was a palmetto tree with a crescent moon.

"That's a beautiful necklace."

"Thanks. My boyfriend bought it for me during a trip we took to South Carolina. It's the state flag of South Carolina." It was a unique piece of jewelry for the reason that it had simple flecks of diamond or glass surrounding the moon. This made the necklace seem to come alive and dance in the sun.

"What's your name?"

"Liz," the woman replied to Emily.

"So, what brings you to Cumberland?"

"I'm a budding author who is putting together my first book."

"That's exciting. What's it about?"

"It's a compilation of all of the ghost stories from Cumberland Island that have been passed down through the years. I'm calling it *The Ghosts of Cumberland Island.*"

Emily just about pushed Trent off of the bench in her excitement. "Do you know anything about the disappearance of Jackson Jones?"

"Absolutely. That's the most famous ghost story that I have uncovered during my research. There were a few other good stories like the father and son who died at Dungeness. But, this one's my favorite."

"Ok. Now you have to tell us what happened and what you know."

Trent was staring at the distant shore focused on the swaying sage grass that formed a perfect border for the coastline. Emily, however, was all ears.

"You sure you want me to give you the full scoop? I don't want to take up your entire ferry ride with this."

"I insist. Besides, it will help us both from getting seasick," Emily said with a snicker.

"Well . . . it starts back in later 1944, right around the time that the U.S. and Allied Powers were liberating France. The war efforts were finally swinging in the direction of a German and Japanese defeat. The Germans in particular were desperate to change the fading tides by using their submarines to sink Allied supply ships taking supplies across the Atlantic. The U.S. began ramping up its own submarine operations off of the coasts from North Carolina down to Florida, to prevent what was suspected to be a heavy wave of attacks by the Germans. There was always the fear that some of the citizens in the U.S. would align themselves with their mother country. This especially applied to those of German descent."

"So how do Addison and Jackson play into this?"

"I'm getting there. Patience, my dear, patience." Liz loved the presentation of her story just as much as she enjoyed telling it to her new friend.

"Sorry, keep going."

"Ok, where was I? Oh yes. Jackson Jones was born poor to a family of six. He was the oldest and carried the burden of helping his father provide for the family. They owned a small farm just north of St. Marys. According to my research he never made it past the eighth grade, but he was brilliant. He could fashion things and ideas that others could not even fathom. He spent hours sitting under a tree after his day was over each day to jot down ideas in a small tattered book that he owned. It was mostly notes and pictures, not a novel or anything like that. When he turned seventeen, he started working at a nearby paper mill to make extra money for his family. The owner started from simple beginnings as well and had no children. He took to Jackson and mentored him. Jackson was born with a slight club foot, which prevented him from military service. Despite his physical obstacle, Jackson was the hardest working person at the mill.

"How did he meet Addison?" Emily could hardly stand the anticipation.

"I'm almost there," Liz smiled and said.

"After about a month or so at the paper mill, Jackson had a pretty steady routine of heading into town with a couple other guys from the mill. They mostly just grabbed a few drinks and played some checkers or fished for sheepshead or sea trout off the docks. According to the broken pieces of information that I have uncovered, Addison worked at one of the local general stores. Jackson ran into Addison at the store one day, and I mean actually ran into her. He was coming around the corner looking down at a newspaper when he about plowed her over. The bond that they formed was one for the fairy tales. They probably could have been married that night, for each of them had that feeling from the soul right then and there that their missing half was found."

Emily's mind wandered for a moment, as she remembered the passage from the journal about how the girl met Jackson in the store. Even though she certainly did not need it, this made her feel vindicated even more, since there was now no doubt in Emily's mind that Addison was in fact the rightful owner of the journal of which Emily came into divine possession.

"Any description of what she looked like?" Emily asked Liz.

"I haven't found any pictures, but I would presume she was a brunette. Probably the type of beauty that would not wear makeup these days even if she could."

"Sorry, back to the story, please."

"All right . . . They dated for what seemed like a lifetime. Jackson wanted to make something of himself to give Addison the type of life that he believed she deserved. That brings them to Cumberland Island. There was some sort of gala or ball or just a really fancy party at Dungeness. It was hosted by a close acquaintance of the Carnegies. Some snooty socialite or that sort. Jackson's boss was well known in the parts, and he tended to rub elbows with the higher-class from St. Marys up to the South Carolina Low Country. He obviously got an invite for this event. He managed to acquire a couple other invitations, which he graciously gave to Jackson and Jackson's new fiancée, Addison.

By this time, Trent began to find himself captivated by the story as well. He had been enjoying people watching on the boat with the occasional glance at the fading shoreline. Now, however, he was being entertained by this storyteller.

"Why would a simple guy like that even want to go to a stuffy ball?" Trent asked.

"From what I found in some old notes, Trent had invented some sort of magnetic device that was decades before its time. He believed that it would revolutionize factories since it could be used in all trades, from paper mills to steel factories. He had fashioned together one device from crude parts that his boss let him have from the paper mill. A few weeks before the Dungeness party, Jackson applied for a U.S. Patent on the device. Again, with the financial support from his boss. The only two people who knew of this were Addison and his boss."

"Sounds like there were two people with a motive to murder him." Emily was proud of her quick deduction.

"That's what I thought in my first impression as well. Problem is that the device was never put into production or even sold after Jackson's death. From all accounts, Addison never saw Jackson's boss after that night, and neither she nor he ever made a dime from the device. Jackson's boss had information about the invention, so he could have easily made millions from the murder. But, he didn't even try. Jackson's disappearance probably hit his boss just as if he were losing a child."

Trent interrupted the story again. "Maybe Addison had him murdered."

"I looked into that one as well. After Jackson's disappearance Addison was truly heartbroken. Jackson was her kindred spirit, and a part of her died the night that he disappeared. She never re-married or had any children. She passed away in her sleep about ten years after Jackson disappeared. Just slipped away without any known ailment. Just a broken heart by all accounts. There was some speculation that she committed suicide. Back then, medical examiners couldn't trace certain neurotoxins or common poisons in the body. Folklore is that she still roams the island searching for Jackson, and that she cannot rest until his body is found. Several people have claimed to see her walking the trail near where he disappeared. She doesn't say anything. She just looks at them with cold dead eyes, as if confused and scared."

"Any chance that Jackson left Addison and made a new life?" Trent asked.

"It's not likely. From the eyewitness interviews around the time, Jackson adored Addison. Any future he had involved her. It was almost like the island just swallowed up Jackson without leaving any trace. The soldiers from the Georgia State Guard and the local Home Guard who were stationed on the island a mile or so from where he disappeared did not see or hear anything. The police and local soldiers spent three weeks combing the island for anything. Nothing was ever found. No blood, no sign of a struggle. Not even a single broken sapling branch to suggest a fight of any kind."

"Were there any other theories?" Emily inquired.

"There was one theory that seemed interesting. Just to the south of Cumberland Island there was an old abandoned Civil War fort on Amelia Island, Florida called Fort Clinch. The fort jutted out on the tip of the Florida coast. On the night of Jackson's disappearance, an old crop farmer saw a small flatboat crossing the jetty from Cumberland to Fort Clinch on the Florida side. He swore that he saw two lanterns bobbing from the boat as it fought the waves. The water was rough that night, which is why it stuck out in his memory. He could not figure out why anyone would risk the mile or so journey from Cumberland to the Florida coast on such an ominous night. Even the Coast Guard, who routinely patrolled the waters, was staying off of those angry waters that night. There was some sort of nor'easter forming that was bringing in driving wind and large swells. As the boat got closer, he saw a couple of shadowy figures get out and push the boat into the thick brush just off of the sand dunes. The crop farmer was a former slave. For this reason, he did not venture too close to the men or the boat. He still maintained a certain set of survival skills, the most important of which was to not poke into a stranger's business affairs."

"Did anyone ever find the boat or figure out who the men were?" Emily was mentally trying to piece together this puzzle.

"Nope. I am not sure whether anyone ever really followed up on that lead. Most just dismissed the farmer's account since he was a ninety-four-year-old former slave. This poor soul was justifiably weathered from decades of being inhumanely controlled and beaten like an animal. The locals dismissed him as being an uneducated fool whose aged eyes deceived him. So far as I know, the boat was never found, and the mysterious occupants never located. They simply disappeared into the Florida night near the fort."

Trent could not resist to ask Liz, "What's your theory? Surely you have one."

"Honestly, I think he was murdered, and that there was some sort of connection between his death and the fact that he was of German lineage, and also that he had this new invention. I would bet my life on it. He's still on this island somewhere, and he won't be able to rest or reconnect with Addison until his remains are properly buried."

"Wasn't he born near St. Marys?" Emily was still trying to keep it all straight in her mind.

Liz brushed a piece of hair from her eyes, which got caught in the wind, and responded, "You are correct. But both of his parents came straight over on the boat from Germany about seven years before Jackson was born. They resided in New York for a year or so before heading south to Georgia for work. It's for this reason that I think that there has to be a link between his invention, his German heritage, and the war. There's something there. Someone did not want his invention to get out. I just know it. Problem is that I can't figure out why."

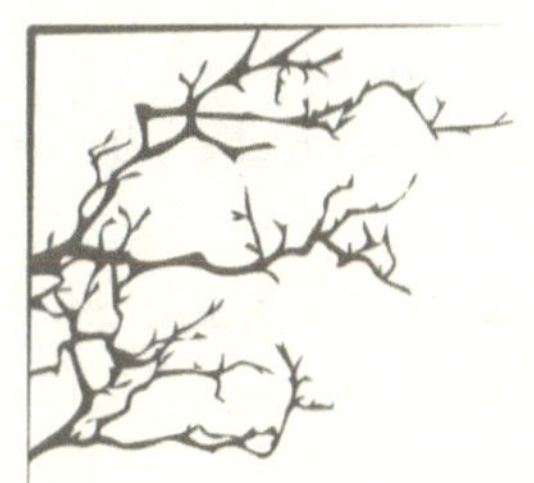

Chapter 11

By this time, the ferry had completed most of its journey up the St. Marys River. The bow of the boat was starting to make the leftward turn into the Cumberland Sound. The boat slightly listed to the right side and bobbed as it made its turn over the waves. Fort Clinch was becoming more apparent off in the distance to the right. Trent couldn't make out any details on the fort, but he could see the basic outline of the once mighty fortress. Looking back at the island, both Trent and Emily could not help but respect the sheer size of Cumberland. It seemed to go on forever. There was something inviting about the island, while at the same time chilling from its isolation. On the east side of the island, any sounds would be lost to the vast Atlantic Ocean. The remaining shores did not offer much refuge either. Any screams would be captured by the surrounding marshes and die out before making their way to any civilization.

The ferry dock was still not visible through the twisting inlets and trees that engulfed the island. Trent looked across the left side of the ferry.

"Look over there on the port side." He pointed to the left side of the ferry. He used the nautical term since he thought it would impress the ladies. It did not. However, their eyes were trying to focus on what he was looking at in the distance.

"It's just a tiny island," Emily said.

"It's actually Drum Point Island," Liz responded.

"No, beyond Drum Point. Look down that way. That's Kings Bay."

Emily was still trying to see what Trent was pointing to. "Are you talking about those oversized storage sheds out there on the edge of the river?"

"That's Kings Bay Naval Submarine Base. It's the home port for the U.S. Navy's fleet of Ohio-class ballistic missile nuclear submarines."

"Are those the big subs?" Emily asked.

"Those are the nuclear subs that carry the Trident missiles. It's the home base for the Navy's nuclear subs."

Liz asked, "What are those sheds?"

"That's where the subs are docked when they're in base. Those things may look like sheds, but they are actually very fortified storage units for the subs. The subs stay submerged and surface once inside the storage units. Top-secret stuff.

"I only know because I had to visit the base a couple of years ago with my bosses. We work closely with the Navy since we are working on technology for their aircraft. A naval commander, who was our liaison, took us to the base to address a couple of issues that they were having with the training program. I guess they figured that we had the know-how to work on a few glitches. My security clearance let me get close. Not close enough, however, to place any eyes on the subs themselves. We were shepherded straight from the main gate to a training building about a hundred yards from where the subs were docked.

"In the facility we went to, they had this mock-up of a submarine command center set up to train the young officers to operate the subs and arm the missiles. We spent the day in there working with a few higher-ups at the base to figure out a problem they were having with the equipment. I'll tell you this . . . the submariners who we met were tough as nails. Very professional with no tolerance for failure. I suppose you have to have that type of bravado to lock yourself in close quarters and spend months circling the globe underwater."

Emily cut off Trent mid-sentence. "So right now, there could be a massive sub underneath us?" Emily started to peer over the side of the ferry on the off chance of catching the shadowy outline of a sub traveling beneath the boat like a Great White shark stalking its prey.

"Yep, I suppose. But I'm sure that they move in and out of the river when they know that there's no traffic on the water. These things are so classified that they take every known measure to keep satellites from snapping shots of them entering and leaving the port."

While Liz showed some polite interest in Trent's knowledge of Kings Bay, she was not as enthralled as others might be with the idea of the submarine base being so close. She was focused on recounting ghost stories from the island and trying to solve a mystery. This did not go unnoticed to Trent, but he dismissed it given the fact that she lived near the area and had probably heard about the base a million times before this trip.

Trent politely looked at Liz. "Please finish the story for us."

He did this not only out of his own interest in learning the rest, but to express his courtesy since he had jumped on a soapbox and had taken the focus from her story. Emily and Trent both smiled and looked back to Liz.

"Yes, Liz, please continue." Emily was all ears again.

"Well . . . I was almost to the end of my knowledge anyway. Let's see . . . nothing of Jackson's was ever found on the island, which is why it is so intriguing."

"Are there any caves on the island?" Trent asked.

"Nope. Too close to sea level. Enough people combed every inch of the island that something should have been found . . . a piece of clothing or some clue. Nothing ever appeared. This is why I'm so interested in this story. There is that obvious attraction of the ghost story, where you have two lost souls in some form of limbo until they can reconnect to be together in their afterlife. Imagine the torture of being bound to an island and looking every day for the missing piece of your soul, knowing that you cannot rest until you are reconnected."

"Has anyone ever seen the ghost of Jackson?" Trent was starting to get into the story now.

"A few have claimed to have seen him on the beach like I mentioned earlier, but other than an occasional glance, people mostly see a woman who is presumed to be Addison. The park rangers get a visit once every couple of weeks from some camper who saw a woman walking the trails. Each time the camper thinks that the woman is alive and breathing until he or she gets closer. Each time the figure disappears as a white mist into the thick palmetto-covered areas. There was one camper who got close enough to touch her while hiking the trail by himself. As he went pass her, his blood went cold. He saw the cold, black eyes. Lifeless and without emotion. Then she was gone, as if she never existed except in the smoke from a dream. Others have claimed to hear noises at night near their tents. They hear footsteps that they cannot explain since the steps are clearly human. The problem is that when they get the courage to look for the intruder in the morning, the area is too dense for anyone to have made such steps."

"How far along are you in your book?"

Liz responded to Emily, "About halfway through. I still have some research to gather from the local museum and the Sheriff's Office in St. Marys. Each has given me great stuff so far, but I need some more information to try to solve this mystery for my future readers."

"Do you camp by yourself out here?" Trent could not believe that Liz was so fearless after the stories she'd told them about ghosts lurking in the bushes near the tents.

"Yeah, I have been coming out here so long, it's like a second home for me. I figure that I know every inch of the island by now. Besides, I like to sit by the ocean and write. There is a serenity about the coast of Cumberland that clears my head so that I can finish bringing Addison and Jackson back to life, even if just in the pages of a book. I am at peace with this place. There is a mutual respect."

Just then, the captain of the ferry came over the speaker. His voice was raspy and faded in and out as he spoke through the boat's old microphone.

"All right folks, we are approaching the dock. Please start heading toward the lower level of the boat to gather your gear. I hope you enjoyed your journey. We'll see you all in a few days."

Liz stood up and shook Trent's hand. "It was nice to meet you."

"It was great meeting you as well. Thank you for the fantastic story."

Emily was a not a handshaker. She went in for a hug with her new friend.

"Liz, thank you. That was so interesting. Who knows, I may have to drag Trent around the island for some investigative probing to see if we can help you solve this mystery." The women hugged, and Emily could not help but to enjoy the subtle smell of Liz's perfume. It offered a mild sensation of lavender. Emily only knew because her grandmother used to rub a dab of lavender oil on her neck.

"Are you staying at Sea Camp?" Emily said as she and Liz pulled back from the hug.

"No, I typically stay north on the island at one of the primitive backcountry campsites. It helps me focus on gathering my thoughts."

"Well . . . maybe we'll venture up that way after a day or so at Sea Camp."

"I hope so. I would love to see you both again."

Emily and Trent shared a quick kiss as they started to gather some of their personal items. They turned to make their way down to the lower level and lost sight of Liz through the other people. At this point everyone aboard was up and shuffling their way to get their gear. It was still about a half-mile hike to Sea Camp once everyone checked in at the ranger station.

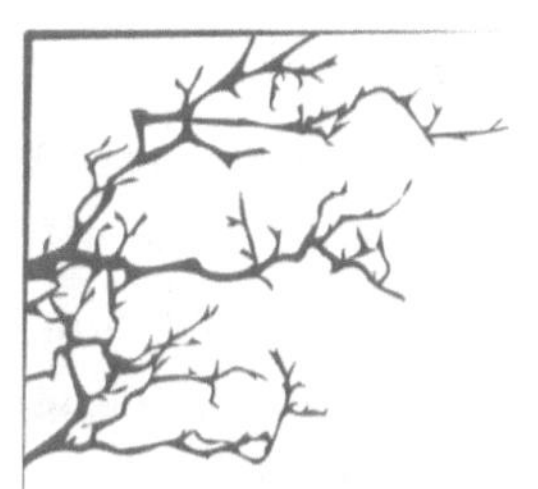

Chapter 12

Eventually, everyone made their way off of the ferry. Trent and Emily put on their backpacks, and Trent started to pull the cooler toward the ranger station. Everyone on the island was required to check in so that the rangers knew who was on the island. They liked to have a head count. Besides, the park required everyone to listen to the rules for the island. As they approached the station, they saw a group of carts lined up. They looked like rickshaws, with two long handles and wooden slats up three sides.

"What are those for?" Emily asked Trent.

"Those, my dear, are how you take your gear to Sea Camp if you don't have backpacks." Trent had seen them while researching the island for the trip. "There are no cars on the island." Emily thought that they were not much to look at, but she figured that they could get the job done.

They approached the station and noticed how welcoming it appeared. There was a painted sign that said, "Sea Camp Ranger Station." It was not what they had expected, if in fact they truly had any expectations. There was a long porch with rocking chairs for people to use while waiting for a ferry. There was even a barrel that was flipped upside down with a checkerboard on top of it. The pine smell was quite pleasant.

"Welcome to Cumberland!" A large-boned woman of about six feet tall welcomed them to the island. She was a pleasant person who appeared to be a veteran at her job. Every piece of her olive-green uniform was perfectly ironed like she just got out of some sort of military boot camp. Trent was definitely intimidated and was not planning to challenge her to an arm-wrestling contest, or a mustache-growing contest for that matter. The ranger looked like she could reach right into a patch of bushes and pull out a snake with her bare hands. She seemed very comfortable with her surroundings and had the visitor-welcome spiel down, as if she'd been doing it for thirty years. For all they knew, she had been there that long.

"If you don't mind, please sign the register over here. We want to keep the numbers straight, so we have a good idea of how many people we have on the island at any given time."

Emily pulled the thick binder and put her name down, as well as Trent's name next to hers. Trent was admiring the Native American artifacts that were in a glass case. There was everything from old pottery to arrowheads.

The ranger looked over at Trent. "We're not sure which tribes those came from, but we are pretty sure that various tribes used this island for fishing at least seasonally."

"They are beautiful moments from history, that's for sure," Trent replied.

The ranger started to gather a few others into the meeting room.

"All right everyone. If I may, I am going to show you brief introductory movie and give you each a map. You should all be on your way in about fifteen minutes."

There were about twenty others crammed into the room with Trent and Emily. No one minded since they did not want to wait for the next movie. These were the people who wanted to start enjoying the island. The movie started, offering a brief history of the island. From there, the narrator discussed the delicate nature of the island, especially during sea turtle nesting season. The overall theme was the same as any instructions that they had been given at other points in their lives. Respect the plants and animals on the island and be sure to keep a vigilant eye on campfires to avoid a wildfire.

As the movie ended, the lights came back on, and Emily was studying the map. Trent and Emily made their way back to the entrance of the station to gather their gear. Several others, who were not as prepared, stuffed all their loose belongings into the carts and started to pull them down the trail to Sea Camp. Trent and Emily started the walk as well. The ranger had assigned them a campsite.

"You folks just need to take that main path to the left, outside of the building, and follow it all the way to Sea Camp. About a half-mile down the path, you will start to see crossings where other smaller trails meet the Sea Camp path. We had all of the paths restored several years ago by taking sand that was dredged from the sea floor just off of the coast."

Emily asked, "Any Spanish gold stuck in the path from the dredging?"

The ranger laughed. "Probably not, but if you keep your eyes peeled, you might be able to find a shark's tooth or two. Every few weeks, someone finds one. No gold yet though."

They exited the ranger station and took the left down the trail. As they took each step down the trail, the sound of shells cracking and moving could be heard. It was a crisp crunching sound. The trail, or nature path as it was, had a light-brown topping of broken shells and crushed sea rocks embedded over the sandy soil beneath. Luckily, their cooler was equipped for such terrain with its oversized, hard rubber wheels. Each step and roll of the wheels from the various trail goers created a natural cadence. It was nature's musical in its purest form.

Everyone on the path slowly put distance between each other, as pairs of people veered off to side trails. Soon, Emily and Trent found themselves alone on the path. There wasn't a cloud in the sky, but the dense foliage blocked out most light. It created a nice cool breeze with much-welcomed shade. On each side of the path there were thickets of palmetto plants that fanned out with their large sturdy leaves. Above them, oak trees tangled atop the path like twisted fingers reaching out to touch the other side of the path. There was an eerie silence to this place even though there were so many others on the island. For this moment in time, it was like the island was theirs without another soul for hundreds of miles.

A few moments into the walk, they each heard some rustling in the bushes. Trent tried to ignore the sound at first by dispelling it as a small bird in the brush. But as they continued to walk, the sound got louder. Both Emily and Trent knew that this was no bird. Maybe a wild boar. It became clear that whatever was in the bushes just off of the trail was nearing them and was actually matching them step-for-step. This became somewhat unnerving. It had a clear step and was not characteristic of a smaller animal, which would have been clumsy as it struggled to form a path through the thick palmettos.

Just then, Emily put her hand on Trent's chest to stop him in his tracks. "Look over there!"

Trent's heart was in his throat at this point. "What is it?"

Before either could focus, it came out on the trail. It was beautiful. A wild horse that stood over six feet tall, even on all fours. It had gentle eyes and a dirty white mane that softly blanketed over its caramel-colored body. It gently bowed its head down to the ground to eat a patch of wild grass. It almost looked like it was welcoming the newcomers to the island. They just stood there in awe admiring the cream stripe that went down the distance of its nose. They knew that the island had feral horses, but they never expected to see one. At least not this close.

After a few minutes of eating grass, the horse slowly walked back into the dense foliage that bordered the trail. Within minutes, it disappeared, and its footsteps were muffled out by the forest. The couple continued down the path to Sea Camp. There was a sweet smell as they approached the outskirts of the campsite. There were wild lilacs everywhere, which radiated the most-inviting smell. They made the final turn on the trail, which had narrowed at the camp area. Each campsite had its own private area. There was a narrow opening off of the trail at each camp location.

Trent was tired from walking and pulling the cooler. He said with exhausted breath, "Camp fifteen, that's our site right there."

They walked through their narrow entrance way, which was marked by logs pressed against the bushes that were cleared for the site. As they walked into their site, it opened up into a huge private area. To the left there was a huge fire pit equipped with an old rusted metal grate to cook canned goods on or to boil water. Straight ahead there was a flat, clear area for a tent. The park rangers had taken special care to ensure that there were no exposed roots or bushes popping out of the ground that could poke through a tent or a sleeping bag. All around the individual site was thick brush that kept privacy for each group.

Trent immediately cracked open a couple of beers for them. They each unfolded the travel chairs that they brought with them on their backpacks. It was a relief to sit and enjoy the sounds of the birds and the wind playing through the trees. That first beer seemed to last for hours, even though it was only ten or fifteen minutes. Trent took his last sip and started unfolding the tent. It was an easy tent to put up. He simply snapped together the poles, and then slid each pole into the tent. Once he had the poles pushed across the tent, he and Emily began to place the ends into the woven ends at the corners of the base. As they placed them into the ends, the tent formed its shape. A perfect dome with an extra piece of fabric to act as a makeshift porch cover.

Emily began to unpack the dry goods from the cooler to place some in the tent. She had crackers, bread, and trail mix. She left all of the perishable foods in the cooler with the ice and cool packs. They had to make this cooler last for a week. The guy at the sports store assured her that at least two of the cool packs Emily purchased were for heavy-duty camping and could keep anything cold for at least six days. The sun was starting to drop in the sky. Emily looked at her phone. She had a couple of bars. The signal was not great, but there was at least something registering.

Emily looked at her watch. It was 3:30 p.m. The shadows off the trees seemed to confirm her watch's reading. At least this trusty old friend that she got from her parents at her college graduation would never fail her. It took about an hour to get everything set up the way that they wanted it. By this time, the sun was hanging on by a thread out over the vast Atlantic Ocean. The two began to explore the area immediately outside of their campsite. As they walked down the path that led to the beach, they came across a restroom and shower area. It was a simple but sturdy concrete structure. They explored it just to see how bad they would be roughing it for the week. It was extremely clean and seemed to have all of the essentials. Near the restrooms there were a few covered, communal picnic areas with grills that were large enough to cook half a side of beef.

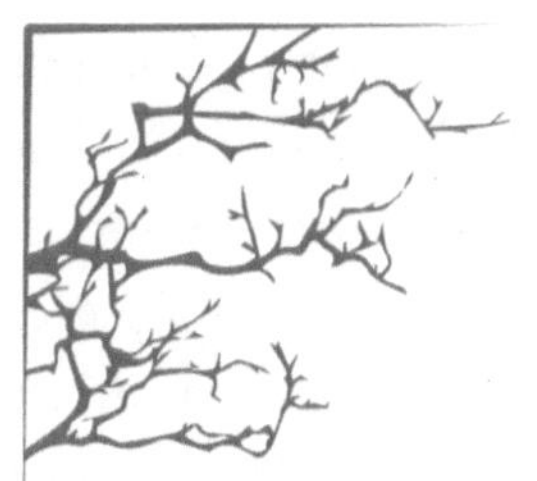

Chapter 13

They continued to trek down the trail around a bend to the beach access. By this time, the sun was slipping into the sea for its nightly rest. There were a few clouds visible in the sky that had a dazzling pink-orange hue to them. It was the type of scene that one would expect to see on a postcard trying to entice a family to the Georgia shores. They took a moment to soak in the feeling of the sea breeze and the soft, cool night scene. Soon Emily realized that the wind was beginning to pick up on the beach. Every minute or so, a fresh batch of ocean mist hit their faces as if it were coming from a quick pull of a spray bottle.

They turned and started to head back to their campsite, holding hands the whole way. The trail had no lights. Even so, they could sparsely make out the border of the trail as the night set in by the camp fires and flashlights of other campers. By the sights of the fires and flashlights, there did not appear to be many campers on the island. Finally, they reached their site. Any light from the trail quickly disappeared as they entered their own private camp area. Trent began to look around for some kindling to get a fire started. It did not take him long to find enough to get the fire going. However, in their excitement to get set up and explore, they forgot to find a couple of logs to burn for a fire.

Tonight would be cold for sure, and they needed it for food and heat. Trent put his flashlight in his pocket.

"I'm gonna track us down some firewood."

"Do you want me to go with you?"

"Nope, beautiful. I can handle it. You just start pulling out something for us to grill up." Trent was not the bravest person, but he wanted to appear to be a tough husband for his new wife. Inside, he was somewhat apprehensive about exploring the woods for pieces of firewood. He felt like a scared child, but he could not let Emily catch on to this. Emily knew that Trent was not the burly, outdoor type, but that's why she loved him. She knew that he was scared, which made her appreciate the fact even more that he was willing to go off into the dark woods by himself. She did not want the macho, brainless hunk who cut down trees with his bare hands. Lord knows there were enough of those guys throwing themselves at Emily in her early twenties. Trent had much more to offer her, and she knew it.

Trent began heading down the path away from Sea Camp to track down a log or two. The path was uneven, and each step made some sort of noise, whether from cracked shells, limestone rocks, or twigs. He knew that he needed some old, dry oak or cedar since the pine wood was not suitable for making a fire. He was wearing some old hiking boots and a tattered pair of jeans that had seen their share of outdoor adventures. The trail was silent, cold, and pitch black expect for the sliver of light that came from the flashlight. If there was to be a perfect night for a murder, this was surely it.

There was the lone sound of an owl in the distance, but nothing else. It was eerily quiet. He would have welcomed any sounds, even from a bunch of obnoxious drunks playing some word game around a nearby camp fire. He positioned his light periodically at the side of the trail in hopes of finding a piece of wood near the edge so that he could just grab and go. Finally, after about twenty minutes of searching, he found his treasure chest of wood. About twenty feet off of the trail there was a huge, half-rotten tree stump with pieces scattered all about. He started to make his way into the area. The ground was soft with the rotten leaves and mushy soil. He could not tell whether his feet were sinking into soil or whether he was following large trail of animal droppings. Trent bent over to grab a piece of what appeared to be oak or hickory. Either way, it should be suitable. He knelt and leaned the light against a tree stump. His hands were shaking from the cold, as well as his fears.

He began to reach for a thick log covered with moss. Just then, the flashlight flickered, which he found odd since he put new batteries in it only days before the trip. He picked it up and shook it. The light stayed on this time. Trent went back to rummaging for wood. At this point, there was dead silence. He noticed it because even the faint, occasional sound of the owl was gone. It was just there, and now it was gone. Nothing but cold blackness around him. The stillness was suddenly broken by the sound of footsteps coming from somewhere in front of him. He was sure that the noise was coming from the middle of the wooded area and not from the trail behind him. It sounded different than the noise from the horse he had heard earlier that day. There was no mistaking this sound. He could make out each step as it crushed down upon the pieces of fallen bark and moved the leaves covering the ground with each drag of a foot.

Trent's body went ice cold. The night air had a nip in it, but this was a new cold that he had not felt before that chilled him to the bone. He had never experienced this type of feeling before in his life. It was as if something had just passed through his body, taking every ounce of warmth from him. The flashlight flickered again for a moment, and then it died. Trent was officially terrified at this point. The only sight he could see immediately in front of him was the foggy mist that his breath was creating in the cold air. He held his breath for a minute, to not give away his location to whomever was approaching him. There was a sense of vulnerability not being able to use the most vital sense that he possessed. His eyes were useless.

The noises continued to get closer. He could not yet make out how close the person or thing was getting to him. He stood there motionless, in hopes of letting his eyes adjust with the help of the moonlight. Now the steps seemed to be within about ten feet of where he was standing. Whoever this person was had found the very location where Trent was positioned. He could sense that someone or something was watching him. The hairs on his right arm were standing straight up, as if someone had just rubbed a balloon over his arm. Then, as quick as they started, the footsteps just stopped. There was no fading of the sound, and not so much as a snapping of a twig. Just silence. The flashlight came back on, and Trent began to frantically shine it in every direction. Surely if there was an animal or person out there, he would see the culprit. There was nothing. He could not make out any fresh trails.

He grabbed the two logs he had managed to locate near his feet and got back on the trail as quickly as he could. His walk turned into a steady jog and then into a fast-paced run as he tried to get back to Sea Camp with haste. The flashlight was in his back pocket, and he carried the logs under his arms like a football player. Within minutes, he saw the familiar comforting lights of the campfires and flashlights again. Trent found camp fifteen and let out an exhale that he had been holding for several minutes. He began to rationalize what he had experienced.

Trent thought to himself, *It had to be a crane or some other large bird that was walking through the brush to find food. This island has to have large birds that can make that noise.*

"Hey babe, good looking logs." Emily was unaware of what Trent had experienced or how he was feeling at this point. She was just happy that he had returned to provide her with a warm fire. The hotter the better at this point so as to cut through the damp night.

All that Trent could muster up in response was a breathy "Thanks." His mind was too scrambled to give his typical witty comeback. He thought for sure that someone was out to find and kill him. He could not explain his feeling, but something was not right.

Over the next hour he managed to justify what he heard and experienced so that he could keep from driving himself into a frantic, nervous episode. He kept busy to keep his mind straight. First was the fire. Once the fire was going strong, he and Emily pulled out some hotdogs and some beans. The food tasted so inviting after a long day. They washed down the hotdogs with a few bottles of water. Trent dispelled the experience as being a bird or another camper foolishly looking for firewood after dark. There was something transcendent as Emily and Trent took deep breaths of the crisp air while being entertained by the full blanket of stars above.

Trent was using a stick, which he had previously fashioned into a hotdog poker, to draw circles into the soft sand next to his foot. Emily got up to head toward the restrooms.

"Do you want me to go with you?"

"Nope. I'll be ok. Just have a blanket ready when I return. You owe me some cuddle time."

"Ten-four, beautiful."

Trent watched as she faded into the darkness. He could barely make out her flashlight as she exited their camp area. He saw it for a moment as she walked down the trail, and then it went black. He could not see or hear her. He continued to poke the ground with his stick. After a few moments he went to the tent to get the old wool blanket that they had brought with them to wrap themselves in around the campfire. As he was rummaging through the tent, he heard footsteps. "Back so soon? That was quick."

There was no response, which was not like Emily, since she always had a quick, witty comeback. He jerked around and exited the tent. There was nothing around. No one could be that quick to walk right behind him and then vanish like they were never there. He nervously looked around the backside of the tent. This area was not exposed to the light from the fire, so it would be a perfect place to hide. He flashed his light around the tent, but there was nothing.

Just then he heard Emily coming back into the entrance of their camp area.

"Miss me, sexy?" Emily quickly noticed the disheveled look on Trent's face. "What's wrong?"

"I could have sworn that I heard someone coming right up behind me a few minutes ago." It was eerie.

"It was probably the natural acoustics playing tricks on you. There were several people on the trail, so as they walked by, you probably heard the noises coming in and out of the trees, which made them sound like they were right next to you."

"Yeah, you're probably right."

Trent wanted to believe Emily's theory, so it was settled. That's what he heard. They wrapped the blanket around each other and snuggled as they enjoyed the warmth of the fire. As the fire slowly faded for a night's rest, the couple retired to the tent. Trent slowly kissed Emily on her neck. Emily knew exactly what this meant. Trent was predictable when he was in the mood. He always started with the neck and then slowly caressed her in the area between the shoulder and breast. Just like clockwork. By this time, he was unbuttoning her flannel top. As they kissed, he began to forcefully run his hands through her hair and give it a tug. She liked that he was getting dominant. Within minutes, they were one sensual naked being wrapped tightly into a sleeping bag.

Emily kissed Trent on the chin and touched the tip of her tongue just below his chin and neck. Trent began kissing her ear. Emily rubbed her hand across his scruffy three-day beard. Trent's hands began to find their way across every inch of Emily's body while his lips slid their way across her neck. Tonight, there was something different about the way Trent made love to Emily. He was displaying a ruggedness about him as he used his hand to cover her mouth with each moment. This was a turn-on for Emily as she lay there letting her husband show his dominance. Any noises of nature went silent, and the only sound that each heard was the heavy breathing and occasional sensual moan. There was no sense of anything in their world except each other's needs at that moment.

After a complete climax, they both lay motionless, still locked together as one in the sleeping bag. After a few moments of touching and loving whispers, they let themselves drift away to sleep. They awoke in each other's arms. Trent slightly rolled toward Emily and began to kiss her lips.

"Good morning, beautiful."

"Good morning to you as well, sexy. I'm going to keep a few snapshots from last night in my mind for a while."

Trent smiled and kissed Emily. He started to blush. By his nature, he was somewhat embarrassed. He typically used a tiny bit of liquid encouragement to become the sexual stud that made his appearance last night. Emily knew this and actually enjoyed watching the other meeker side of Trent come out on mornings after a good night of pleasure. They slowly gathered themselves and put on their clothes from the night before, which were scatted about the tent like a scene from an erotic movie. The clothes smelled of smoke, but they didn't care.

They took some fresh clothes and walked down the path to the showers. As they passed the other campsites, they saw others slowly gathering themselves to start the day. There was one group playing beer pong or something like that. These were definitely a group of diehard partygoers. Probably old college buddies who managed to get one week a year to relive glory days with their wives, away from their kids.

They cleaned up in the showers. At least for Emily. the water felt amazing. It was not too hot, but definitely better than lukewarm. She managed to bring a small bag of essentials, which included a travel bottle of her favorite shampoo and some leave-in conditioner that she swore by to keep her hair its best. The warm shower felt like a wonderful lifetime to a couple of grungy, chilly campers. All-in-all, it lasted about fifteen minutes. Trent was dressed in his bathing suit and made his way out of his shower area. He was ready for the beach, with his old tan flip-flops and yellow board shorts with purple flowers on them.

Emily looked like she could jump right on the cover of a fashion magazine. She wore a two-piece, midnight-blue bikini with some sort of frilly edges. She had an old pair of short khaki shorts over her bikini bottom. It was from her former college days, when she dared to wear her favorite skimpy shorts around campus just to feel relaxed and sexy. Now, they were relegated to her lower dresser drawer, which was filled with beach shorts and bathing suits.

Emily gave Trent a loving slap on his asset. "Looking hot, honey!"

"Looking yummy yourself," Trent said with a wink.

They gathered their smoky clothes and their shower gear and packed them away for another day. Trent jogged over to the campsite and dumped the things next to the tent. Emily stared at the nearby trees as they danced in the wind. She also enjoyed the sound of the waves hitting the beach. She could not yet see the ocean, but she knew that it was just over the sand dunes, within about fifteen feet of where she stood. Trent was back before she knew it with their folding chairs, and a cloth mini-cooler. They were ready for a beach day and followed a path through a man-made clearing to get it started.

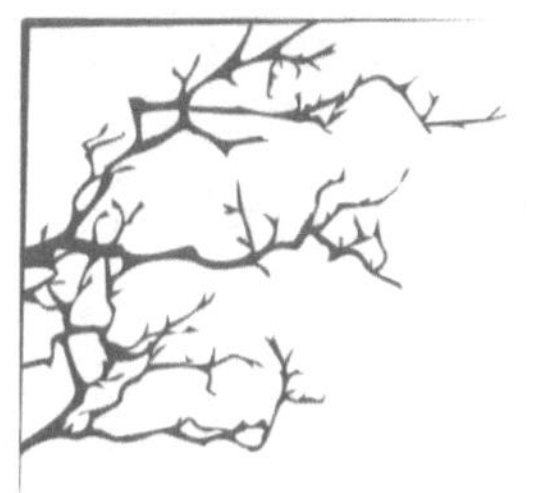

Chapter 14

As they exited the dune area, they could see it. The infinite Atlantic. There was no end of it in sight. They took a moment to soak it in and enjoy the sounds of the seagulls above, calling out as if on cue. The ocean seemed to be in a good state of mind this day with her gentle waves and deep-blue hue. The beach had only a few people wandering the shores. There was a couple reading about a hundred yards to the north. There were also a few people playing paddleball.

They found their section of sandy paradise somewhere about fifty yards to the south of the dune path. The chairs were swiftly unfolded, and the pair let their bodies draw them back into the mesh lining of the chairs. It was like a pair of masseuse hands cradling their necks and backs. Emily adjusted her chair to put it back as far as it would go so she could catch some much-desired rays from the sun. It was not a cloudless day, but they were scattered just enough to keep from getting that uncomfortably cold feeling as a cloud passes across the sun. Emily pulled out her book again to try to find any clues to solve the mystery of Jackson. She was determined, especially after hearing the riveting tale from Liz on the ferry ride over to the island. She kept going back over pages she had read before. Maybe there was a sign of some sort that she could not see before because she hadn't known the full story.

Trent just sat and gazed at the ocean. It was almost like meditation for him. He just focused on a part as far out as he could see. He occasionally closed his eyes and let his ears take over his primary senses, enjoying the sounds of the waves and sea birds. At one point there was a ship passing that caught his eye that took him out of his Zen moment.

He turned and leaned over Emily's shoulder. "Any luck finding the golden key to solving the mystery?"

"Nope, not yet, but I just know that there's something in here I—"

Before she could finish her statement, a familiar smell came across through a passing breeze. It was undoubtedly the smell of peaches. They both looked toward the direction of the smell and could see Liz strolling up the beach toward them. She was wearing a floppy straw beach hat, which had a lemon-chiffon colored ribbon just above the brim.

"You both look like you're enjoying this gorgeous day."

Trent was quick to respond. "We sure are. It's magnificent out here, almost like we have our own private island."

"I know what you mean. That's the lure that draws me to this place. Do you mind if I park my chair just down the beach from you? I want to continue my book. This spot seems to be the best place for me to think, for some reason. My mind stays clear, and I can focus my jumbled thoughts into some semblance of rationalization."

Emily chimed in, "So have you found anything else about the mystery of Jackson Jones?"

"As a matter of fact, I did find something interesting in some tattered notes that I copied from the St. Marys local archives office. During the war, there used to be a local army station toward the northern area of the island, right next to the lighthouse."

Emily provided her two cents and said, "Yeah, those were the soldiers from the Georgia State Guard and the local Home Guard you mentioned the other day, right?"

"Bingo. Apparently, during a routine weekly equipment inspection a week after Jackson disappeared, it was discovered that one of the small flatboats was missing. It was never located. There was no record of it being checked out, and to this day, it has never been located. No soldiers went AWOL. The army had to create the typical paper trail to try to determine what happened to the boat, or at least create the presumption that it had exhausted every means available before closing the file. There is an official memo signed by some private who was stationed on the island. From the looks of the paper, he was an eighteen-year-old equipment clerk. The memo is hard to make out since it appears to have been partially burned. From what I can make out, however, he reported that two officials showed up looking for the captain or lieutenant who was in charge of the company stationed on the island."

"Real life men in black, huh?" Emily's eyes were as large as a child listening to her favorite bedtime story. This mystery was growing by the minute.

"Something like that. No names, no known purpose for being on the island. From what I can tell, there is no record of them at all, which is strange considering that the army kept a pretty close eye on anyone who stepped foot on the island. That's where I am at right now with the mystery and story. I've been camping up at Halfmoon Bluff near Christmas Creek. That's near where that army station was located. Not much there anymore. Just the old guard house and some remnants of the areas fortifying the station. There has to be something up there that can provide the missing piece for me."

"Sounds like you could use some extra sleuths to help you out." Emily was ready to get her hands into whatever mystery was laying under the century-old brush. Trent was not as excited about solving any mystery, but he did have a slight interest in the story, at least in. the way that Liz could paint the picture in their minds.

"If you both want to come up, please do. The more the merrier. We can also head to the northernmost point of the island to see the old abandoned lighthouse."

Emily and Trent looked at each other and agreed in unison. "Sure, we'll stop by late tomorrow afternoon, if that's ok."

"Just follow the Bunkley Trail, and you'll see my tent. It's the ratty old blue one. I don't think there are any other campers in the backcountry, so you can't miss me."

"Tomorrow it is. I think Trent and I are going to explore the river trail near Dungeness later today."

Liz smiled, nodded, and gave a friendly wave as she made her way to her beach area to work on her book. Trent and Emily continued to chat for a few minutes before falling back into their prior activities. Emily continued to read her book like a trained detective trying to solve a cold case. Trent, meanwhile, just enjoyed his surroundings. Emily did get up a few times to cool off in the ocean. She just dipped her feet in a small channel in the sand that the waves had created. This small trench had cut off a pool of water from the rest of the sea, which gave it a refreshing, warm feel. It might have been the fact that they were on vacation or the fact that it was still the fall season, but for whatever reason, the day flew by as if it had some place else to be. Trent looked at his watch and realized that it was already two-thirty p.m. He knew that they needed to start down the river trail if they wanted to see the Dungeness ruins today.

They left their chairs and beach belongings, since they figured that no one was going to steal them. Besides, there was barely anyone on the beach to steal their stuff, anyway. The only thing Emily took was Addison's journal. She would never let that leave her side. As they headed south on the beach, they realized that Liz was gone.

"Probably headed back up to her backcountry campsite," Trent said to Emily.

"Yep, it's probably a good three miles to get back up there."

As they walked down the beach, they rarely took their eyes off of the sand below them. Emily was looking for shark teeth. Every time she thought that she had scored one, it turned out to be a broken shell or a tiny sea stone, which was polished by the constant pressure of the water washing over it. Trent, though, was fascinated with the occasional jellyfish or horseshoe crab shell that they came across. There was also some small crab variety on the island that made miniscule holes in the sand. After passing what seemed to be a hundred of these holes, Trent finally saw the small creature pop itself out.

They walked about two miles to the south of the beach. Just when their feet were about to reach their point of complaining from the hard sand, the pair saw the river trail marker. They made their way from the beach and through another set of sand dunes. They were now on at the beginning of the river trail. The sun was still shining high in the sky, but this area had a nice shade from the large cypress trees. All of the trees surrounding the trail had a blanket of moss hanging from their branches, like something that you would see on a postcard for Savannah or Charleston. It was nature's chandelier in its purest form.

The path that they followed wound in and out between wooded areas and barren, sandy fields. The sounds of nature were alive this day. Birds of all kinds were chattering high in the trees. Soon they came upon a small area surrounded by a dilapidated concrete wall, which was covered in a blue-green algae. The wall was made of large stones fashioned together in a concrete mixture. At any other time of day, this sacred area would have had a more ominous feel to it. However, with the sun as their ally, the place had an inexplicable charm. By its appearance, they could make out that it was a cemetery before they even got to the edge of wall. There was no gate, just an opening where a gate had once been. They made their way inside and noticed two raised tombs. Trent bent down to see the names. Being a history buff, he was more interested in the dates than the names. However, as he approached the second tomb, Trent's eyes widened with excitement.

He stared at the grave marker, which read SACRED TO THE MEMORY OF GEN. HENRY LEE OF VIRGINIA.

"Do you know whose tomb this is?"

"Nope. But I'm sure you're gonna enlighten me."

"It's Light Horse Harry Lee!"

"The Confederate general?"

"No, you're thinking of Robert E. Lee. This was his father, the revolutionary war hero. He was a well-known soldier for the Continental Army, and I think even served as a governor or congressman for Virginia."

"I swear, you are like having my own pocket encyclopedia on hand. When we get home, I'm putting you on one of those game shows that require useless knowledge. Is there anything that you don't know?"

Trent gently swept away some of the dirt and algae that had built up on the marker. It was his show of respect for this almost immortal soul. He could not believe how small the tomb was. It stuck out to him because he imagined that someone as famous as this historical figure would have a shrine that was fit for a tsar or king. This resting place was small by anyone's means or imagination.

"Want to hear the best part?" Trent asked with a smile.

"Uh-huh."

"His body was moved in 1913 by his son, Robert E. Lee."

"Go on."

"The Lee family wanted his body placed in Arlington, Virginia."

"So, who is in this tomb?" Emily asked.

"No one."

Once Trent had gotten over his disbelief that he was in the presence of the once resting place of an American patriot, he and Emily made their way back to the trail. At this point, the trail was right on the edge of the St. Marys River.

The path was narrow along the river. Emily started to place Addison from the night when Jackson disappeared. "This is where Jackson disappeared! It has to be!"

"Are you sure?"

"Definitely. The dock for the ferry is only about a half-mile or so ahead. Look around. This is the kind of place where a person can get pulled into the forest without a sound. Trent felt the same kind of chill that he experienced the other night while looking for firewood on the trail. There was something ominous about standing in the same spot where someone vanished into the abyss. He played down his fear and joked with Emily.

"Well, if I disappear, you'd better start looking immediately and not hide behind some tree or rock. I don't want to end up lost and forgotten in some old diary that you write."

"They'd probably let you go once you start babbling about your random historical knowledge." Emily knew how to make even a moment like this lighthearted.

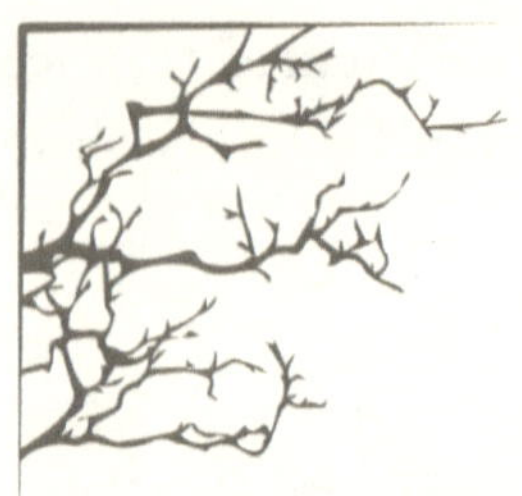

Chapter 15

They continued to twist and wind with the trail. The paths through the island were imperfectly perfect, as if an artist were commissioned to paint and clear abstract paths with her hands. There were the occasional squirrels and some small animals that paid no attention to the newcomers walking on their island. After about ten minutes, they finally came to the clearing where it appeared. The Dungeness ruins came into sight like a majestic castle. It was a shell of what stood in the past. It burned down in the 1950s. The rumor was that it was arson. Now, all that remained was the massive foundation with all the brick chimneys still reaching for the sky. In Emily's mind, she saw the proud majestic centerpiece of the island in all of its splendor, as if time had not chipped away at its face.

They approached it and imagined it back when the Carnegies hosted parties there. Emily immediately felt a connection to this place, as for at least a moment she could picture Addison walking into this place holding the arm of her one true love. She saw the walls with ornate furnishings. There was music playing and a grand party in her version. Addison was smiling, still unaware of what horror would transpire in just hours. Jackson was in a happy bliss as well, his future still ahead of him.

Then, with a blink, the image was gone, as if he never existed. The setting sun again outlined the skeleton of the mansion. They realized that it was getting late, and Dungeness was preparing for the night. Trent tugged at Emily.

"Come on babe. We can come back tomorrow, but we need to get back to the beach to get our chairs and stuff. The sun will be down soon."

"You're right. Let's get back."

They started to follow the same twisting path that had led them to the ruins. Within a few minutes, Emily had a sense that someone was watching them. She turned to look back at the ruins, and the shadows from the trees were playing tricks on Emily's eyes. She could have sworn that she saw the figure of a man standing on the second floor of Dungeness. She knew that this wasn't possible since the floor was burned in the fire. She quickly closed her eyes and refocused. As soon as she did, the figure was gone. She did not tell Trent, since she was obviously letting her mind have some fun with her. There was no way anyone could have been where she saw it. They would have to have been standing on a floor that did not exist anymore.

They made their way past the cemetery, which at this point was not quite as inviting as it was with the sun's full light. It had a different feeling for both of them, although neither would admit it out loud. The bend back to the beach could not have gotten there quick enough. It took about another ten minutes before they finally reached the turn for the beach. As they turned, they could see the opening between the dunes. Their minds were at ease with the thought of having the narrow woods behind them for the openness of the beach. The light on the beach was scarce, since the sun was almost completely beneath the horizon at this point. The moon did provide some comforting light. However, not as much as the sun.

They walked briskly up the beach, making small talk along the way to put each other at ease. Neither wanted to admit that there was something wrong. They were about a mile from their chairs when they heard a scream. They could not tell whether it was human or whether it was some animal or another camper fooling around. They did know one thing. It came from behind them. They both looked back at the same spot at the same time. It was the spot just through the dunes near the cemetery.

"What was that?" Emily was visibly shaken.

"Beats me. Don't worry. It was probably some animal." Trent knew full well that it was not, but he had to keep up a strong façade for his wife. There was nothing visible behind them. No one running up the beach. They kept a fast pace. Not a run, but about as close as you could get without actually getting into a full jog. Finally, after what felt like six hours, they reached their beach chairs. They grabbed their gear and made their way back through the familiar sand dune opening to the Sea Camp.

"What's for dinner?" Emily was trying to lighten the mood and change the subject.

"Let's see, hotdogs or . . . oh yes, hotdogs." Trent's mind was still running that scream like a movie replay. However, he knew that they had to dismiss it, or it would drive them nuts. Besides, they were back in comforting surroundings with the other campers. They could hear all of the others talking around the various campfires and see the flashlights walking up and down the trails. They both made their own internal promises to themselves that they would forget that bloodcurdling scream and chalk it off as nature's way of spooking the island's visitors.

Tired and hungry, they made their way back to their camp area. There was little light penetrating through the trees, so they could hardly see anything. Trent found his way to the tent and grabbed the flashlight. With a click, they had light. Trent also lit a small, battery-powered camping lantern that he brought with them on the trip. Emily rummaged through the cooler to get some hotdogs to cook on the fire. Neither of them noticed that their camping backpacks had been moved to the other side of the campsite, as if someone were snooping through their things.

Soon Trent had the camp fire burning full blaze. The warmth of the fire felt inviting to both of them after the walk up the beach and back to the campsite through the cold, night air. It felt warmer this evening than it did the night before. Trent and Emily enjoyed the charred taste of their hotdogs. They also ripped open a bag of potato chips. The salt and vinegar from the chips seemed to complement the taste of the hotdogs burned over an open fire. This was the most elegant meal that they had had today. All that was missing was a Solo cup filled with cheap box wine.

Trent slowly pushed his tired legs out of his chair, and he snuck away to the tent while Emily was starting to doze off from the sounds of the crackling and popping fire. He reached into a small bag that he had brought with him. Soon he was back by Emily's side. She leaned over and grabbed his arm. He gave her a kiss and then tenderly opened her hand. He rubbed her palm with his forefinger. She melted into his shoulder and let her body lean against his. Just then, Trent gave her a long, passionate kiss. This was one for the books. Her eyes were closed, and she was unaware of anything at that moment except for the softness of his lips. As she opened her eyes, she realized that Trent had slipped something into her hand.

Emily looked down and noticed a beautiful necklace in her hand. It was one of the necklaces from the old shop in St. Augustine. She used her thumb to feel the curves and markings on the old Spanish coin. The coin was a dull, European silver, which was cradled by a polished silver ring to hold it in place and attach it to the necklace.

"I love it! And I love you!"

Trent did not say anything. He just leaned in, and the two began to kiss as if they were going for the Oscar for best on-screen kiss. Soon, they were on a blanket in front of the fire rolling around like a couple of college coeds on a weekend getaway. Emily sat up and pulled Trent toward her. They pulled a blanket over them, and soon they were enjoying each curve and feel of the other's naked bodies. There was something about the possibility of someone walking up on them that made this more intense for Emily. They could not care less about the occasional stick that they rolled over with each passionate-filled moment. It was nature and sex in its unalloyed form. It did not matter whether they were penniless on a floor or millionaires in some fancy hotel. This type of animalistic passion transcended everything else that man could create.

They lay there for about a half an hour until the fire had dwindled down to nothing more than a few embers trying to hold on with each passing breeze. They soon retired to the tent and held each other tight in the sleeping bag. It took no time at all for them to fall asleep. Trent awoke hours later to the sound of footsteps outside of the tent. At first, he thought that Emily must have gotten up for something. He moved his arm and immediately realized that she was out like a light next to him. He looked down at his watch and could make out that it was three a.m. Now, he was concerned.

He thought to himself, *Who is stalking around the tent? Is it an animal or a human*? He did not want to wake Emily since he did not want to frighten her, and he did not want her to make any noises to alert whomever or whatever was outside of the tent that they were awake. He slowly pulled his arm from next to Emily and then quietly slinked over to get his camping knife. Not that he had special-forces skills with a knife, but he wanted to have something to be safe. He grabbed the flashlight. He did not turn it on yet. He just lay there staring at the walls of the tent.

The moon was full that night, so there was some light shining through the tent. Just as his eyes were about to adjust, he saw it. On the backside of the tent there was a shadow of a person. Not a large person, but a person. He was sure of it. Whatever it was, it was moving around, so the silhouette kept fading and then getting more precise as the figure got right up to the tent. Trent about lost his breath when he realized that the person's face was pressed against the tent. The wall of the tent was slightly pushed in from the pressure. Then, he saw a hand press into the tent like someone was trying to reach through the fabric to grab him. The hand slowly worked its way down the tent as Trent watch four distinct fingers drag their way toward the bottom. The sound was almost worse than the sight. He could hear the nails scrapping the fabric of the tent as the hand moved its way down the side.

He knew that he had to protect Emily, so he leaped up and quickly unzipped the door. As if a crazy man, he flew out of the tent with his knife poised up and out. He flashed the light to the side of the tent where the person was and lunged into the area. His heart was pounding like it was already out of his chest. He had no idea what he would do if confronted. As soon as he clicked on the flashlight, it died. Trent could not believe it. He had personally checked this flashlight and even replaced the batteries to be safe. Luckily for him, the moon provided a natural bright light for the open camp area. There were no further sounds. His analytical brain could not comprehend how someone could get away so fast. They would have had to run around from the backside of the tent that was facing the woods and then go a good twenty feet to make out of the campsite entrance. Every other area was covered with palmettos and prickly thorns. Within a few minutes, the light came back on. He flashed the light into the woods, but there was no sign of any fresh path from an intruder.

There was no way possible that someone could run that fast, and certainly Trent would have heard the sounds of the footsteps leaving the area. It was as if whoever was watching them had simply floated away on a bed of mist. Emily had emerged from the tent.

"What's going on? Did you hear something?"

"Not sure. I swore that I saw someone outside of our tent, and when I came out to check, there was nothing."

"Are you sure you weren't dreaming it or sleepwalking or something?"

"No. I am positive that I saw someone."

They both continued to look around the tent area. It could have been a drunk camper from a neighboring site who got disoriented and thought that this was their camp. That still didn't explain how the intruder just disappeared. Emily saw an impression of a face that was smack on the side of the tent, as if someone had been pressed against it. She knew for certain what this was. Her mind was not playing tricks on her. The morning dew was unmistakably gone from one area in the shape of a face.

Emily was distraught from this revelation. She looked at Trent and said, "Well, whoever it was is gone now, and it doesn't look like anything has been taken."

"Yeah, I guess, but this is really strange." Trent was struggling to make sense of it.

Emily kissed his cheek. "At least we'll be at the backcountry site tomorrow night." Trent's recitation of what had just happened, along with her own discovery, clearly frightened Emily, but she knew that showing her fear would not help the situation.

Trent was comforted by the thought of changing locations, even if just for a night or two. Either way, he was not falling asleep in the tent tonight. He started the fire back up, and he and Emily fell asleep next to the fire on the old blankets that they had on the ground. This way, he could see whatever was coming.

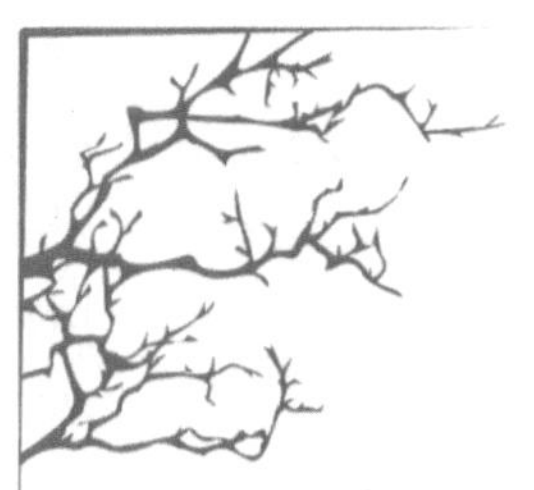

Chapter 16

The next day came early. They awoke to a cold frost over the ground, which made the blades of grass stand straight up like icicles. The campfire was still burning, with a few small flames fighting for survival. By this time, it was more smoke than fire, and it was offering no comfort as they shivered under the plaid wool blanket. They jumped up and inspected every inch of the camp area. Nothing appeared to be out of place. The sun was just clearing the horizon. It was like an old friend coming back to take away the blackness that had consumed the island only hours earlier. It was a stunning scene as the soft shade of amber highlighted the fresh dew on the treetop.

Emily's mind raced with an emotion somewhere between the polar extremes of fear and stimulation. She wanted to continue to explore the island and see the areas to the north near the backcountry. For reasons unknown to her, she could sense that something was happening, and she knew that Jackson's disappearance was at the root of it. It was a feeling that she had, and her instincts were seldom wrong. She convinced Trent to hike down some of the nearby trails to finish checking out the Dungeness ruins, with the goal of having lunch at the beach on their way back. Trent was all for it at this point since he wanted to see what was around the trails that were near their campsite. Now that he could see, he wanted to search for any fresh clearings in the woods.

"If we're going to do this, we might as well pack up the tent and most of our stuff so that we can just hike to the backcountry after lunch."

Emily agreed. "Good point."

As Trent began taking down the tent, he saw it. The tent was still wet with the morning dew, and there was no mistaking the finger impressions on the tent. His knees went weak. Still, he just rationalized it as being a drunk neighbor who got lost on the way back from a late-night stop to the restroom. Surely it had to be a lost camper who realized her mistake and scuttled off to avoid the embarrassment. He placed his hand over the imprint at the top of the impression just above the dragging marks. The hand was larger than his hand, so he deduced that it had to be a drunk man. There were plenty of guys camping adjacent to Trent and Emily's site. The other day, he noticed all of the beer cans strewn everywhere and the remnants of drinking games. That's what it was. A group of hearty, non-threatening partygoers.

It took them about twenty minutes. They managed to get their tent and sleeping bags rolled up tight. They packed everything into their backpacks. The cooler was too much to drag miles around the island. They tucked it away toward the back corner of the site with a few miscellaneous items that they did not want to pack up just yet. They figured that they would be back to this site in two days to finish out their trip.

They packed a lunch and made sure to pack extra water bottles. They walked past the other campsites, and there was no movement anywhere. They peered into the sites as they walked past, and they noticed the typical early-morning scenes. Beer cans on the ground with the smell of burned fire wood from fires that had gone out just a few hours earlier. One site had what had to be fifty assorted beer cans stacked in a perfect pyramid. Before they knew it, they reached the turn from the Sea Camp toward the ranger station. There was a quarter-mile hike to reach the fork in the paths. As they walked, they saw a few cinnamon-colored, speckled quails. The island was waking up with each chirp and each sound of shuffling leaves from squirrels.

Soon they reached the fork. They turned to the left trail and saw the morning fog still blanketing the trail. The sun was still making its way through the trees, and it had not reached this area of the island yet. There weren't as many sounds on this trail.

Emily gently jerked her hips toward Trent to hit his side, and she said, "Isn't this the part of the movie where the fog sucks us into the abyss?"

Trent laughed, albeit with a little hesitation. "Nope. That's just for those fools in the movies who try to run from the fog and always trip over nothing the entire time that they are running. The fog probably wouldn't even know you were there if you just stayed put."

"Good point. I doubt the fog would get a couple of idiots who voluntarily walk right into it." Emily knew that on certain things she could never one-up Trent. His imagination was too strong. Emily's mission in life, however, was to find a way to beat Trent at his own game by the time that they were sitting in rocking chairs outside some retirement home in rural South Carolina. As crazy as it was, she had already planned where she and Trent would spend their golden days. Emily's grandparents on her mother's side lived in a beautiful but modest retirement community just outside of Spartanburg, South Carolina. It had the scenic beauty that Emily enjoyed and was only a ten-minute drive from Cowpens Battle Field, which she knew would lock the deal for Trent.

A couple of minutes later, Emily was looking down the path to see if she could make out the Dungeness ruins. She couldn't make out the remains of the mansion, but something was at the end of the trail.

"Do you see that, Trent?"

"Where?"

"Just off to the right, over there on the trail?"

Trent focused, and he noticed something. It looked like a woman standing on the edge of the trail. With the fog, they could barely make out any features.

"She must be a fool who gets up early to hike and walks into the creepy fog, like us."

Emily smiled, but there was something she could not make out about the person. As they got closer, the person did not get any clearer. They could see the long hair but could not make out any hair color or features. Then, she was gone. It was as if she just turned and walked down an adjacent path. They reached the point where the woman was standing, and there were no paths. In fact, the brush was so thick that there was no place to enter the woods. They both stopped and looked into the area just off of the path to see if there was any sign of a fresh trail, but there was nothing.

"What the heck was that?"

Trent looked white. "Beats me? This is starting to get really weird. My vote is that we make our way to the beach as quick as we can. I'm not really excited about exploring some old mansion that may be occupied by some residents who don't know that they don't live there anymore."

Emily, who was typically brave, agreed. "Let's just check it out quickly, and then we can make our way back to the beach for some sun and sanity." Emily had dismissed Trent's early sightings as being something from his lively imagination. With this recent experience, however, Emily could not ignore what was happening. They were in the presence of something that was not human, at least not anymore. This was unnerving to Emily, who always tried to find a rationalization to every mystery.

As they passed the place where the woman disappeared, they each independently looked back periodically, as if to be sure that someone was not following them. They turned at different times so that the other would not see. Each had the same instincts and emotions, but there was still that pride of not being a paranoid coward.

They finally reached Dungeness. They looked around, but neither had a deep desire to explore with the same level that they did the day before. They began to make their way down the river trail, and then noticed someone else quickly coming toward them.

"Is this the morning of mysterious shadow figures or what?"

Trent grabbed Emily's hand. "Hold on. No, that's a ranger."

"Hey folks." They immediately realized that it was the ranger who they met when they got to the island. "How's the trip going?"

Emily replied, "It's been great, but we just saw someone disappear on the trail over there."

"Let me guess, you saw a woman on the trail, and when you got close, she was gone."

"Yes!" Trent shouted.

"That's what several other campers have reported over the years. It seems to be getting more active as the years pass. Heck, it could just be that I am becoming more aware of it as I age with this island."

"Maybe we just saw you walking the trail?" Trent said.

"Wasn't me. I have a small boat that I use to patrol the island. My boat is docked just past those trees over there on the south end of the river trail. The ranger pointed in the opposite direction from where they saw the apparition. Anyway, before I forget, I'm glad I ran into you both. Xavier has turned into a category two hurricane. It should pass by the island, but we may be closing the island in three days if it makes a turn too close to us. It's still going pretty slow, so there is no immediate risk. We will post signs at every camp area if we need to close the island. Just keep your phones handy. We have a head count of the number of people on the island, so we can double check to be sure everyone get off safely."

"So, we just call the number for the ranger station?" Trent wanted to be prepared.

"Yep. If you want, I would go ahead and program it in your phone now while you have a chance."

The ranger gave Trent the number and he imputed into his phone under "Emergency."

"Well . . . enjoy the day, looks like it's going to be a nice one."

Emily gave a wave and said, "Thanks."

They explored a few of the older buildings around Dungeness. These were the old quarters that were used by servants and various others over the years. Now they were mere remnants of their youth. Shells of old wood with rusty peg nails. Not much to look at, but historically they were beautiful moments of time that survived storms and the destructions of men.

By now, it was around eleven o'clock in the morning. Emily pressed forward like a general leading her troops, and Trent followed his orders.

"Onward, babe. Let's get to the beach," Emily said with a determined voice.

"Ten-four, beautiful."

They started to make their way past the cemetery that they had just visited the day before. There was something that drew Emily to this place. Nothing that she could put her finger on, no specific noise or anything like that, just a sense. It wasn't a good sense either. This place gave her an unsettled feeling. Just as they passed by the perimeter of the old walls, there was a loud thud. It sounded like something fell over about twenty feet from them. They stopped for a second to listen, hoping it was just an old, water-soaked log finally giving in after years of fighting to stay upright.

After about twenty seconds of silence there was another sound. It was someone walking through the woods. There was nothing mistaking the sound of feet and hands pressing their way through the thick brush. They looked in the direction of the sound, but there was nothing. They could not even make out any bushes moving.

They both looked at each other with odd disbelief. The person had to be within a few feet of them by now, but there was nothing. Then, without warning, a bloodcurdling scream blared out. Emily and Trent froze. It was the same sound that they heard the other day, but this was all around them now. It came from every direction, but there was nothing anywhere, just trees and forest.

After what seemed like five minutes of non-stop screaming, it was just gone.

"What was that?" Emily was visibly shaken.

"I'm not sure, but we're not sticking around to find out!" Trent grabbed Emily's arm and guided her down the path toward the beach access. Within minutes, they reached the familiar site of the beach access. The sun was bright, and the beach was empty except for a couple of sunbathers up the beach. They made their way up the beach about three hundred yards just to put some distance between themselves and the cemetery. They were exhausted, both physically and emotionally. Trent just dropped his backpack onto the sand. Emily unsnapped her harness and gently set it next to Trent's gear. They fell onto the beach and looked up to the sky to focus. They did not speak, just let their bodies sink into the soft, warm sand.

Emily scanned the sky above. It was remarkable, as if it were alive. There were bright white, fluffy cumulonimbus clouds everywhere. Each had soft, dark shading outlining the edges, making them look like pieces of popcorn to Emily. She imagined that they were popping right in front of her eyes. In her peripheral vision, she also caught an isolated off-shore storm that appeared to be at least five miles out over the Atlantic. There was a clear line where she could see the rain streaks in contrast to a perfect blue sky next to the storm. It was as if an artist had taken a broad paint brush and had made one swipe of the wrist in the sky.

After a few minutes, both Emily and Trent began to focus on something coming up the coast from the south. It was a pair of kayakers in a two-person kayak. It was bright orange and had some camping gear tied to the middle of it in between the paddlers.

"That looks like fun." Emily said, trying to take their minds off of the morning's weird events. "I wonder where they came from?"

"Probably from the Ft. Clinch area on the Florida side of the St. Marys River. Man, they are crazy."

"Why do you say that?"

"That's open water with bull sharks and an occasional great white. Those kayaks look like tasty fish to a hungry shark. It wouldn't eat them whole, but it would take a massive bite before it realized that the kayakers weren't fish."

Within minutes, they were up on the beach. There was a young brunette woman, probably in her early thirties, and a blond male of the same age range. Their fascination with watching the paddling duo take each stroke in unison to beat past the current and waves running parallel to the island made Trent and Emily almost forgot the unexplainable events from earlier in the morning. Even though Trent would never do it, he did have a healthy respect for those who put all caution to the wind to endeavor on brave adventures like that. He sometimes wished that he possessed a more reckless gene in order to do things like that occasionally.

Emily thought to herself that the kayakers were definitely not novices. They had their gear tightly stowed for the trip and landed the vessel on the shore like they were in some sort of race. The blond was making his toward Emily and Trent as he dragged the kayak. Soon he was within about ten feet of the pair.

"Hi there. Sorry to encroach upon your space here. This is a great spot to store our kayak up on the dunes over there." The man pointed to a space about twenty feet behind where Emily and Trent were lounging.

"No problem at all," Trent said.

"I'm gonna get this beast tucked away up on the dune, and then if you don't mind, my girlfriend and I will have a drink with you."

"Sure," Emily replied.

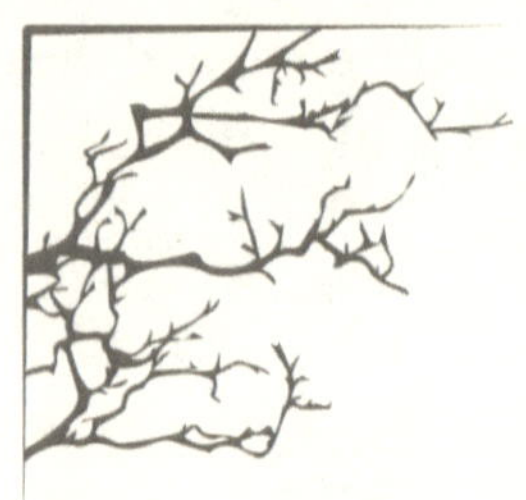

Chapter 17

As the blond man finished placing the kayak behind the dune, his girlfriend came up to Emily and Trent. She was a beautiful woman with olive-colored skin. Her dark tan told a story of a person who loved to be outdoors. She took her off her sunglasses, which allowed the light to hit her emerald green eyes. She smelled of coconut tanning oil.

"Hi, my name's Amanda. My boyfriend over there is Dan. Sorry to crash your party over here." Dan was a tall man who obviously worked out and kept himself in good shape.

"Don't be silly," Emily responded. "We always enjoy meeting new people." Emily truly did like to meet new people and was not just being polite. She always believed in her heart that people were brought together for some reason, and she enjoyed every chance meeting and adventure, whether it was something like this or simply chatting with a stranger on a park bench while letting her dogs play at a local dog park. There was a moment of solitary dissolution that came with each new person who Emily came across during her adventure of life. She figured that she would learn and gain something special from each person, and for the most part, she was right. Even the most trivial information or other mundane conversations with strangers always seemed to provide some piece to the puzzle of her life, even if it wasn't for years down the road. This was Emily's mantra of existence ever since she had her first bout of depression. Every day that the sun was shining and God gave her an opportunity to meet someone new was a defining day as far as she was concerned.

Trent was fixated on the kayakers, and he was curious where the pair had paddled from. "So . . . where did you shove off from to get here?"

"Amelia Island, just near Ft. Clinch."

Trent smiled at Emily as if to say, "I told you so" without actually saying anything.

By this time, Dan had made his way to the others. Emily noticed that he had several tattoos down his forearms. He seemed to be a blue-collar guy who enjoyed the free time that the weekends offered him. As he approached closer, Emily could see the calluses on his hands and the tiny wrinkles that the sun had prematurely placed upon his face. She had no doubt that Dan was a roofer or a landscaper. It made no difference. White collar, blue collar, no collar, she could not care less. People were people so far as she was concerned. This was just another spice in the mixture of life.

"Hey, thanks again for letting us post up here for a while," Dan said to Emily and Trent.

He reached into a small cooler that he pulled from the kayak and pulled out some fruity concoction. It looked like an orange or peach mixture of some sort.

"You want to try my tropical creation? It's delicious, if I do say so myself. It took me a couple of years to perfect."

"Really?" Trent asked as if he was impressed by the conviction of a man who would spend so much time working on the perfect beverage.

"Nope, I'm just pulling your leg," Dan responded with a laugh.

"What's in it?" Trent asked.

"A splash of raspberry vodka with tangerine juice and schnapps. Not too strong, just a little victory drink that Amanda and I partake in after a few hours of hard-core kayaking."

"Poor them up!" Emily exclaimed. She was ready for a drink or two or three after her recent experiences. Her mind was still trying to wander back to her ghostly encounter, and she welcomed a sun-filled day with drinks. This was her honeymoon, and she did not want to spend it fearing everything that lurked in the shadows of the woods.

The four sat back and enjoyed their drinks against the perfect tropical setting. There was nothing in front of their chairs except for the endless Atlantic Ocean. To their right off in the peripheral vision sat Ft. Clinch marking the northernmost reach of the Florida coast. Emily closed her eyes for a split second just to listen to the waves crashing and lapping on the soft white sand. This was the same sound that this island had made during Addison's time here. The conversation flowed between the four new friends like they were old college buddies who knew each other for years. As it turned out, Dan was a computer programmer for a large investment firm in Jacksonville, and Amanda was an emergency-room nurse practitioner. They were high school sweethearts who managed to find love and make it last through a couple of short-term breakups along the way.

Emily, being the darling nosey busybody that she was, had to let Dan know that she was way off on her prediction of what Dan did for living. "Dan, I have to say, I had you pegged for a roofer or someone who worked outside with as tan as you are?"

"Nope, but that's funny. I actually get that a lot. I think it's because I have a side business refurbishing old furniture. It started as a hobby, but now I'm actually making enough to make it a legitimate part-time gig. I do all of my work in my backyard, hence the worn hands and deep tan."

After a couple of hours of great conversation, Dan realized that he needed to secure a campsite.

"Sorry to be rude, but we need to get moving, or at least I do, to get us a campsite. I need to check in at the ranger camp. They're pretty strict over here about making sure that no one is trying to get a free ride when others are paying to stay and play."

Emily looked at Trent, and they had the same idea as if two light bulbs turned on just above their heads in unison.

Emily said, "Why don't you guys save at least a couple days' worth of fees and just stay at our campsite? We're heading up to backcountry for a couple of days."

"Are you sure?" Amanda asked.

"Positive. It's yours until we get back in two days."

Trent agreed. "Yes, mi casa es su casa."

Amanda, whose parents were Cuban, was fluent in Spanish, so she followed up with a humorous comment in her parents' native tongue.

Trent laughed. "Sorry, that's all I have. My Spanish is tapped out. To be honest, I'm not even positive that what I said was correct."

Amanda winked at Trent to acknowledge that Trent was correct in what he said. Emily almost spat out her drink and just about fell out of her chair from laughing so hard at Trent.

Trent gave Dan and Amanda the camp number and pointed out the direction. After some more guffaws and fact-finding by all as to their new friends, the couples parted ways. Neither Emily nor Trent felt the necessity to let Dan and Amanda know what they had experienced in the camp the night before or earlier in the day. It wasn't that they had some ulterior motive, they just wanted to forget about it. In addition to that, there was absolutely no need to spook these new arrivals to the island. Nothing positive could come from placing an unknown fear in the psyche of the kayakers. Even if Emily or Trent wanted to say something, what in the heck would they have even said, "Hey, we've been seeing and hearing ghosts for the past two days." That would undoubtedly go down like a lead balloon.

Emily and Trent finished lunch. Emily had a ham sandwich with a crisp slice of lettuce, and Trent polished off a plain turkey on rye. They each took some needed gulps from a water bottle to rehydrate. After lunch, they started making their way up the beach toward the backcountry camp area. Trent pulled out his map of the island just to verify where the beach entrance was to get to the trail that Liz had mentioned. The map was wet from Trent's sweat since he had it tucked in his back pocket all day. It didn't matter though. It would still serve its purpose.

They walked for about thirty minutes. The sand on this part of the beach felt hard, and it began to wear on their feet. It felt like walking on a concrete sidewalk as opposed to a soft, squishy beach. Finally, Trent recognized the entrance for the trail by the markings.

"There it is," Trent said with tired but excited breath.

Emily read the trail sign. "Roller Coaster Trail?" she asked Trent. Neither she nor Trent could figure out why someone would name it that, but they didn't care. It was one step closer to their destination.

"Yep. Let's get on the ride!" Trent's humor still needed work, but Emily was amused, and that was all that he cared about.

They started to walk up the trail that wound in and out parallel to the beach. They continued up the trail for another hour. This was by far the longest stretch of walking that they had made on the island thus far. It was about five in the afternoon at this point. The trees seemed thicker in this area, and the light was having difficulty piercing through the old oak trees. After another ten minutes of walking, they came up on a tent, which they knew had to be Liz's camp since there was no one else as far as they could see. Trent looked at the map.

"This is Half Moon Bluff. We're finally here."

Emily headed toward the tent and called out, "Liz, are you there?"

There was no response.

"Liz?" Trent called out.

Still nothing.

They set down their gear and walked the perimeter of the place to see if Liz was gathering firewood or hiking a nearby trail. Without snooping too much, they briefly looked through the backpack on the ground. In it they saw that distinctive necklace that Liz was wearing on the ferry. There was not much else in the way of food or supplies.

"Liz sure does pack light."

Emily responded with a crafty smile, "She probably keeps it minimal since it's just her toting the stuff across the island. She doesn't have a big strong man like I do."

She waited for some form of response from Trent, but he seemed preoccupied with the sky.

"What's the matter? What are you thinking about?"

"Listen." Trent said.

"Listen to what . . . I don't hear anything."

"Exactly. Just hours ago, there were sounds all over this island. Now, there's nothing. No birds. No rustling."

As if on cue, a flock of black birds came rushing by just above their heads. Then, minutes later, several other random birds made their way north of the island. Neither of them was by any means an expert with wildlife; however, they both knew that something wasn't right. These birds were fleeing the island for some reason.

By this time, the weather was turning for the worse. Emily could not hide her typical strong demeanor as she looked at Trent. They both knew that this was not just a typical fall storm. This was much stronger. The type of winds that hinted of a hurricane somewhere, rising above the edge of the horizon. Just then, an old oak, which had probably battled for years against the Atlantic's temperamental nature, came crashing down over the trail. Several large branches shattered completely, blocking access to the trail. It was as if some divine event was preventing them from turning back or making a belated attempt to keep the pair from venturing farther into the unknown forest ahead.

There was still no sign of Liz. Trent knew from looking at the map earlier that the old guard station and lighthouse were only a hundred yards ahead on the trail. Emily and Trent dropped their backpacks and just took a few items to make it through the night in case they didn't make it back to camp until morning. By this time, a heavy wave of rain came from nowhere and began pelting them. They each grabbed a travel poncho, which provided little salvation from the beating that Mother Nature was unleashing. It was that eerie, driving type of rain that came before the worst of the storm hit. Each raindrop felt like a soft punch as it landed on their bodies. Trent took Emily's hand, and the pair quickly made their way north on the trail. They knew that needed a more secure shelter than their tent could provide. Besides, it was doubtful that they could even get one of the tents pitched in the face of this wind.

They could hardly see anything. The sky at this point had a light hue of yellowish-green, even though it was pitch black all across the forest around them. Emily could not put logic to this. It was as if the sky and forest were in conflict. One was as bright as an early dawn, while the other was as cold and dark as any nightmare she had experienced as a child. Finally, after what seemed like thirty minutes, Emily saw the shadow of the guard station ahead of them.

"Look! Do you see it? That's got to be the guard house."

"Yeah, that's the abandoned army guard station all right," Trent replied.

It wasn't much of a structure, but it had a roof and appeared to have intact walls. It was an old wooden two-story station with sleeping quarters on the second level. Emily and Trent fought the winds that were now blowing directly at them. Trent pulled Emily onto the guard station's porch. It appeared that this piece of history had not been touched by human hands since the last guardsman left his post when the station was decommissioned. Each board creaked with every step. Several had signs of termite damage. Just as Emily went to make her way into the musty old structure, her foot crashed through a board.

"Are you ok?" Trent asked as he pulled her up.

"I think so."

She fell through, almost a foot down on the raised porch. As Emily looked down at her leg, she noticed a gash. Trent shined his flashlight on the wound.

"It's deep," Trent said with a squeamish glance. He did not like the sight of blood.

"Think I need to get stitches?"

"No, I think we can wrap a piece of cloth around it to keep it from bleeding out. It should heal fine since it's got a clean cut-line. Almost like a paper cut on steroids."

Emily was not amused with Trent's joke this time. Trent tore off a piece of his undershirt and tied it to Emily's leg.

"Let's get you inside." Emily was not as repulsed by the sight of blood. She took over and made sure that the makeshift bandage was tight.

They pushed through the old door without much effort. It seemed to swing open with the mere presence of the two, as if someone or something was just waiting to let them in. Trent used all of this force to push the door closed against the will of the wind that was traveling through the doorway like a freight train. He finally got it shut and used the old wooden latching system to keep it locked.

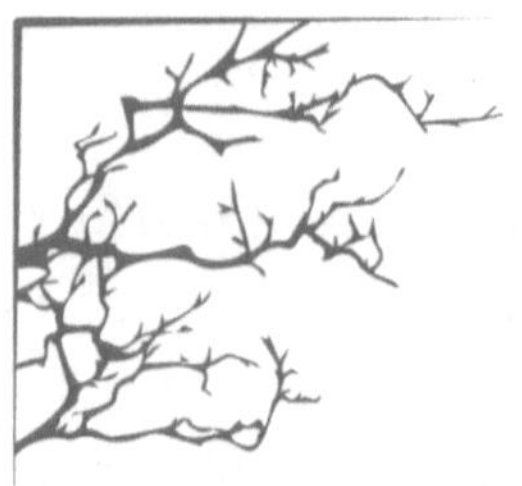

Chapter 18

As soon as the door was shut, both Emily and Trent had the unsettling realization that they had not even bothered to check the area before sealing themselves into it like a tomb. Trent quickly turned on his flashlight and frantically began scanning the area for signs of any animals or other unspeakable myths, which his mind was creating with each second. After several minutes, the two realized that they were alone in the building. It was comforting, yet still offered little in the way of easing all of their fears of the unknown. Something still did not feel right about this place—or their situation in general. The sound of the wind against the fragile wood shakes that lined the walls and roof of the guard station sounded like a massive supernatural creature clawing to get its way to the pair. Emily began exploring this capsule of history to keep her mind off of the unnatural sounds that were coming from outside.

She knew that she and Trent were safe from the storm, at least for a while.

Trent found a few pieces of old floor boards that were just dry enough to place in an old, half-collapsed fire place. He struck a match and got the wood to catch. He found a few other dry pieces of cloth and old pieces of paper to keep the blaze as hot as possible. Emily explored a corner and found what appeared to be an old footlocker. It seemed to have remained untouched for years. Emily figured that it was because it blended perfectly with the wall structure, so it could easily go unnoticed. She pried open the old brass buckle-lock, and all of a sudden there was an aged smell of mold. Before Emily realized what she was doing, she was reaching into this dark box. It paid off since she found a wool blanket with a federal emblem on it. Somehow, this treasure survived years of visitors and artifact scavengers.

"Em . . . see if you can find some more paper. I'm going to break off some more pieces of this old desk over here."

"Be careful." Emily was not one for destroying a piece of history, but she also knew that she needed to stay warm if they were going to make it through the night.

Emily found a few odds and ends to burn and took them over to a pile that Trent had started forming next to the fireplace. As she turned to look over at the desk that Trent was working to break apart she saw something shining in the light of the fire. Something had fallen out from within a side compartment from the desk.

"What is that?"

Trent looked over where Emily was pointing.

"Not sure, but it didn't come out of a drawer. It must have been tucked away in some secret compartment from the side of the desk. There wasn't even so much as a hatch or handle on the side where this came from. This was not meant to be found."

Trent reached into what appeared to be the hidden drawer that he uncovered while dismantling the desk. It was a diary or book of some kind with a metal seal on it. Trent gently took his thumb and brushed the dust off of the cover. He and Emily sat next to the fire mesmerized by the quality of what Trent had in his hand. They basked in the warmth of the old, smelly blanket. Luckily, the smell of burned embers from the fire masked the scent after a while. Emily was stuck by the fact that the book's soft leather binding had fared so well through the years.

Emily gently reached over and slipped the book from Trent's hands. She placed it closer to the fire, so she could see the seal. The top had markings that read *Department of the Army*, and below that on the bottom half of the round seal was *United States of America.*

The picture in the middle of the seal was faded, but they could still make out a pair of riffles crossing, as well as two flags.

Emily opened the book and quickly realized that it was the army log for the guard station. She immediately knew the significance of this find. It had specific dates with meticulous notes of each activity that any soldier took. If anyone was leaving for the day, or if any equipment was being taken from the premises, it was in there. This made sense to Emily since the U.S. Government was not the type of boss who would let an employee slide.

"What is it?" Trent asked like an impatient child waiting for a surprise.

"It's the daily log for the guard station. It was probably used to keep tabs on everything to ensure that no one was entering or leaving without permission."

Emily began scanning the dates and realized that this one book probably contained every entry for this outpost from day one until the last soldier left. They read the entries for over two hours without even the slightest desire to put down the book. They each knew that the last time that the book was probably touched it was in the hands of one of the servicemen from the station. Emily and Trent both appreciated the pure historical significance of this fact.

Without warning, the fire went out. There was a whoosh of wind pouring down the fireplace, creating an almost lifelike rolling plume of smoke. Just then, a top piece of the window sill nearest to them peeled off of the building like it was nothing more than paper. Wind and rain began to penetrate into the station through the small hole surrounding the window. Emily and Trent were in disbelief and shock but managed to keep as calm as possible under the circumstances. Emily tucked the book under her shirt and into her pants to keep it as dry as possible. She knew it had to have clues regarding the mystery she felt a connection to.

Just then, there was a loud crash from the second story. It sounded like something from inside the house came crashing off the wall. Emily and Trent remained motionless in order to let their senses get a bearing.

"Maybe the force of the wind knocked over a picture?" Trent said, as if to comfort himself.

"Doubtful." Emily knew that whatever fell was massive.

Emily looked over to the right side next to the cast-iron oven and saw a narrow staircase that hugged the wall up to the second floor.

"Let's go check it out," Emily said.

"Why? Besides, you shouldn't be moving on your leg," Trent replied with a shakiness in his voice.

"We're stuck here for a while, so we need to figure out if something is about to come crashing down on our heads through these old floors. My leg feels fine." It really didn't feel all that good, but Emily could walk on it if she needed to, and in her stubborn nature, this was one of those times.

Trent, while scared, could not argue with that logic. They carefully made their way up the stairs and were each expecting to find a cluttered room full of junk. To their surprise, there was nothing at the top. As Trent flashed the light across the room, they could see every wall. Not one thing was up there except for bare wooden floors—not even one piece of loose board sitting against a wall.

"What could have made that sound?" Emily asked in frustrated fear.

"Beats me," Trent responded.

It did not take Emily long to get that uneasy feeling again. She grabbed Trent's sweaty hand, and she dragged him downstairs so that she could get away from the death that seemed to surround them upstairs. He gladly followed without any pushback at all. They regrouped by the fire and placed the blanket back over them as if they were children again searching for a sense of security. Trent wrapped Emily's leg again, cleaning it with some fresh rainwater that he collected in a water bottle by the open area of the station. Within about five minutes they started to get heavy-eyed from the walking and stress. They rested their heads on each other and slowly dozed off.

Emily was a light sleeper and was awoken about thirty minutes later by what sounded like footsteps coming from the second floor. Initially she thought that she was just letting her mind get the better of her, but she knew what footsteps sounded like, and there was no mistaking the sound. Someone was in the guardhouse with them. She nudged Trent, and he immediately looked at the ceiling. There were flakes of wood and dust lightly falling from above their heads. This gave credibility to the fact that someone was walking just above them.

Emily whispered to Trent with a strained breath. "How could this be?" Trent looked at the door, and it was still locked from the inside.

Trent could not make sense of this either. There was only one door, and they were just feet from it. Trent went to turn on the flashlight and within a minute, it died. Trent knew for sure that he had placed new batteries in it. Regardless of any rhyme or reason for it, the fact remained that he had no light except for the fire. Emily and Trent never once took their focus from the stairs. If anyone was going to make a go at them, they were going to see them head-on.

Emily could not stand playing the victim any longer. She shouted as loud as she could,

"Who's there? I have a gun!"

Emily hated the thought of guns and would not be caught dead holding one in her hand. To the best of her knowledge, no one in her family owned one. Trent was startled by Emily's unannounced statement to the intruder. However, he was so frightened that he just froze, staring at the staircase.

The steps did not stop. With each beat of the heart, Emily could make out a step, like they were in perfect cadence. The only light was the fading fire from the fireplace. Then, without warning, there were no more steps. Not even a slight drag of a foot. Emily and Trent fell asleep from shear physical and emotional exhaustion. It was about seven in the morning when they awoke. The wind and rain was eerily calm. As Emily got up from the floor, she looked over at the door.

"When did you get up and go outside?"

Trent looked perplexed. "What do you mean? I didn't go outside."

Emily pointed to the front door. The door locks were unlatched.

"How is that possible?" Trent asked.

Emily was stunned. "I have no idea. We were the only ones who could have been in here last night. There was nowhere for anyone to hide. We looked everywhere."

The pair began to explore the station one final time. The light of the morning sun made the place less ominous than the night before. Sure enough, there were no secret passages or nooks in which someone could hide. It was a basic wooden structure with minimalistic features.

Emily gathered her belongings, including the new station log that she found, and she and Trent left the station without any hesitation. She was not a believer in ghosts, but this island was starting to make her understand that something was not right. Trent was already ahead of the curve on his supernatural beliefs at this point, since this was just another string of spooky events since he landed on the island.

As soon as they made their way to the porch, Emily's adrenaline was starting to subside. This fact, coupled with having had her leg motionless for hours on a hard floor, gave way to a pain she had never felt before. She knew that her leg wound was much worse than she first realized. She removed her homemade bandage and saw a good-sized gash. The good news was that it did not appear to be bleeding.

"Can you walk on it?" Trent asked with concern in his voice.

"Yeah. It hurts, but I can manage. I don't think it's broken, just stiff from being in one place for a few hours." Emily wasn't really sure how bad it was, but she didn't want Trent to worry about her. There were more important things to deal with—like the storm outside.

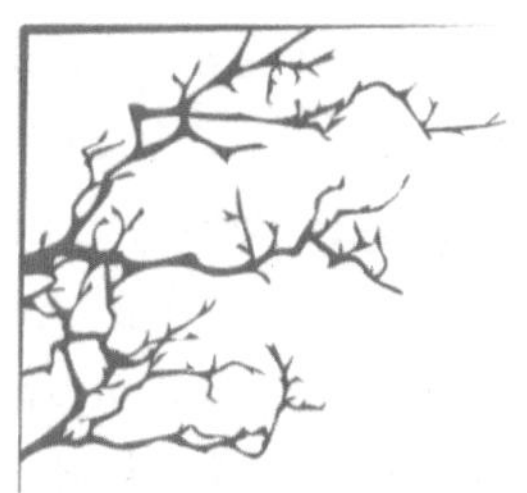

Chapter 19

Trent pulled a piece of broken two-by-four from outside the station. It was most likely a piece of the building that blew off during the storm. He fashioned it into a rudimentary crutch. Emily did not care what it looked like or that its hard edge dug into her shoulder a bit as she walked. It made her leg feel a thousand times better, and that was all that she cared about at this moment in time.

Trent looked up at the sky, and he immediately knew that this calm was a deceptive enemy waiting to pounce. This was not the end of the storm. Emily and Trent were smack in the middle of a hurricane.

"We're in the eye of the storm," Trent said.

"What is the eye of the storm?" Emily wasn't much of a meteorology enthusiast and was really hoping that it meant something positive, like the storm was giving them a symbolic wink and was turning away from them.

"It means we are safe for about three to four hours tops before all hell breaks loose. This is the middle of the storm. The other half makes what we just went through seem like a mild summer shower."

As he explained this to Emily, the wind and rain began to pick up again. This was the eye wall closing in on Cumberland Island.

"We need to find the lighthouse. That guardhouse will probably not be there in the morning. We need something that is clad with titanium, but at this point, I'll settle for brick."

Emily could barely hear Trent over the wind that was picking up with each second. Trent yelled over the sound of the wind and rain.

Emily reached out for Trent, and with her hurt leg, she mustered all of her energy to follow Trent into the unknown again. As they walked, day became night. The eyewall had covered every bit of the sun's rays and left the world a dark gray. Emily knew that she could not make it back to their camp in her condition, and given the weather, she wanted the security of something stronger than a tent. Neither Trent nor Emily were willing to brave the guard station again. Something was not right in there, and Emily believed Trent when he said that it wouldn't likely make it through round two of Xavier.

Trent followed his map, and after a ten-minute walk, they saw the Cumberland Island lighthouse. As they approached, they saw a faint light shining at the top.

Emily asked, "Do you see that? Is that someone with a flashlight standing at the top of the lighthouse?"

"I'm not sure, but maybe it's Liz. Either way, we have to get over there."

They moved as fast as they could under the circumstances. Emily's leg and the relentless wind pressing them backward with each step made the seemingly short distance seem almost impossible. The greenish light that they kept seeing was flickering in and out with each glance. They finally reached the lighthouse after what seemed like an hour. They walked the perimeter of the magnificent structure to try to find the door. With the rain and dark conditions, they relied upon feel. They both brushed their hands across the weathered brick wall to try to feel for a door. As they drug their fingers across, they could feel the imperfections of the brick, which gave away the age of this once spectacular piece of art.

"Here it is! I found it," Emily shouted.

"Thank goodness. It's like this stupid storm Xavier has some vendetta against us. Like we cheated him in poker or something."

Trent used all of his might to pry the door open. It was rusted shut, as if it had not been open for decades. Surely, if Liz was in there she had found some other means of entrance. The door made a God awful screeching sound as Trent pushed it in. It was the type of sound that you would expect to hear before some grotesque creature or an ax murderer in a horror movie jumped out to kill unsuspecting passersby. The inside of the lighthouse offered some warmth and dryness but afforded no sense of protection.

Truth be told, Emily was considering going back to the haunted station. She was almost more willing to take her chances in the straw hut versus the sturdy brick lighthouse at this point. Both Emily and Trent looked at each other, and neither had to say a word. Each knew that something did not feel right about this place. It wasn't even anything that they could explain. It was just death. Nothing more, and nothing less. There was a smell and feeling that smacked of lost souls. It was so dark that they could barely see each other, despite the fact that they were only inches apart. Moreover, it made uneasy creaking and knocking sounds from the rain and wind pelting it from all directions. They each slowly dragged their feet across the floor to avoid stepping on a nail or on some other broken object in the dark. With each swoosh of their feet across the dirty floor, they caught small rocks or shards of glass that got swept to the side with each shuffle.

Emily looked at Trent and said, "Let's go to the top and see if we can find that person with the flashlight?"

Trent agreed with Emily but with little enthusiasm. He was not excited about venturing to the top. Nor was he enthused with the thought of his hurt bride walking those steps. Nevertheless, he knew that once Emily made up her mind, he had no say in her decisions. His flashlight was their only source of light. He reached into his backpack and found the last of his spare batteries. He loaded it up. Just then, there was a loud boom from the top of the stairs, and the flashlight went dead. The sound of the wind traveling down the walls of the lighthouse sounded like a thousand ghosts screaming into the darkness of the cold building. Trent's mind raced, and he knew that this place had to be haunted.

"What the heck was that?" Emily asked Trent with an all-too-common sense of panic and fear.

"I'm not sure. Stay next to me. I saw an old lantern on the floor over by the door when we walked in. Maybe it has some oil left in it."

They walked hand in hand to the spot, and Trent reached down to pick it up. He gave it a slight shake.

"We're in luck, it has some kerosene left in it."'

"How do you know that it's oil and not something else that will blow up in our faces once you light it?" Emily did not like how this scenario was going, and she was starting to lose her optimism for realism.

"I don't, but we don't have much of a choice. We need to get to the top to see if we can find Liz, and then find some place against a wall to ride out this storm."

Trent reached into his pocket and pulled out one of his camping matches. Luckily, he'd packed well and always kept a couple close at hand since they were waterproof. He struck it against the brick wall, and with a rough swipe, it ignited. He carefully touched the rusty lantern's old wick with the match. It lit up as quickly as it probably did decades before when the lighthouse keeper would use it to find his way up the old staircase. At first, it provided a comforting bright flicker, but it quickly faded into a soft-pink light, like the kind that would soothe someone sinking into a soft leather chair on a cold night. This night, however, the light did not provide that same calming feeling. It was quite the opposite. Trent and Emily would have preferred a large, Hollywood-style spotlight to create a sense of daylight in every direction.

Using the lantern to guide his way, Trent scanned the area at the base of the stairs to see if there was anything of use or if potential objects that needed to be avoided were on the floor. Aside from a few old metal soup tins, there was little around. As he scanned the light toward the wall, he did, however, come face-to-face with one of the old lighthouse keepers. Trent shook and took a huge step back as his light lit up a picture on the wall of the old keeper. He was so startled that he almost knocked over Emily, who clung to his back as if the two were attached with Velcro. The framed image of the older gentleman had to be between three to four feet in height and was hung at eye level. The image of the unknown man stood out in the picture against the smooth gray background. It was almost as if someone had taken the picture and then carefully brushed some coal around the image in contrast.

Both Emily and Trent were entranced by the man's face. Although terrified, they realized that they could not turn away without studying every inch of the picture. For a brief moment, Trent found himself analyzing a piece of history, which fascinated him and took his mind off the current setting. The keeper had a well-groomed gray beard that started over his mouth and went just beyond the edge of his cheeks. It flowed down about three inches below his chin. He was dressed in a black coat, complete with vest and tie. He appeared very stoic.

On either side of his coat there were emblems of some sort. His flat-brimmed hat sat perfectly straight on his head. It had an emblem as well, and it reminded Trent of a hat that a Civil War soldier might have worn with its straight, squared-off brim and cylindrical top. His eyes, though, were the most telling about this man. They appeared to be tired and worn from age. They were not large and were beady, with a noticeably white accent point on the upper right of each, from where the light caught his eyes during the capturing of the shot. Trent's intrigue grew as he pictured the process that would have taken place under the old wet plate collodion system of photography. His mind could not help but quietly ponder how long this poor guy had to stay still in that wool suit while the photographer went through the endless process of preparing to take the image.

"Come on, babe, let's get up the stairs to be sure that Liz is ok." Emily was nudging Trent forward as she tried to get him from his historical-minded trance.

"Gotcha. Let's go." Trent realized that he was wasting time staring at a picture that had been in this spot for probably a hundred years, a picture that would still be there in the morning. Somewhere in the back of his mind, Trent knew that he was stalling. He had no desire to come face-to-face with an apparition at the top of the lighthouse. Reluctantly, he pressed forward with Emily.

Emily and Trent made their way to the cast-iron spiral staircase. Trent led the way, and Emily was attached as close to him as she could get. They could hear the rails and steps clatter with each step. It was as if the stairs were some living, breathing thing that despised each step they took. After a few minutes, they had reached the halfway point, and they could see a sliver of moonlight through a tiny window. The moon was fiercely trying to break through the darkness of the clouds and rain that continued to grab control of this island.

Without any warning, a gust of freezing-cold wind came crashing down upon both of them, nearly knocking them back against the wall. The lantern went out. It was pitch black. This wasn't the type of force from a natural event. It felt like a person violently pushing them out of the way. Trent, beyond terrified, reached into his pocket to get another match. He struck it against the wall and tried to light the lantern. Nothing. Whatever remnants of oil that were left on their old companion was spent.

"Are you out of matches?" Emily asked in alarm. She knew full well that whatever brushed by them was not made of Mother Nature.

Trent mustered up all of the courage he could so as to not give Emily more reason to be concerned.

"I have a couple more in my pocket."

He reached into his damp pocket and grabbed one of his last matches.

As he had done before, he struck it across the wall. With one motion he dragged it from behind his shoulder toward his face. The match lit with success, and as soon as it lit in front of his face, Trent came to the horrifying realization that there was someone standing within inches of him on the stairs. Trent and Emily both gasped at the same time as they starred directly into the face of someone who was looking right back at them.

Trent put his hands out in defense, but he knew that he was in a bad position since the person was standing above him on the steps. Besides, Trent was not the sort of man's man who could put someone in a wrestling chokehold on the fly. He was more of a slap-box kind of guy. Just then, there was a familiar voice.

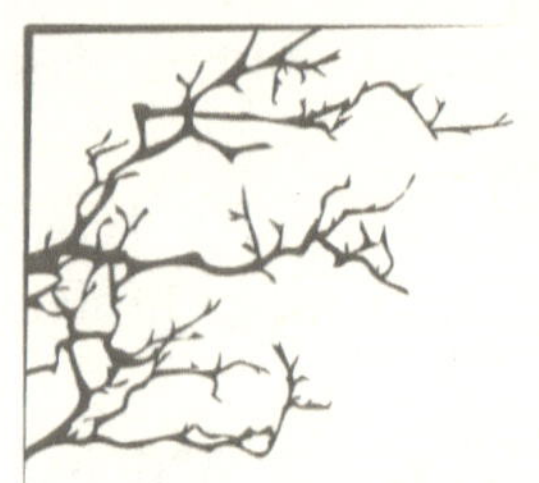

Chapter 20

"Whoa, guys. It's me. It's Liz."

Trent and Emily slowly began to regain their composure. Luckily for Liz, she identified herself since she was about to get the slap of the century that would, without a doubt, leave a mark for an hour.

"What the heck are you doing here, and how did you even get into this old thing?" Emily asked. Asking questions helped take her mind off the creepiness of the surroundings and the pain in her leg.

"I was hiking up the trail and heard a man's voice calling out for someone. I kept getting closer to the sound and realized that it was coming from the lighthouse. He sounded weary, like he needed help, so I found my way in to try to help out. Once I got inside, the voice stopped. I looked everywhere, but I couldn't find anyone. This hellish storm came in so quick that it trapped me at the top of the stairs. It got so dark that I could not find my way, even with my flashlight."

All three of the wanderers stepped carefully down the spiral staircase, the occasional strong gust of wind pushing down around them as it raced to the bottom. These blasts of air felt different than the portentous one that greeted Emily and Trent as they ascended the lighthouse. It took them about ten minutes to finally reach the bottom of the stairs.

Trent took charge and said, "We need to stay here for the night to ride out this storm."

Emily and Liz had no argument to that. This island was in nature's mixing bowl at the moment, no one inside that lighthouse wanted to be the topping sprinkled across a plate of uprooted trees.

"Agreed," Emily said.

Liz nodded her tired head in agreement as well. Emily and Trent could see that she was drained. Although they did not know why, Liz seemed disappointed that she had not found the person calling from the lighthouse. Personally, Trent was just fine with the fact that the person was not there anymore.

Trent grabbed that old wool blanket from the guard station and placed it over the girls, who huddled to stay warm. He took one final match that he managed to dig from the bottom of his pocket to light some loose kindling on fire. With the help of the flickering light, Trent started scooping up loose pieces of wood. He knew that some of these items were probably historical artifacts, which on any other day would have mattered to him, but not today, however. He was in survival mode. The fire grew steady and seemed to be good enough for the time being. Emily propped up her leg. Liz pulled out a small bottle of hydrogen peroxide from her tiny first-aid kit and wiped down Emily's leg. It bubbled, which indicated that it was cleaning the cut. Emily thanked Liz, and then she placed a new clean bandage on her leg courtesy of Liz's first-aid kit.

By this time both girls were nearly asleep from sheer exhaustion. Trent was still terrified since he knew that something was not right about this place. Even still, he enjoyed the fact that Emily and Liz felt safe enough in his presence to let their guard down and relax. Trent slowly took a seat next to them. He let his back rest against the brick wall of the lighthouse and rested his hands on his knees, which were filthy. He took his right hand and scratched his face and realized how bushy his unshaven face felt. Then he reached into his backpack to find his cell phone. As he had suspected, it was completely dead, just like everything else on this island. After several minutes, his eyes began to succumb to the night. His head felt as heavy as a bowling ball, and he knew that he could not fight to stay awake any longer.

Several hours passed. The wind howled, and random objects could be heard striking the side of the lighthouse. All three were so used to the sounds by now that it resonated like a child's sound machine. It was early morning, around four o'clock. Trent awoke for some reason. He couldn't figure out why and was pissed off that his body chose this exact moment to starve him of sleep. He looked over and saw that the girls were still sound asleep. Emily and Liz were cuddled together like two best friends at a slumber party. He stood to stretch his cramped legs. No sooner did he get to his feet when he heard a man's voice coming from up the stairs of the lighthouse.

"It can't be," he said. "There's no one else here."

He heard it again, and this time there was no denying that this was a person's voice.

He could not make out what the words were, but he knew that it was a man's voice. He knew for sure that this was not the wind. The fire was still burning, so he could see about twenty feet or so up the spiral staircase. The noise was just beyond the light's reach.

"Who's up there? Why are you harassing us? Just leave us alone, you sadistic bastard!"

The voice went silent. Trent could hear someone or something walking toward the top near lantern room.

"Is someone up there? Get down here, you wimp!" Trent could hardly believe that he was taunting whoever this was and that he was actually daring this mysterious person to respond. It almost did not even seem like it was him asking such a ridiculous question. What if this was a serial killer or some crazed cult member trying to earn a murder badge to add to his cult sash. For some reason, Trent's mind had this guy dressed like a screwed-up girl scout with a dozen badges attached to his uniform. He probably had one for his first stabbing, his first abduction, and then another one for his first sexual assault.

The lighthouse was silent for a few minutes. Then, Trent heard a voice right behind him. He spun around, but there was nothing there. The air was dense and thick from the cold. He found himself face-to-face with the lighthouse keeper's picture again. He scanned in every direction. He was waiting for the eyes to move like in one of those old seventies movies. The eyes never moved. They just stayed fixed on Trent.

"Who are you, and what do you want? Is this your house? Why are you doing this?"

He felt someone touch his shoulder. By this time, he was petrified to the point of not being able to move. Trent was helpless and would no doubt accede whatever evil was about to thrust itself upon him. He could hear each beat of his heart working in conjunction with his cold breath. It was as if Trent were a machine running in rhythm with some programmed sequence.

Just then, he went dead cold and gave a quick shiver, like a brisk breeze found its way through his body. This snapped Trent out of his frightened trance. He immediately heard the voice again. The man cried out in a soft, raspy voice. "Help." He knew this for sure. The voice traveled a few feet from Trent and was fading up the stairs until it just got beyond earshot. It just kept saying, "Help." A few times, he thought he heard, "Help, Lee." Before Trent could let his mind unravel that phrase, he felt a soft nudge on his back.

"Hey, are you ok? You look like you've seen a ghost." Liz was up and trying to calm down Trent's excited state.

Trent was relieved that someone else was up.

"There's someone else in here with us. I heard the voice of a man who came down the stairs and then went back up to the top."

"Are you sure?" Emily was now up and wanted to solve this mystery. She used the crutch that Trent had made for her to keep as much weight off of her foot as possible.

"Let's check it out!" Emily exclaimed. By this time, Emily was flat-out incensed that someone was continually messing with them. She was just about ready to go toe-to-toe with whomever this was and kick the sadistic sense of humor straight from his or her mouth.

"I'm in too," said Liz.

Trent, being the man of the group, was not going to be shown up by these two. Besides, he felt safer with two women with him. He felt sorry for anyone who got in Emily's way when she was upset.

The three slowly started up the stairs to the top of the lighthouse. Liz was in front, then Emily, and then finally Trent. As they climbed they could still feel the cold night air whipping past them like they were in the inside of a tornado. About three-quarters of the way up, they noticed a green light at the top. It appeared to have a human figure. As they tracked it, the figure disappeared out the door to the top of the lighthouse. Liz and Emily popped their heads out once at the top. Every sound seemed to be accentuated. They could hear footsteps on the metal grate walkway that circled the top of the lighthouse. As they leaned out to peek around the corner, they saw him. They were not crazy. There was a man standing right there. They all saw the same thing.

They each took an excited, yet anxious gasp. The green figure was not as defined as a living, breathing person. However, it was clearly a man. He was looking out over the island and did not seem to realize that there were two women staring at him in disbelief.

"Are you ok? Who are you?" Emily asked the soul.

There was no response, and he continued to look for something below on the island.

"Liz, what should we do?"

"Beats me? I don't even think he can see us. But I think he's trying to get us to find something for him. Something that he needs to cross to the other side."

"How so, if he can't even see us?" Trent asked.

"From my research, spirits can sometimes come in and out of a realm that allows them to see and hear us. Typically, with lightning storms. This storm may have been the catalyst that he needed to connect with us, even if just for a brief moment in time."

Emily wiped her face with her hand to push away some water that was dripping from the eve overhang above her head. She asked Liz, "So you think that this person was hearing us without being able to connect since he was caught in some other dimension? And then with this storm, he could finally unite his place in time or space with ours to communicate?"

"That's exactly what I think."

Emily responded, "I'm game. After everything else that I have experienced on this island, why would I question that theory?" Emily, Liz, and Trent were still watching the phantom with a watchful eye.

As quick as a gust of wind, the ghost turned directly toward Emily and Liz and walked right through them. He had no defined eyes and no specific shape to his face. He wasn't ominous, just absent of any emotional features that would comfort a warm-bodied human. They each had the cold shiver as he passed through their bodies. It felt like someone was stabbing them with ice shards. Trent was behind them in shock, yet again. The apparition went around the corner of the walkway atop the lighthouse and vanished. As quick as he appeared, he was gone, as if he was never there. They each had some sense of peace. This person or soul or whatever it used to be, did not appear to be trying to kill them or even harass them. There was a different feeling around him. A sensation of loneliness and endless searching for something that could not be found no matter how hard he looked.

It was almost dawn outside. The dark clouds were being cut through by the early signs of the sun piercing the remnants of the storm. It appeared that the worst of the storm had passed. The three remaining persons on Cumberland Island knew that they were alone in the human sense, but they each had no misconception that they were truly alone on this slice of land that seemed so isolated now. Xavier's fury appeared to be over as he passed north to play with the Carolinas.

"Do you think the storm has passed?" Emily said.

"I think so, but we'll still have a few hours of potential tornados," Trent replied.

Both women looked at each other with a sense of fear.

Emily was always the planner. "Let's get back to camp while we can to grab more supplies, and then get back to the lighthouse."

Trent and Liz agreed. They all knew that they needed to stockpile the lighthouse like a bunker just in case they were stuck for a longer period than they expected.

They opened the door and found that the world outside was a collage of torn and tattered landscape. Oak trees lay on their side. The guard station was almost completely gone, aside from a few fragments of the stone foundation. It looked as if someone had taken a bulldozer and cleared the island. They all were in shock. None of them expected it to be this bad. Xavier was one nasty son of a bitch. In fact, the only sense of security that was within miles was the lighthouse. The fresh scars were visible from the trees that had hit the side the night before, but it remained in place. Not one brick appeared to be out of place.

Emily used the crutch and led the group through and around the carnage of fallen trees and uprooted bushes. There was clearly no path to anywhere on this island anymore. Emily, however, appeared to have the best sense of direction of the trio. She was on a mission to find what was left of their belongings. Emily was shocked to see a perfect line of palm trees that had a uniform bent to them, as if someone had walked by and hit them down the line. She knew that this hurricane was serious.

Trent was concerned and asked Emily, "Are you sure that you're okay to walk on your leg?"

She smiled at Trent and replied, "You bet your ass." Emily was taking charge like an Army Ranger leading her troops. At this point with what she had been through, her mouth might as well have belonged to a merchant marine after a seven-month stint overseas. She didn't care if she cussed or how she looked. She just knew that she needed supplies for her troops. After what seemed like two hours of working around and over trees, they reached what was left of the campsite. Everything was scattered. No tents remained, although they did eventually spot one about thirty feet up in a tree.

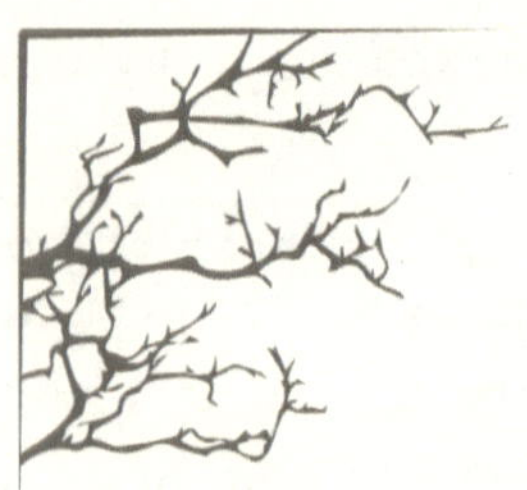

Chapter 21

As they searched for what was left of their travel lives, Emily saw Liz grasp her necklace—the same one that captured Emily's attention on the ferry.

"That's pretty special, huh?"

"Yep," Liz replied. "It's a family heirloom that rarely leaves my neck unless I'm doing something where I think that it may fall off. It connects me to who I am, who I was, and who I plan to be one day."

"We saw it at the campsite the other day. Why did you leave it?"

Liz looked somewhat perplexed, like she had been caught in a lie. She grinned, and said to Emily, "I was looking for wood. I never like to take it with me when I'm searching off of the trail. It could get snagged on a tree or catch a bush when I'm leaning down to pick up some wood."

Emily seemed content with Liz's answer and didn't pry any further. Moreover, Emily appreciated Liz's sense of pride and commitment to her lineage. Liz's philosophy on life was in line with the way that Emily saw life as well. These two women might as well have been twins. Their convictions and fight-to-the-end attitude were aligned.

"These are the fragments of life that make us who we are," Emily replied.

They each shared a moment of respect for each other's sense of being.

Then, Trent broke the moment. "I found our cooler, and it appears to be unharmed."

Trent and Emily did a quick inventory, and everything appeared to be in there. This would be enough to get all three of them through a least another night on the island. Liz was not so fortunate in locating any of her belongings. Nothing remained but scattered clothes.

"I can feel the wind picking back up. The other side of the storm is approaching. Let's get this stuff back to the lighthouse," Trent said.

Emily and Liz agreed with Trent's logic, and they all started the trek back to the safety of the brick walls. Emily took a few breaks to rest her leg. It was throbbing, even though she wouldn't let Trent or Liz know. Trent dragged the cooler as best he could. It had wheels, but given the terrain, they almost seemed useless. As far as Trent was concerned, they could have been in the shape of squares. Wheels or no wheels, dragging that cooler was just that, dragging it across the mud and muck. There was no rolling of the wheels. It took a good hour and a half for them to reach their newfound place of refuge. They all had a strange look, as if they knew that they were heading back into a certain haunted location. All of them saw that apparition, and none had yet found a reasonable explanation. However, given the dangers outside, they all seemed to approve of the risk inside. It was either this or make a makeshift hut from fallen trees and palm leaves, which meant that they might as well have just thrown themselves into any passing tornado.

Emily pulled open the door to the lighthouse. It creaked even worse than the night before, when they first found the courage to enter that ill-omened place. Even though the sky was clearer than yesterday, this place had a more ominous look than before. By Trent's watch it was five thirty. The clouds, however, did a brilliant job of masking any sense of true light. The lighthouse was as dark and gloomy as the night before when they followed that lost soul up the spiral staircase.

Trent reached into his cooler, and low-and-behold, his preparation paid off this time. He found a clear baggy containing matches. Trent wasted no time striking one of the matches against the grainy wall to spark the flame. Without any hesitation, the flame took, and he quickly used it to start the pile of scraps from the prior night. The picture of the old lighthouse keeper was the first thing that Trent noticed. There was just something about this image that gave Trent a cold, dead feeling. Trent couldn't stand it anymore. He reached up and pulled it down and turned it around.

Emily tried to lighten the mood. "That will definitely keep the spirits away from us. So, what do you call three people hanging on to life in a centuries-old lighthouse?"

Trent and Liz looked at Emily as if there was some good answer.

Emily shrugged her shoulders in the air with her palms pointed upward and answered with, "Screwed."

They all laughed to try to mentally remove themselves from the situation at hand.

Emily pulled out her book of Addison, as she was now calling it.

Liz sat next to her to absorb any tidbits of information.

Trent was still standing guard as the quintessential husband should do. He nibbled on a granola bar to ease hunger pains, which were now at the forefront of his mind. It wasn't even the kind he liked that was dipped in chocolate and had peanut butter chips in it. This one was pretty plain, but as it hit his mouth, it might as well have been a piece of filet mignon.

Emily found just enough light to continue her journey into the psyche of her journal's author. Emily and Liz talked for hours about who this girl probably was and how she was becoming a part of their lives through this adventure.

"How does such a passionate love story end so abruptly?"

Liz nodded, as if to indicate to Emily that she had no idea. "As far as I can tell, the only way to truly know what happened is to find

Jackson's body. That may help put some closure to this story and ease Addison's pain," Liz said.

"How can one island swallow up the body and soul of a person?" Emily asked, as if to actually get an answer from Liz.

Liz quickly corrected Emily. "Oh, my dear, his soul walks this island. I am convinced of that."

Emily put down the journal and pulled out the station log.

"What's that?" Liz asked.

"It's an old station log that Trent and I found at the old guard station." Liz was mesmerized by it. It was so detailed, almost down to each time one of the soldiers wiped his nose.

Liz's curiosity was killing her.

"Do you mind if I take a look at this for a minute?"

"Not at all."

Liz thumbed through the pages. Each day of each month of each year was meticulously chronicled. Every smoke break was in there. Liz was not sure what type of operation the state guard or the army was running, but she knew one thing for sure. This was not just some podunk Georgia outpost. There was something important happening on this island.

"Here it is!" Liz exclaimed to Emily.

"What?"

"Look. Right here. It's the entry for 1944/08/21. That's how the military writes their dates."

"Gotcha. So, this is the entry for August 21, 1944."

"Smart girl. Now look, there are two names listed as being present at the guard station."

Officer on Duty: Lieutenant Mitchem

NCO: Private First Class Solinski

"What the heck is an NCO?" Emily asked Trent.

"It's a Non-Commissioned Officer . . . like a sergeant or other enlisted guy in the military as opposed to an officer like a captain or major."

Liz redirected Emily's attention to the entry.

1300 - Meeting between Officer on Duty and NCO to address visitors from 1600, who are arriving today for meeting with Officer on Duty to address recent U-boat contact on Atlantic. NCO instructed to implement top-secret status as to all written and verbal communications.

Trent was intrigued enough by the talks of U-boats that he was now sitting next to these two female sleuths.

"What is a U-boat?" Emily asked.

Trent replied. "It's the name that was given to German submarines during the war. There must have been some sightings, or even a secret skirmish or two near Cumberland Island. Looks like Washington sent down a couple of heavy hitters to strategize with Lieutenant Mitchem."

Emily was quick to point out that all of the other times after 0300 were left blank, except for a notation "TSO."

"Let me guess, that's the acronym for *Top Secret Operation,*" Emily said with a confident grin.

"That's correct, my dear," Trent replied. "Also, that notation to 1600 is probably referring to someone from the White House, since that is what military guys say when someone high up on the chain of command makes a visit."

"Why 1600?" Liz asked.

"1600 Pennsylvania Avenue is the address for the White House," Trent replied.

Emily chimed in, "So this whole day after three o'clock was one big secret."

Trent nodded affirmatively and said, "Yep, it sure looks like it."

Emily continued to peruse each page of her journal to try to find some link between the two books. The biggest clue, however, was already solved. There was some form of top-secret meeting on the Island on the same day that Addison and Jackson made their ill-fated visit to the Carnegie mansion.

Emily continued to read entries to Liz and Trent. She found several where the NCO on watch actually conformed spotting a U-boat on a clear night.

1944/05/07

0300 – NCO Solinski has made visual confirmation of a submarine off of the coast about three clicks. Solinski followed protocol and called in the sighting to be sure that we had no units in the area. Washington confirmed that there were no Allied submarines patrolling that area. The closest unit was in Norfolk. Solinski took a picture of the submarine. The image was cloudy. However, it confirmed that there was an unauthorized submarine off the coast of Georgia. This was reported to HQ in Washington, since there were several supply ships moving from Miami to New York over the next week. This sighting and this entry were authenticated by Lieutenant Mitchem.

Emily found several subsequent entries discussing and confirming that the United States Army had taken proactive steps to counter this imminent threat. There was no doubt that this area of the coast was a hotbed for naval activity. In fact, according to the log entries, two destroyers were sent south to patrol from Savannah to Melbourne, Florida. The theory that Jackson was murdered over an overzealous fear of German U-boats was starting to take more shape. The world was in state of paranoia.

By this time, the night began to wear on all three of them as they nodded off to the faint sound of light debris brushing by the walls of the lighthouse. Trent was the first to nod off. As much as he tried to stand guard, he just could not stand any longer. He curled up against the wall near the fire for warmth. Liz was not far off as she began to fade as well. Emily, while tired, was still very keen of her surroundings and any potential danger. It could not have been but forty minutes or so when she heard a loud thump on the stairs. She couldn't make out anything. It was pitch black up there.

She was terrified, but above all, she was tired of being afraid. She got up while the other two slept and made her way up a few stairs to peer up the spiral of unknown sounds. Her leg might as well not have even been attached at that point. She couldn't feel the pain over all of the other emotions that were racing through her body. There was nothing. No further sounds. In fact, the outside seemed to be at peace as well. She could no longer make out any tree branches hitting the walls of this brick fortress.

She turned to make her way down the few stairs that she dared to explore. She had not fully turned when someone pushed her abruptly against the wall. She was pinned without the ability to move or scream. She was screaming as loud as she could in her mind, but no words would come out. She felt the hard, cold hands of someone pressing her against her will. Just then, a cold breath pierced the back of her neck. Every hair on her body was standing up. A gruff tortured sounding voice said, "Help, Lee." It repeated that exact phrase five or six times, and then as quick as it happened, it was over.

Emily was free from the person and ran to Trent. She dropped her crutch and didn't even think twice about it.

She screamed. "Someone just pinned me against the wall!"

Trent and Liz were confused and startled since they were fast asleep until awoken by Emily's scream.

"Maybe it was a dream."

"No, Liz. This was no dream. I know that this was real."

Trent reached over and pulled back Emily's shirt by her neck. "This was not a dream."

Emily looked over at Trent and asked, "What do you see?"

"You have a visible handprint on your neck." It wasn't black and blue or anything like that, but it was red from the pressure that was exerted upon her skin.

Liz looked as well, and she had a sense of panic on her face at the sight of the bright read mark in the perfect outline of a man's hand.

Needless to say, no one was willing to sleep anymore this night. Emily shook off her fear and replaced it with tough anger.

"Whoever you are, you messed with the wrong girl, pal!" She made sure to yell this as loud as she could up the stairs.

Liz put her arm around Emily and asked, "Did he say anything?"

"Yes. He said, 'Help, Lee.'" I have no idea what that means.

Trent leaned over. "Are you sure he did not say, 'Help me?'"

"Positive. I'm not crazy."

"I know, babe. I just mean . . ." Trent stopped himself before he put his foot in his mouth any farther.

Emily grabbed her journal and the station log to find solace in her written world. As she picked up the station log, she noticed that it was open. This was odd because she knew that she shut the book.

"Hey, did either of you read that station log?"

"Nope," Trent replied.

"Me neither," Liz said.

That's odd that the book was open. She looked closely at the page. At first glance it did not appear to have any words. As she held it to the firelight, she realized that there were two pages stuck together. She carefully pulled apart the pages and found a handwritten notation. *Mechanized unit poses risk to U.S. Atlantic Fleet and must be destroyed. Origin must be destroyed as well.*

Emily knew exactly what this meant.

"Liz, come over here."

Liz sat next to Emily, and Emily read the passage.

"Do you know what this means?"

"What?" Liz asked with a child-like curiosity.

"The U.S. government killed Jackson."

"What makes you believe that? That's insane."

"This entry clearly talks about Jackson's invention. The government thought that it was going to be used for espionage and wanted to not only destroy it, but also the person who created it. Think about it, this would stop the use of the invention and the mind that could recreate it."

Liz's face had a sober look. "Why would our own government kill one of its own? Why kill such an innocent person?"

Trent was eavesdropping. "Liz, you have to remember that this was a darker time. The world was paranoid. Just think, our government created camps to keep the Japanese Americans in one place to prevent what was feared to be mass espionage. This makes perfect sense. Kill the German American who created the single weapon that could destroy the Allied subs on the Atlantic front."

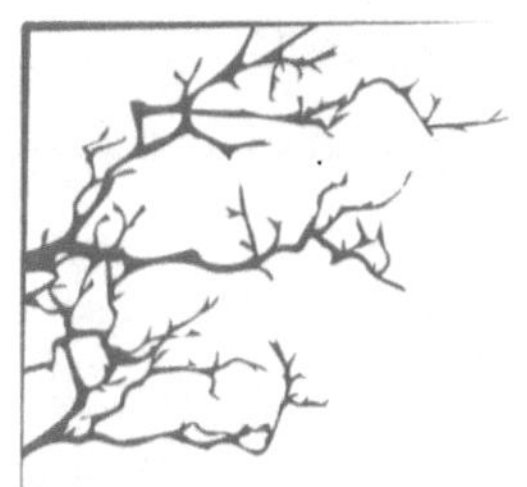

Chapter 22

As morning broke, Emily was overtaken by the revelations of the night before. She figured out what happened. Now, the mystery remained as to what fate came upon Jackson. Even if he was killed, how did he just disappear like he never even existed? Trent was pacing back and forth trying to put the pieces together, since he marveled over the puzzle pieces coming into place. As he passed Emily, she yelled out with an epiphany.

"I know! I know!" Emily yelled.

"You know what?" Trent asked.

"I know where Jackson is."

Liz asked, "How do you know?"

"Liz, how far is the cemetery from the Dungeness mansion?"

"Maybe a quarter mile at most. Why?"

"Trent, remember the other day when you said the body of Light Horse Henry Lee was moved by the Lee family from the Cumberland Island cemetery to Virginia."

"Go on." Trent stated with proud astonishment. He thought he knew where Emily was going with this but was pleased to know that this time she was the one with a conspiracy theory to prove.

"It would only take about two guys to shimmy off the top of his tomb and place a body in there. No one would even suspect it since everyone just presumed that any body found in the casket was that of Light Horse."

"How do we even know that there is a body in there?" Liz asked.

"We don't for sure."

Emily chimed in. "That makes perfect sense. That's why the ghost kept saying, 'Help, Lee' and not, 'Help me.' He wanted to lead us to Mr. Lee's tomb."

The three were now on a mission to hopefully put this lost soul to rest in peace. They packed their gear and made their way outside. None of them knew for sure that there would be any corpse in the tomb, but at this point, they all knew that they had to prove or disprove this theory. The sky was bright blue, and the surroundings looked like a war zone. There were hundred-year-old oaks toppled over, as well as a few dead birds lying around. Xavier had given Cumberland Island a pretty severe right cross and followed it up with an uppercut.

It took twice as long as yesterday for the three to pave their way through the weather-beaten trail. Part of this was due to Emily's leg. She had been good about keeping it clean and bandaged. Even still, it had a pretty nasty gash. As Emily looked around her on the trail, she noticed that it was as if nature had systematically restored all of the man-made penetrations through the forest. To say this was a trail anymore was a stretch by any means of the imagination. When they arrived back at the campsite, Emily noticed a series of footsteps all around the area where the tents once sat. Trent and Liz noticed these as well.

"Look at these boot prints. They are erratic," Emily stated.

Trent kneeled down and looked closer.

"It looks like at least two people were here."

"But who?" Emily pondered.

Trent's imagination began to run away with fantasies of ghosts or psychopaths walking the campsite in order to find some victims. This was partly due to his sleep deprivation. Emily quickly brought him back to reality. She surely didn't need Trent letting his brilliant mind going off on tangents right now. They needed to stick to the plan.

"I don't know if it's ghosts, but I don't want to find out who has been snooping around our campsite," Emily said.

Emily pointed toward the coast area and began to lead Liz and Trent down toward the path along the coastline. Emily reasoned that it was better to walk in an open area versus fighting nature and whatever else was looming within the heart of this island. With each step toward the coastline trail, they had to maneuver around broken tree limbs and wade through standing water that went just above their shoes. Emily's shoes were so saturated with water that she could hear a *squish* with each step, like she was walking with two sponges on her feet. She wanted to desperately cut off her leg by this point. She despised her leg for hurting and keeping her slowed down.

After what seemed like hours, they could finally see the St. Mary's River. They had reached the coast. Emily was leading the group. She was on a mission to solve this mystery, and she put all of her ailments aside to get it done. Even if she fell to her knees as they reached the tomb, she was certain that she was going to complete this journey.

"How much farther do you think it is, Em?" Trent asked with tired breath.

"If I had to guess, I'd say about another mile."

Liz was patiently following, with little to say. At times, Emily forgot that Liz was even still with them. Liz was just quietly looking around at her surroundings and the devastation that the hurricane had caused to this natural treasure. The conditions on this coastline trail were becoming worse with each step. This was most likely the result of some tidal surge thrashing and mixing the coast like a blender. The smell of dead fish was all around them in the air. It was almost unbearable. The Georgia mud mixed with the fine silt sand made each step feel like they were treading through quicksand. Emily's homemade crutch kept getting stuck each time that she jolted it in front of her and let her weight rest on it.

The day was passing, and by Emily's watch, it was now three o'clock in the afternoon. The temperature was brisk, which made the journey somewhat more pleasant considering the less than desirable walking conditions. And to make it even better, there were no mosquitoes biting at them. It wasn't for another twenty minutes that they reached the cemetery. By this time even Liz was noticeably exhausted. They each took a minute to sit and rest on an old concrete bench next to the cemetery wall. There was still no sign of anyone else on the island. The only noises that Emily could hear was the sound of the small waves hitting the broken wooden trail from the river, as well as birds chirping in the distance.

Emily enjoyed the much-deserved rest. She propped her leg as high as she could get it on the top of bench to let the blood circulate. It immediately felt better. She let her head fall back on the bench for just a moment. After a few minutes, she was ready to move on like any good soldier would do. "Well, folks, let's do this," Emily ordered with a smile to the other two, as if she were the officer in charge of this mission.

"Are we sure that we want to do this?" Trent asked, to give one last way out for everyone.

"I need to know," Liz replied.

"Me too," Emily said.

Trent nodded his head since he was outvoted. Emily, Trent, and Liz all approached the grave of Light Horse Henry Lee. The concrete block had survived the storm better than a couple of the other ones, which had broken concrete pieces surrounding them. Emily noticed a chipped corner on the grave. She motioned for Trent to help her leverage that corner with a large broken tree branch. Trent found a nearby branch and forced it into the corner. Emily and Liz pushed the top of the grave as hard as they could. Nothing happened.

"Trent. Let's give it everything that you have on this one, babe. Use that untapped muscle," Emily said to lighten the mood and encourage the team.

"You got it, Em. I'm all in for this push."

Emily directed Liz to another corner of the grave to help give more leverage.

"One, two, three, push!" Emily yelled.

All three pushed and pried the thick concrete top until finally it moved. They continued for another three attempts until they ultimately got just enough pushed aside to see inside. As soon as they cleared it, the smell of death overtook the air. It was a pungent smell of mold and decay. Emily thought that it smelled like a dead animal on the side of the road, only ten times worse. They all took a step back for a minute to get a breath of fresher air.

Trent was so overtaken by the smell that he began to throw up next to a log by the river. He heaved and fell to his knees. He then heaved again. Trent was so pale that it looked like every bit of blood from his head had completely left his body. Emily grabbed Liz's hand.

"Come on, Liz. Let's get this over with."

Liz followed Emily, yet did not say much, presumably from her own battle with the smell. Emily and Liz peered into the grave and saw the skeletal remains of a human. The clothes were still on this poor soul. They were tattered, but they could clearly see he was dressed in nice clothes.

"It's Jackson!" Liz cried out.

Emily was shocked. She was not fully expecting to actually find anybody in the grave. Emily agreed with Liz. Based upon the remains of the clothes, this had to be Jackson Jones.

"We need to get to the ranger station to report this to the authorities," Emily said. She could hardly believe that they had located the long-lost soul of Mr. Jones.

Liz agreed with Emily but wanted to cover the tomb first to protect this poor man's body. Liz grabbed some thick branches and covered the open portion of the grave to keep the elements out.

Emily went to Trent's side. In all of the commotion, she forgot that her husband was about to fall into the St. Marys River from sickness.

"How are you feeling, babe?"

"Better now, but that was touch and go for a minute. Was there a body in there?"

"Yep, and I'm pretty sure that it was Jackson Jones."

Trent was shocked and said, "We need to get help."

As Trent stood up, and started to make his way up the embankment, his foot got caught in a muddy hole. As he turned to wiggle his foot loose from the thick boggy clay, a dislodged cypress tree fell over and landed squarely on his leg just below the hip. Trent screamed with pain. Emily turned and ran to his side.

"Trent! Are you okay? Can you move?"

Trent's mouth was moving as if he was trying to respond, but no sound was coming out. He was almost immediately turning a pale color from the shock and pain. Emily grabbed his hand, and it was clammy with little grip to it. Emily brushed away some of the mud and could immediately see where a portion of his femur was forcing its way out of his skin. Liz came running down to Trent as well. Emily and Liz tried to move the tree, but it was useless. It was too heavy. This was a full tree that probably weighed all of five hundred pounds, if not more.

Emily tried to stay composed for Trent and said, "I'm going to get help at the ranger station."

Liz interrupted Emily. "Stay here with him to comfort him. I'll run to the station to get help."

Emily reluctantly agreed. She wanted to be in control, but she also knew that she needed to keep Trent from going into shock. His eyes were becoming unresponsive as they periodically rolled back in his head.

"Please hurry, Liz!" Emily shouted with fear.

Liz nodded as she began to run. Liz ran off as fast as she could down the trail, and tripped several times over fallen limbs. Emily lost sight of her after a few minutes. Trent was in and out of consciousness from the loss of blood and the pain. Emily knew that she had to try to stop the bleeding from Trent's leg. Emily reached into her pocket and pulled out a Swiss Army pocket knife from her pocket. Had the moment not been so emotional and unnerving, she would have certainly found more irony in the fact that Trent bought it for her a couple of years ago for her birthday. She hated the knife at first, but it eventually became a staple in her camping gear. She used it every time she and Trent went camping. She even liked to use the spoon extension just to say that she had lived like a true mountain woman.

Emily took the knife and cut off a portion of her sleeve. She quickly reached down into the bloody, murky water and tied this makeshift tourniquet around Trent's leg. Trent smiled as best he could, but he was fading fast.

Emily kissed Trent and said, "Betcha never thought this birthday gift would come this much in handy, did ya?" She would say anything at this moment if it would keep him alive.

Trent was unresponsive. Emily knew that this was a serious situation. She tried her best to keep the mood light, but Emily's own injury was starting to become worse. Emily could barely see from the water and sweat coming off of her temple. As Emily brushed her blistered fingers across her forehead to wipe away the night mist and her sweat, she immediately came to the disquieting revelation that it was blood. Somehow during this ordeal, she had sliced her head on a branch. She tried to scream, but there was no sound. Emily had finally succumbed to exhaustion and fear. She felt imprisoned in her own body. The darkness of the night provided little comfort, and the air around her was bitter and stagnant with death. With each labored breath, Emily was coming to the realization that this island was going to be her tomb.

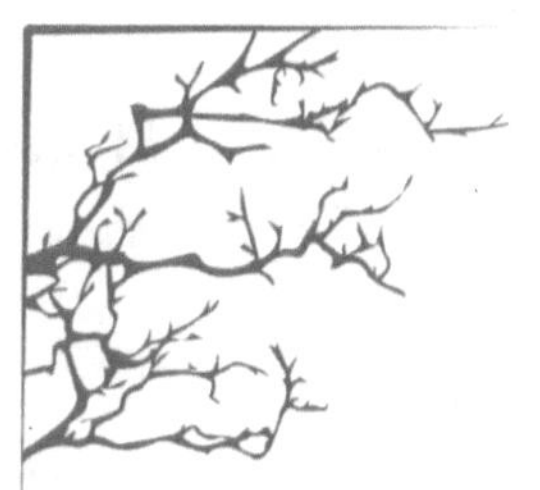

Chapter 23

Emily was on the ground next to Trent, almost as if they knew that they might be finishing their journey in life together here in this desolate moment. After about an hour, she heard a noise. Emily barely had energy left in her body or soul and forced herself to look up. She was sure that at this point it was probably some animal coming to finish off the wounded prey. Emily could make out a figure coming directly toward her. Even though her eyes were blurry, she could make out a human form.

She shouted, "Liz!" with a raspy voice.

The figure did not respond. It was not until the person was within a foot or so of her that she realized that this was not Liz. It was the ranger from the ranger station when they checked in on the island. She was noticeably out of breath and was running off adrenaline.

Emily looked up at the ranger, and said, "Thank goodness Liz found you."

The ranger looked confused. "Who's Liz?"

"Wasn't she the one who told you where we were?"

"No. We have had teams looking all over the island for you for the past two days. We had a miscount on the ferry numbers since two kayakers who were not on the original manifest list were on the last ferry off of the island before the hurricane hit. Apparently, they told one of the deck hands that they did not have a chance to check in, but the hand forgot to tell the ferry captain due to all of the mayhem. I was searching the southernmost paths near the Carnegie ruins. I was about to make a left turn to Sea Camp, and for some reason I knew that I had to go to the right to the southern dock near the cemetery. Once I saw you I started running as fast as I could. Liz must have just missed me on the other path. I'll let the other group know that she is heading their way."

Emily was beginning to worry for Liz now as well.

The ranger could see that this poor girl was giving her emotional-all to everyone but herself.

"Don't worry, my dear, I'm sure that Liz is fine. This island is swarming with police and rangers looking for you all. We probably just missed each other on the fork up by Dungeness. There was a group of searchers in that area."

The ranger pulled out a survival first-aid pack, but she knew that there was nothing that she could do. It was almost just to invoke an emotional adrenaline rush in Trent. From the looks of his condition, the ranger was not certain that Trent was even alive. She dared not indicate that to Emily, since Trent was what was keeping Emily alive. The tree had to be moved. She called in their location on her radio. She gave Trent a strong, powerful pat on the back, and said, "Son, you're going to be just fine."

She knew, however, that his life was in a fragile balance, and that he needed to be flown out to a hospital as soon as possible. By this time, the water around him was bright red from his blood. This also gave the ranger additional concern—alligators. They were known to frequent the brackish waters of the St. Mary's River. She made a barrier around Trent in the water to protect him from an attack. She also placed some repellant in the water to ward off any reptiles looking for easy prey. The ranger kept a brave face for the benefit of Trent and Emily. However, she knew how grave this situation could really be if no help came soon.

It only took about twenty minutes until a massive spotlight was shining on Trent. A Navy SH-60 Seahawk helicopter was hovering. Two thick, twined ropes dropped, and two sailors from a nearby

Navy base repelled down from the helicopter. They immediately began to assess and take control of the situation. One was a Petty Officer Second Class, and the other gentleman appeared to be the officer in charge - a Lieutenant Commander.

They removed their flight helmets so that Emily and Trent could see their faces. The younger enlisted sailor appeared to be about twenty-five. He had short blond hair with a muscular build. The officer was almost completely bald except for a couple areas of hair on the side by his ears that he had shaved skin close. It was actually comforting for Emily since they had eyes that were set on a mission. These guys were professionals, and they kept themselves very controlled and calculated so as to not allow Trent to go further into shock. The petty officer pulled out a small gas saw to cut away the tree, and then began to assess Trent's injury. Emily was looking on at Trent's leg, not even thinking about her own injuries. The sailors were obviously combat medics, who luckily were training off of the coast of Fernandina Beach, Florida, only miles away. They got the SAT-Call from the park ranger due to the fact that someone had to remove a tree, which the local Medical Air Evac from St. Marys, Georgia did not have the resources to do this quickly.

By this time, a third sailor repelled out from the helicopter. He was a short, stocky petty officer first class with eyeglasses. He took Emily to the side and began giving her fluids to counteract the dehydration. He also placed a butterfly clip on her head to stop the bleeding from a gash that she had near her ear. It was likely from a branch that she had scraped. Emily didn't even cringe from the alcohol as the sailor wiped the wound. She could barely feel anything. As she began to get more fluids, Emily became more aware and responsive. The flight officer debriefed her on the situation. Emily tried to stand up and immediately fell to the ground. Her adrenaline had masked her other wound—the laceration to her leg. The sailor who was tending to her pulled out a large first-aid kit that made all others look like a toy. This had compartments and more organization that Emily had ever seen of anything in her life. He cleaned the wound with some type of iodine, and then gave Emily a shot in the arm to get some antibiotics into her. Finally, he unfolded a metal splint to put on her leg.

"This should do the trick, ma'am. It doesn't appear to have any infection. Just really dirty. Actually, I'm surprised how good it looks given what you've been through. This antibiotic that I just gave you will kill any infection that might be in there."

Emily thanked him for the attentiveness to her wound but wanted to focus on Trent. She pointed over at Trent and asked, "How's my husband? He's okay, right?"

"Ma'am. He has a compound fracture. Luckily, it missed the femoral artery by two inches. However, this break is a nine on a scale of ten, ten being the worst. We are going to move him to a clearing two clicks down the trail. We gave him some pain meds to keep him from going into shock. Please follow me to the helicopter."

Emily kept her composure and reacted like a soldier under stress. She followed the men as they carried Trent on a mobile stretcher to the Seahawk. The pilots were making some last-minute preflight preparations. Within seconds, Trent and Emily were aboard the massive gray helicopter. All of the soldiers put their flight helmets back on so that they could communicate white in route to the hospital. The pilots flipped down their night-vision goggles on their helmets and roared the engines. The co-pilot tapped two toggle switches in the center above his head. There were four massive monitor screens in front of the pilots' seats, which were glowing in green with radar images. Just then, this great metal beast took off like one of those rides that shot straight into the air. It took Emily's breath away at first.

The officer in charge put a headset on Emily. He began to speak.

"Ma'am, we have a direct clearance for Southeast Georgia Health System Camden Campus. Our ETA is ten minutes. The doctors there are awaiting us on the Tarmac."

Emily was shaken up but nodded her head and gave a thumbs-up to thank the officer. The Seahawk was moving low and fast with the side door open to give Trent much-needed air. It swayed occasionally as it followed the river. By this time, he was completely unconscious. Emily could see the concern in the seasoned corpsman's eyes as he tapped his superior officer for some experienced guidance. Emily wanted nothing more than to squeeze Trent with every essence of her exhausted body. Just to feel his touch in this moment. However, she knew that she needed to let these trained professionals do their job to keep him with her. Emily clenched the Spanish medallion necklace that Trent had bought for her in St. Augustine. She rubbed the worn engraved symbol in a circular motion with her thumb. It brought her comfort. It was her bond to Trent.

Emily's mind wandered to a house that she imagined she and Trent would own. It would be a two-story, Charleston-style place with a huge wrap-around porch extending out from the master bedroom. She could see herself drinking coffee as she sat across Trent's legs on a swinging loveseat that creaked with each soothing swing. The harvest moon would be peaking over the hills in the distance, and there would be a gentle summer breeze. The only sound would be the crickets who were starting their soft, nighttime serenade paired with the occasional distinct sound of a northern bobwhite in the distance.

There was a sharp movement as the helicopter cleared a batch of trees. Emily could see the lights of what appeared to be the hospital's helipad below. As they got closer, she could see the red lights that surrounded the big *H* that was painted in the middle of the Tarmac. The pilots swiftly dropped the metal bird from the sky and made a smooth, soft landing.

Two doctors, one male and one female, as well as a trauma nurse, came running up to the open door and took control like a scene from a prime-time television show. They immediately transferred Trent to a wheeled stretcher so that he could get into the OR stat. One of the nurses gently grabbed Emily's hand and placed her in a wheel chair to have her wounds looked after as well. She broke away for a moment to give Trent one last kiss before he was whisked into the operating room. The nurse tried to make some small talk, but she knew that Emily was preoccupied.

Another doctor met Emily inside and began to diagnose her injury. Emily could tell that this physician was probably coming down to the end of his shift by the scruffiness of his face and the bags under his eyes. His breath reeked of coffee, probably maximum strength Colombian, straight black. He also kept cracking his neck from side to side to occasionally to wake himself up. He appeared to be in his mid-forties and had a distinctive surgical cap with a Superman emblem on it. In a weird way, this comforted Emily. There was an arrogant confidence that exuded from this man.

"Miss, you are going to be just fine. I am going to give you about six stitches, and you will be good to go. It's a clean cut. It's deep, but it's not bleeding so you won't have to worry. It shouldn't scar too bad either. Just be sure to keep some vitamin E on it as it heals." It only took an hour to get her cleaned up and stitched. The doctor put a boot brace on her leg, so she could walk while it healed.

Emily tracked down a nurse to get an update on Trent. The station nurse advised Emily that Trent was still in the OR and that they didn't have any updates yet. Emily's eyes started to water up, and she asked where she could find the chapel. Emily knew that she needed some solace in the only place where she could reach higher than her humanity could take her. She needed to speak with an old friend. Emily weaved her way around the corridors of the hospital and finally saw the cross. The room was small with a few lit candles. It smelled like vanilla, which was soothing. She fell to her knees and began to cry. She spoke to God like she was just having a conversation with a lifelong girlfriend. She prayed for twenty minutes and cried more than she had cried ever in her whole life.

"Please, God, you can't take my soul mate. I need Trent to stay with me. Please! I'll do anything and give anything, just don't take him from me."

The room was dim and silent, but in her body, she felt at peace, as if there was an answer. She just knew that he had to be okay. She sat back in a small pew to rest and compose herself. Between the stress, the peace, and the flickering candles, Emily began to fall asleep. She tried to fight it, but her body was exhausted. She couldn't fight it anymore and succumbed to all that she had been through in the past week. She was awoken two hours later by the tender touch from that nurse who had helped her get into the ER earlier in the night. The nurse's face was sullen, and Emily did not have an easy feeling.

"Is Trent okay?"

"I need to let the doctors speak with you. I'm sorry, I just can't explain. They asked me to get you, but they did not tell me anything."

Emily lost her cool. "What in the hell do you mean? Why are you here if you can't tell me anything? What use are you?" After realizing her behavior, she quickly apologized to the nurse, and then also gave an apology to her divine maker under her breath for using such a profane term in His chapel. She began to walk briskly down the hall and worked up to a slow jog. She made a turn and ran smack into the surgeon who was heading her way to give her the news. The collision was forceful enough to knock the stethoscope from the doctor's neck.

"Whoa. Sorry about that," the doctor said apologetically, as if she had caused the collision. It was more of just a polite lip service to appease Emily since the doctor knew full well that she was not the guilty party in this head-on accident.

"Are you Mrs. Decker?"

"Yes. Yes. How is he? How is Trent? Please tell me."

"My name is Dr. Riley. I was the chief surgeon overseeing your husband's surgery."

"How is he? Can I see him now, please?"

Dr. Riley took her hand to comfort her and smiled. "Mrs. Decker, Trent is fine. The surgery was successful. He had a complete break of his femur and narrowly missed the femoral, which is great. We were able to make a clean connection of the bone, so it should heal without any complications. Mr. Decker is resting in his room. Given the trauma and the anesthetic, I would not expect that he will wake until morning. I'll take you to his room. He was really lucky that the naval team got to him when they did. It was probably their quick reaction to control the bleeding that kept him alive. Most people in his condition never make it to the hospital."

Emily exhaled with relief. As she walked, she took a moment to look at the doctor since she was caught up in the moment of stress when first conversing with her. The doctor appeared quite young. She had strawberry-blonde hair and was attractive in the way that she carried herself. Emily could see that she had her name sewn onto her scrub top, *Stacy O. Riley, M.D.*

Emily tried to assuage the mood by making small talk now that she knew Trent was okay.

"So, doctor, how old are you if you don't mind me asking? You seem quite young."

Dr. Riley laughed and said, "I'm actually thirty-seven. I'm the youngest chief surgeon ever at this hospital."

"You must be a prodigy."

"Well, I don't know about that, but I did graduate high school at seventeen. Then, I made it through Clemson undergrad in two years before embarking on Harvard medical school. I don't call myself a genius, just a hard worker who is focused on a goal."

"Well said. Thank you again for saving my husband. We've only been married for a week, so I can't afford to lose him yet. I'd end up in some tabloid as the black widow wife or something like that. I'm just lucky that another Clemson Tiger found him."

"You went to Clemson as well?" the doctor asked.

"Yep, I'm a Tiger through and through." At that moment, Emily's emotion took over and she gave the doctor a huge hug, like they were now relatives.

Both women laughed. Before long, they arrived at Trent's recovery room. It was just an ordinary looking room from the outside with a removable name plate that said *Trent Decker.* The doctor gave Emily a pat on the back and advised the nurse to let Emily stay in the room with Trent overnight. The nurse on duty was a short, elderly woman with bad posture. She was as polite as she needed to be for her job, but Emily could tell that she would prefer to be back behind the main check-in desk watching some re-run on the small television behind the desk. Before she left the room abruptly, she quite awkwardly pointed Emily in the direction of the linens. There was no doubt why she was on the midnight to seven shift.

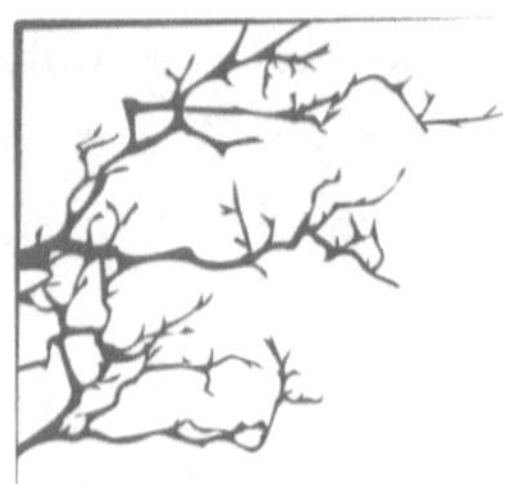

Chapter 24

Emily made her way to Trent. He was out cold. Behind him, she could see the heart monitor and other vitals beeping softly. He had two IVs in his arms dripping some form of fluid, no doubt pain medications and an antibiotic. He was tucked nicely under the covers and had his leg raised in a huge sling hanging above the bed. The cast on his leg went nearly to his waist and was as bright white as she had ever seen anything in her life. Emily leaned in and gave Trent a huge kiss on the lips before settling in for the night on the hard couch in the corner of the room. She fell asleep to the sound of the distant voices from doctors and nurses in the hallway coupled with the hypnotic beeping from Trent's machines. This was the first good night's sleep she had got in a while.

In the morning, she was awoken by the sound of Trent's voice. It was raspy from his tribulation, but he was in good spirits. Emily jumped up and went to his side.

"Am I glad to see you, babe!"

"Back at ya, beautiful."

Trent reached over and grabbed Emily's arm as best he could with the IV still stuck in an outer vein.

"So, did we solve the mystery of Jackson Jones, Em?"

"I can't say for sure, but I definitely think we did it. How are you feeling?"

"Like I got hit by a truck, then a bus, and then a frying pan. My leg is starting to hurt like hell. I think the meds are wearing off."

"Good news is that the doc said the surgery was perfect, and that you'll make a full recovery. Now, if I could only get them to do something about your horrendous sense of humor," Emily said as she kissed Trent again for good measure.

Trent asked Emily about the details of how they got off of the island since he was unconscious from the time that his leg broke. Emily filled him in on the adventure. He was jealous that he missed the Seahawk flight, since he had always dreamed of flying in one of those. They also talked about Liz, and how they hoped she made it safely off of the island. Neither of them had her cell phone number to check up on their friend who had helped with this adventure.

After about an hour of talking, Emily could see that Trent was starting to get sleepy from his medications. It was about that time that Dr. Riley poked her head in the door.

"How's my patient today?"

"Great doc! Thank you for taking care of me."

"My pleasure."

The doctor performed some standard tests and checked her work on the cast once again.

"Everything looks good. The nurse will come see you in a few minutes to give you your breakfast and morning pain medications."

Trent nodded and thanked the doctor, and she graciously slipped out of the room to head home after a long shift. Soon after Dr. Riley left the room, the nurse on the morning shift came into the room. She was much more pleasant than the night shift nurse. She was a young, heavy-set brunette with dark brown glasses.

"Here you go, my dear. The best that we can offer. Eggs, toast, hash browns, bacon, blueberry yogurt, a cup of coffee, and a glass of orange juice."

"Thank you," Trent said with confident grin.

The nurse excused herself, and Trent began to pick through his food with the small plastic spork he had been given. Emily was not much of a fan of hospital food, even when it was as fancy as this spread. It was still hospital food and never had the same appeal as a home-cooked breakfast. Trent knew that Emily was starving and convinced her to go to the cafeteria to at least get a muffin and coffee. She agreed and gave Trent a peck on the cheek as she made her way out toward the smell of the food.

Emily strolled down the hallway, occasionally peeking into the open rooms. She was curious by nature and could not help it. She saw people of all ages in the various recovery rooms. The hallway was filled with every gambit of emotion, like a bottle of pure humanity. There were those people like Emily who were relieved and happy. On the other side of the spectrum, she could see the stress, disbelief, and sadness in others' eyes as she passed them in the hall. It took her two levels and ten minutes to weave her way to the main cafeteria.

There was nothing special about it. The walls were pretty plain except for some standard hospital art on the walls. It had that overly cleaned sanitizer smell that always made her a bit nauseous. She hated the smell of hospitals. There was just something about that smell, but she could not pinpoint what exactly it was that she disliked. It was just a smell that made her nauseated. She could not for the life of her figure out why no one had invented some better smelling hospital-grade disinfectant to use in places like the cafeteria. Today, she sucked it up to get some food in her system since she was starting to feel faint from low blood sugar.

She nibbled down a blueberry muffin and chased it with a mocha latte. Now that Emily was in better spirits, she realized that she had completely neglected to call her parents. They were no doubt worried sick about her and Trent. She reached into her pocket. Her phone was partially charged, so she immediately dialed her father's number.

"Hello? Em is that you? Are you okay? Where are you? Why haven't you called?" Judge said in a frantic state. He had fifty questions that he needed to get answered now. Emily's mom got on the line as well when Judge put his phone on speaker.

"Emily, what happened?" her mother asked.

"I'm okay. Sorry for not calling. It has been a crazy few days. That stupid hurricane ended up hitting Cumberland Island."

Judge chimed in, "Yeah, we saw that. It hit us too, but not as bad. Did you and Trent make it off of the island before it hit?"

"No, we got stranded."

"What! I'll sue the damn government! Can't it even run a fucking national park without screwing that up?" Judge was beyond upset and was turning a shade of red that Marjorie had never seen in all of their years of marriage.

"Dear, hold on. What happened, Emily?" Marjorie was always the voice of reason who could calm Judge when he got into one of those moods.

"Mom, dad. It was just a mistake. There was a miscount on the ferry in all of the confusion. Trent and I let another couple use or campsite for a couple of days and they didn't have a chance to check in with the rangers to give the rangers an accurate head count. This must have thrown off the island count."

"Em, that was stupid. What were you thinking?" Judge said. As the words left his mouth he realized that he was beating her up enough. All that mattered was that she was not dead somewhere on the banks of the island. "Sorry. I didn't mean that. I'm just scared."

"It's okay, Dad."

"So, what happened?" Marjorie asked.

Emily left out all of the supernatural events, since this was not going to make this call easier. That would unquestionably require a full, in-person conversation like at Thanksgiving or Christmas. She took a deep breath. Just the thought of telling this story made Emily uncomfortable. "We were hiking to get to the ferry after the storm hit, and Trent got hit by a falling tree. The branch broke his leg. Luckily, we had a friend with us named Liz. She got stranded as well. Liz went to look for a park ranger, and under God's watchful eye, a ranger showed up. Trent's leg was hurt really bad. We ended up being rescued by a naval medivac team. They whisked us away from the island on their Seahawk helicopter. These guys saved Trent's life."

"How's Trent?" Judge asked.

"He's okay now. He made it through surgery successfully. Now he's resting in his recovery room. He's getting fat off of hospital food, sodas, and bad TV."

"Thank goodness," Marjorie said.

"We'll pack up and head to you." Judge was not one to sit by and remain idle in situations like this.

"No, Dad. Stay put. The roads are probably all torn up from Xavier. It could be dangerous. We're both fine, and we're safe in this hospital."

"Are you sure?"

"Yes."

"All right. I trust you. You've always been pretty smart like your old man." Judge was trying to lighten the mood.

"Do you need anything? Do you want us to at least send up a care package?" Marjorie asked.

"No thanks, Mom. We're good. We'll be home in a week or so once Trent is mobile. I love you both."

"We love you too, dear," both Judge and Marjorie said in unison.

Before hanging up, Marjorie got in one last sentence and said, "Call us before you leave to give us an update. We'll prepare a nice home-cooked meal for you both. Invite that new friend as well if you want if she lives anywhere near here,"

Emily felt reassured after speaking with her parents. They always found a way to bring her to a stable emotional place. This time was no different. Emily placed the phone back in her pocket since it was just about out of juice.

After hanging up the call, Emily watched as an expecting mother came down for a quick bite. The woman looked exhausted, and she nibbled on ice chips from a small, clear plastic cup. The poor woman was obviously ready to be a mother and have this child freed from her body. This took Emily's mind to a joyful place where she daydreamed of one day being in a hospital much like this waiting to have her first child. Maybe she'd have twins and get it done with one shot, she jokingly thought to herself.

Emily's daydream was abruptly interrupted by a large figure approaching her table, and thus blocking the light of the nearby window. Emily looked up and saw a large, stocky gentleman. He was wearing some form of police uniform and had perfectly trimmed, medium-length black hair with flecks of gray. When he reached her table, Emily realized that he was wearing an FBI field shirt with a Kevlar vest. He also had a gun strapped to his side.

"Mrs. Decker?" the man asked with a strong southern accent.

"Yes?" Emily was not sure what to make of this, and she could not handle any more twists of fate that somehow impacted her life. She was not sure whether this guy was going to give her a medal for finding the body of Jackson Jones or arrest her on some misguided claim of destroying a cemetery tomb.

"Ma'am, my name is Special Agent Aiden Callaghan. I'm the head of the Bureau's Louisiana field office out of New Orleans. May I sit?"

"Sure, as long as you're not here to arrest me for something."

Special Agent Callaghan laughed with a huge belly laugh that everyone in the room could hear.

"No ma'am. Quite the contrary. I need your help."

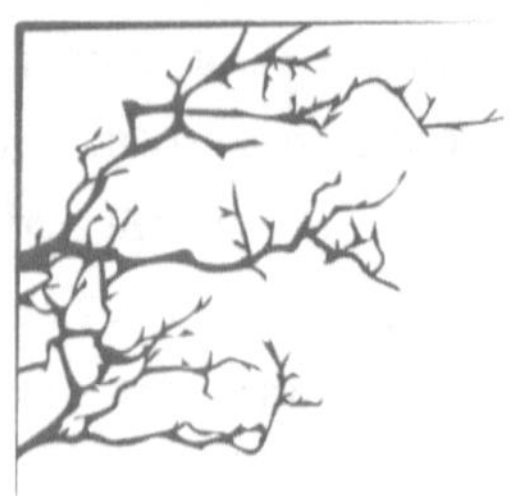

Chapter 25

He began to explain to Emily how his office was in charge of a closed cold case involving the disappearance of Jackson Jones. According to Agent Callaghan, the feds had this case instead of the local authorities due to the fact that it involved a mysterious mechanized invention that went missing. Ever since 1944, there were speculations that everyone from the President of the United States to the mob had something to do with Mr. Jones's disappearance.

In between a few minutes of his story, he would take a sip from a small, cafeteria-issued Styrofoam cup of black coffee. He explained how the local authorities contacted his office when Emily and Trent found the body.

"Ma'am, we have been . . ."

Emily stopped Agent Callaghan and said, "Please call me Emily. There's no need for the formality. It makes me look around for my mother. Sorry, go on."

"Thanks, Emily. Where was I? Oh yeah, we have been combing Cumberland Island for the past day. Our teams have been working around the clock with huge spotlights to continue at night. You could probably see the entire outline of that island from space at midnight. Our forensic team has confirmed through DNA, as well as through identification found on the body, that you did discover the body of Jackson Jones."

Emily was entranced with this story. She already knew in her heart that she had found Jackson, but it made her feel vindicated to hear it from a federal agent. She loved every bit, like a student listening to a teacher. "Did anyone ever speak with Liz?"

"No, ma'am. I don't think we've spoken with a person name Liz yet. However, we have several witnesses who are on our list."

Emily playfully scolded the agent. "First, remember, call me, Emily . . . EM-I-LEE. Second, be sure you speak with her. She was with us when we found Mr. Jones's body. I don't have her cell number, but she is a good source of information as well."

Agent Callaghan laughed. "Sorry, force of habit. We will definitely track her down to debrief her as well. Any help is appreciated since this case could end up a cold case forever given the lack of witnesses."

"So, what is the link between your office in New Orleans and a mystery from Cumberland Island, Georgia?"

Agent Callaghan paused for a moment to take his last gulp of his now lukewarm coffee He pushed his cup to the side of the table and then reached down into a small fabric briefcase that was next to his foot. The briefcase had the logo *FBI* embroidered in the center of it. He pulled out a yellow legal notepad that was covered in his chicken scratch. He seemed to keep his briefcase very organized. Emily was sure that he even had his pens organized with the blue and black ones being separated.

He looked back up at Emily. "This one is our office's Jimmy Hoffa case. Obviously, not with the same notoriety or with the same amount of leads. Nevertheless, this one has been lingering on a shelf in my office before my time and before my former boss's time. It went cold from the beginning. Our office interviewed the army soldiers on the island, as well as every fact witness we could find. No one told us anything of any substance. We did initially manage to get a few nuggets of information from Private First Class Delford Solinski, who was stationed on the island, but it just led to more questions than answers. To my office, this disappearance has the infamy of any case that we've come across. Unfortunately, outside of the purview of the field office, it does not carry the sexy, materialistic appeal like the unsolved crimes that appear every weekend on the cable channels."

You could hear the crinkling of the paper as he licked the tip of his finger to flip each page. According to the field notes, Mr. Solinski, was wishy-washy in his responses. He never went beyond a certain threshold of knowledge in his responses. Agent Callaghan went on to explain how it was hard to gather from the pieces of paper whether Mr. Solinski was a scared young man or some devious co-conspirator. Agent Callaghan's theory was that he knew something, but that he probably was not directly involved with the murder.

Emily took a sip from her coffee since she was now fully invested in knowing what happened on the island and finding out the truth. "So why not just drag him into the station and force him to talk? Can't you strap him to a chair and beat it out of him?" That's the best way she could describe it since her only knowledge of these things was what she saw on the prime-time TV cop shows.

Agent Callaghan gave her an inquisitive look and put down a pen. He had been clicking and twirling the blue pen in one hand in some sort of repetitive quirk that he had. "Typically, we would not hesitate to bring a witness like Mr. Solinski down to our office to question him. However, he is ninety-three years old, and by all accounts is in failing health from prostate cancer. He has refused to voluntarily come down to speak with any of my agents, and he has flat-out told us that he will not speak with anyone from our office. Unfortunately, he holds all of the cards since he has nothing to lose. If he dies, he could very well take the last remaining shred of clues with him to the grave."

"Why are you here if he won't talk anyway?"

"We think he will talk.

"What?"

"I had one of my agents call him yesterday to let him know that we located the body of Jackson Jones. According to the agent, Mr. Solinski was not as obstinate as usual and actually engaged in some limited conversation. He asked how we discovered the body and whether we now know the truth about Jackson Jones. The agent told Mr. Solinski that it was a woman who had been camping who actually uncovered the truth. This was our way to try to personalize this situation more and get him to speak with us. It worked in the sense that we breached his shell just enough to pique his interest. He told my agent that he would only speak with the woman who had uncovered the truth, and upon our request, he did agree that the conversation could be taped. We think he wants to tell this story to release himself from the secret so that he does not carry this burden to his grave. He just won't speak with any of us for some reason. This guy takes conspiracy theory to a new level. He really hates the government."

Emily was stunned. How did the FBI or Agent Callaghan expect her speak with a gentleman in New Orleans? Trent was laid up in the hospital, and she needed to be here with him. Emily began to pull and curl a long strand of her hair. This was her telltale quirk when she was in thought or was nervous.

"I appreciate the offer, Agent, but what exactly did you have in mind? Skype or webcam? This guy probably doesn't even own a computer."

"No, Emily. We would need for you to travel to New Orleans to take his story in person. We need it recorded for evidentiary purposes."

Emily was shocked and said, "I cannot travel to New Orleans. After all that Trent has been through, I need to stay here with him."

"I completely understand, Emily. We are in a bind, and I would not even ask if it was not a last resort. We just have nothing without this witness's statement. This file will likely go back on the shelf forever, and no one will ever know why Mr. Jones was killed. Please at least think about it. Promise me that. We are flying back in three hours, and I promise that I can have you back by tomorrow night. You were obviously intrigued enough to put the pieces together to find his body. All that we are asking is for you to help find that final piece."

Emily shook Agent Callaghan's hand and politely declined. "You're not going to tell me to do this for my country or something corny like that, are you?"

"Would it work?"

"Nope," Emily replied.

Agent Callaghan left the table with a disappointed look, but he understood. He left Emily his business card just in case she changed her mind.

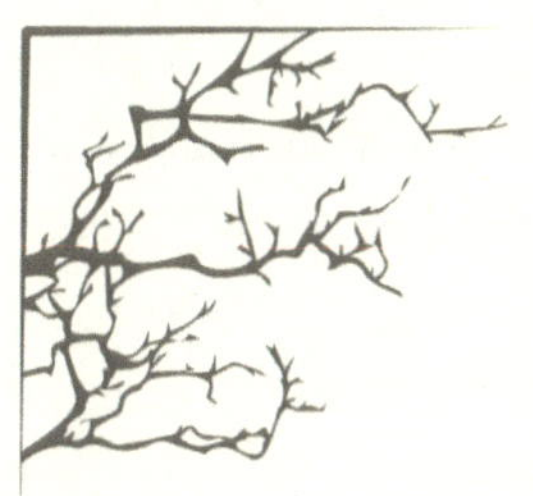

Chapter 26

Emily got another cup of coffee to take back to Trent's room. She slowly sipped it as she walked, wiping a dribble from her mouth. This one tasted worse than the first cup. It was like the cafeteria was trying to make her sick to keep her checked into this place. She was horrible at walking with coffee in her hand. She could not remember a time when she actually made it from one place to another without spilling hot coffee on her wrist or arm. Half of her wardrobe had permanent coffee stains. The walk back to Trent's room seemed nowhere as far as the walk from the room to the cafeteria. When she entered the room, Trent was wide awake looking over some pamphlet about how to treat broken legs after discharge from the hospital.

"Howdy, beautiful! How's that awful hospital food?"

He was in good spirits. With one look at Emily he knew that something was on her mind. He motioned for her to come to his side, which she did.

"What's up, babe? You look like you're desperately trying to solve a math problem in your head."

"I just had a meeting with the FBI.

"The FBI? Why?" Trent asked with a curious half-nod of his head.

"Apparently, they are asking me to take a witness statement from the last reaming soldier who was on Cumberland Island when Jackson Jones disappeared. It's the guy from the entry that we found. That NCO, Private Solinski."

She explained the whole meeting to Trent. He was excited for her since he knew how much she loved these types of mysteries. She went on to tell Trent how the Bureau wanted her to fly to New Orleans later today to meet with the witness tonight, and how she had graciously declined. Trent gently grabbed her arm and caressed the inside of her forearm. This comforted Emily.

He looked up at her and said without hesitation, "You need to do this, Emily."

"How can I do that with you here like this?" Emily was shocked at Trent's reaction to this whole thing. She knew that she had married a supportive man, but this even took her by complete surprise since he was in a hospital with a cast, IV tubes from every direction, and the sort. How could anyone be this selfless of a human being? Maybe it was the medications making him loopy? She leaned in and kissed him and presented her case as to why she could not leave him sitting in a hospital. She put on a convincing case.

Trent, however, taking a page from Emily's litigation mindset, used Emily's own logic to justify the trip to New Orleans. He explained that he was stuck sitting in his bed for another week. He wasn't going anywhere, and he was going to be right here when she returned tomorrow night to fill him in on her adventure. Emily was impressed, and actually agreed with Trent. If Trent wanted her to go, how could she refuse this honest, loving man's soft directive to her. It would essentially be discrediting his point of view and symbolically slapping him in the face.

She gave him another kiss and said, "How did you become such a good wannabe lawyer?"

He smiled and responded, "I learned from the best. All of those years of listening to your logic and losing arguments. I finally took a page out of your manual."

Emily knew what she had to do. She reached in her pocket and pulled out Agent Callaghan's card. She just stared at it for a moment.

"Do it already, babe," Trent said with a supportive grin.

Emily flipped the card a couple of times in her right hand. The ends of the card were frayed and bent from being in her pocket. She went over to the corner of Trent's room, and grabbed the off-white phone that was sitting on small, cheap-looking end table. Emily could feel her adrenaline increasing as she dialed the number. She was excited about this proposition. She could not believe that she was actually doing this.

"Are you sure about this?" she asked Trent.

"Do it. This feels right. With all that we have been through, we all need closure to make what we went through worth it," Trent responded.

The phone rang four times. Each ring seemed like an eternity. Agent Callaghan answered on the fifth ring.

"This is Agent Callaghan, may I help you?" He knew that it was Emily, but he wanted it to sound as formal as possible. Inside he knew that Emily was going to say yes. No one ever called just to say no again. He had been through this drill too many times in his career and was one of the best profilers in the agency.

"Agent Callaghan, this is Emily Decker. I'm in!"

"Great! I was hoping that I would back hear from you. Your husband is okay with you heading over to bayou country for a day?"

"Yep," Emily replied with a smile as she blew a kiss Trent's way. "I've married the best man in the world."

"All right. I'll swing by and pick you up in thirty minutes. We are wheels up to New Orleans in one hour. Please thank Trent for me as well. Not to sound like a cliché, but you both are doing a great service to your country by just allowing us to try to get this mystery solved. Even if we can't find out anything from Mr. Solinski, I will be able to sleep at night knowing that we gave it everything possible."

Emily felt a sense of pride. She was getting ready to hang up and pack her things when she realized that all of her belongings were somewhere on the island or at the ranger station. She had nothing to take.

"Wait, Agent Callaghan are you still on the line?"

"Yes, what did you forget to ask?"

"I just realized that I don't even have any clothes to change into for the trip."

"Don't worry. We've got you covered. Literally," said Callaghan. "We have some spare standard uniform shirts and slacks for two of our female field agents. You should be just about the same size. We'll also arrange for you to get a toothbrush and anything else that you need."

Emily and Trent shared a few final moments of small talk and kisses. Then she bolted as quickly as she could toward the entrance of the hospital. She was trying not to run, but she was a close to a jog as one could get without breaking a sweat. She stood out in front of the hospital and watched as a few ambulances came screaming by to drop off patients in the Emergency Room. The sky was clear, no clouds to be found. Xavier had taken all of the clouds with him as he passed north. After about ten minutes of waiting, she saw two black Suburban SUVs turn into the parking lot. They approached and stopped right in front of her. Each was jet black with tinted windows.

Agent Callaghan opened the door of the rear vehicle for her, and Emily stepped up inside. There were two other agents in the vehicle as well. One was driving, and the other was analyzing something on a small laptop. They each quickly introduced themselves and then went back to their tasks. They were polite, but Emily could tell that she was in the company of professionals. Agent Callaghan had an unlit cigar in his mouth.

"Don't mind this thing. I gave up smoking them about five years ago. Now, I just put one in my mouth every once in a while, to chew on the tobacco."

"Don't stop on my account. I'm not offended. Now if you light that thing up in here, I may have to slap it out of your mouth. Besides, I may grab one from you if we get the answers to solve this mystery. "

Both Emily and Agent Callaghan laughed. He leaned over and pulled out a spare set of clothes for Emily. She unfolded the shirt and slacks. They were standard Bureau issue, with blue and white trim. The shirt said *Federal Bureau of Investigation* and had the FBI logo on it. The slacks seemed to be her size.

"You can change once we arrive at the airport."

Emily was relieved. This was her first government gig, and she was afraid that she may be changing in the SUV to keep time. That surely was not a part of Trent's deal. Callaghan gave Emily a folder. She was reaching down to open the packet. Agent Callaghan stopped her and advised her that he would have to go over some protocol first. Emily completed understood, given her experience as a prosecutor. She looked Callaghan in the eyes, and she awaited his instructions.

"Okay, Emily, I'm going to swear you in for this limited assignment. This way, you will be under our jurisdiction, and we can brief you on specific details of the investigation. Also, it will allow us to use any recorded information that you receive from Mr. Solinski. Any questions?"

"Nope. I understand."

"Perfect." Callaghan began to give Emily an oath, which she recited to him. She was now under the umbrella of the FBI for this investigation. The two then went through the detailed folder. It had several old pictures of Mr. Jones, as well as all of the witness statements. There were statements of everyone, from a local barber who swore he cut Jackson Jones's hair only days after the disappearance to a waitress who said she was secretly married to Jackson. There was one common theme that Emily noticed as she flipped through the pages. Each lead went nowhere. It was as if each lead was a lit fuse that simply went out before reaching its powder keg of truth.

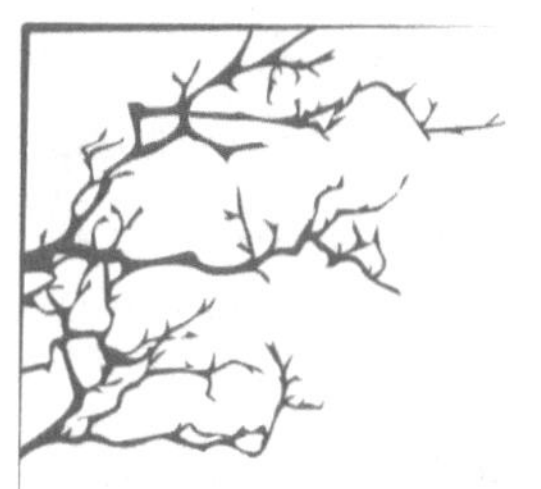

Chapter 27

Emily, because of her perfectionist nature, took notes and asked Callaghan every minute detail that she could think of to be sure that she successfully carried out this assignment. She knew had to depose a witness. If she had to guess, she had about three hundred depositions under her belt. This was different though. There was a level of finesse required to be sure that she did not lose the last witness. To Emily, this would be like fishing. She had to give enough line to make the witness bite at the questions and then be sure that she didn't yank on the fishing pole too soon or she wouldn't have anything to show for her efforts.

Agent Callaghan was impressed by Emily to say the least. He saw how she was preparing, and it made him proud. It was as if she were a new recruit in training. She was methodical in her preparation, looking at every piece of information in front of her in order to fit together the puzzle pieces.

Agent Callaghan kept to himself so that Emily could get the mental image of the items that she was looking over for her mission. He was focused on preparing some general questions for Emily to get her started on the right track. This witness was tricky. No one really knew for sure whether this gentleman was going to be hostile, evasive, or maybe even just absent-minded from old age. He was a wild card to say the least. The Bureau had no real emotional background on him from which they could properly create a profile.

The SUVs were flying down the road with the lights from the front grills flashing. Emily felt important, like she was in a Presidential motorcade. She looked out the windows occasionally and could not help but feel like she was in a dream as she watched people point and wave to the passing vehicles. None of these people knew who was in the SUVs, but they didn't seem to care. They just loved the fact that there was someone important in there. On this day, that person was Emily.

"Do you ever get used to the rush of having people gawk at you in these SUVs like you are some sort of movie star or athlete?"

Agent Callaghan smiled and responded, "Not really. It still feels the same today as it did my first day on the job. Unfortunately, most times we are so focused on saving a life or finding an abducted child that we don't even get to soak in the feeling."

This put everything in perspective for Emily. She felt bad for feeling like an important person on the way to a film premiere. This was a job, and people were affected. How could she allow herself to enjoy this pleasure when these agents were faced with deadly situations each week? Emily put on her game face and focused.

When they arrived at the St. Marys Airport, the SUVs made a beeline straight for an unmarked hangar toward the back of the airport. Emily saw a large twin-engine turbo prop airplane sitting on the Tarmac. It was beautiful. There were two security guards on either side of the aircraft. Emily could not get over how beautiful it looked. It was white with an Air Force blue underbelly. There was a dark-blue pinstripe going across the middle, separating the white from the blue on the plane.

The plane was pristine to the point where you could see your reflection as a shadow off of the white surface. As Emily exited the SUV, she could smell the fuel and tire grease for the aircraft. It was the stout smell that you encountered on a freshly prepped aircraft. She approached closer to the plane, and she could not believe how large the propellers were on each side. She surmised to herself that each had to be at least ten feet in circumference. It reminded her of the planes that her family would catch on their connecting flights in Charlotte on the way to a ski lodge in West Virginia. She loved these planes, the way they bounced with the turbulence. It made most people sick, but not her. It was like riding on a metal bull to her.

Agent Callaghan started toward the stairs, and Emily followed. The door was open, and the stairs were attached to the inside of the door with a foldable metal handrail on each side. Emily and the other agents entered the plane single file up the stairs. Emily let her fingers loosely run across a couple of rivets on the door as she went up the stairs. She had no doubt that this bird was ready to fly. All-in-all, five passengers and two pilots got on the plane. All of the passengers except for Emily were special agents. As best Emily could figure, they were all from the New Orleans field office. The plane was modified and had a small round table in the back.

Emily followed Agent Callaghan to the back of the aircraft. She and Callaghan sat in chairs on either side of the table. They buckled up. Within about ten minutes, the preflight was complete, and the pilots came over the intercom to advise the passengers that they were off. Sounds of ringing bells could be heard as the co-pilot made the final preflight preparations by toggling up various electrical switches. One by one, the engines cranked up to a roar. Black smoke poured out behind each engine as they fired up. There was a smell of burned oil from the initial engine blast. Emily could feel the power as the plane tried to jolt forward, only being held back by the brakes. It was like a metal stagecoach with several horses pulling against the reigns as the driver held them back.

There was a slight cool breeze as the cabin air began to circulate. The noise was almost deafening as the aircraft began to taxi. Emily could hear the pilots as they approached the runway.

"St. Marys Tower, this is November Niner Niner Pappa requesting permission to taxi to runway three-six." The pilots were wearing their aviator sunglasses and looked like they just stepped off of a Navy aircraft carrier. Emily had no doubt that these guys were probably former F-14 pilots. They had that swagger about them.

"November Niner Niner Pappa, you are clear to taxi to runway three-six. Hold short of runway, you have a Gulfstream turning base for final approach."

"Copy that."

The plane swiftly made its way to the runway and stopped just short of it. Emily watched as a massive Gulfstream 650 landed just feet from where the FBI plane was patiently waiting. After a few minutes, she heard the pilots again.

"St. Marys Tower, November Niner Niner Pappa requesting permission to take off on runway three-six."

"November Niner Niner Pappa, you are clear for an immediate take off on runway three-six. After five hundred feet, depart to the left."

"Copy that."

The plane rolled onto the runway, and the engines got even louder as the pilots hit full throttle. Within a minute, the aircraft was in the air. The air was cold today, which made the takeoff smooth. Agent Callaghan was sitting back. Emily could tell that he was not that enthused with the takeoff portion of the flight. She waited until the plane reached its cruising altitude before opening her folder to ask Callaghan some questions.

Emily looked over to Agent Callaghan and said with a smile, "So . . . what are my marching orders, sir?"

Agent Callaghan chuckled and took a breath now that the plane was safely in the air. He got up from his seat and went over to a coffee pot.

"Want some fresh coffee?"

"Sure. I've never been known to turn down a good cup of Joe."

He poured a cup for each of them. Emily was impressed. This cup was not the standard, flimsy Styrofoam cup. This was the real deal: a blue ceramic cup with the FBI logo on it.

"I may have to put this cup in my purse and steal it."

"Emily, if you can get me something from Mr. Solinski so that I may close this file, I'll send you a dozen of these things."

"Do you want any cream or sugar, Emily?"

"Nope. Black is fine for me. I like to savor the pure taste of the coffee no matter how bad it may be."

"I knew that I liked you for a reason. Black coffee tells me a lot about you."

"How so?"

"It says that you're a to-the-point person who does not get caught up in minutiae that bogs down most people. It's actually one of my tests for my new recruits. I always see how they drink their coffee."

"Interesting. I had better keep my eye on your cop tricks," Emily said with a chuckle.

Callaghan took a sip from his coffee and put on a pair of reading glasses. They sat on the edge of his nose.

"You know, I wasn't always afraid of flying."

"I was wondering about that, but you don't have to explain anything to me," Emily responded.

"About five years ago, I was on an assignment in Wyoming. We were working a joint case with the local sheriff's department regarding a biker gang who had been caught up in a string of interstate bank robberies. It was truly God's country. The prettiest sunsets that I had ever seen. A painting could not even do justice to the pure, uncut nature of the countryside and mountains. Anyway, one day we were flying out of a small airport just east of the Black Hills mountain range. The sky was clear, and it seemed like a perfect day to fly. We got up about thirteen hundred feet, and all of a sudden, we lost the left engine. The pilots scrambled to control the plane and turn us back to the runway. We dropped like a rock and fell into a flat spin. The pilots managed to straighten the plane out at the last minute. However, by that time, we were carving up a field just shy of the runway. We had ten of us on that flight. We lost one agent and had two others with paralysis."

Emily was shocked by the details of the story. "If you don't mind me asking, how can you keep flying?"

"It's tough . . . that's for sure. But you know, my love for my job gets me through it. I'd be chained to a desk in D.C. if I did not suck it up and get back in the saddle."

Emily took another sip of her coffee and shook her head in an understanding nod. Agent Callaghan took a gulp of coffee.

"Now, back to work. We should be on the ground in about two hours. We'll get there about six-thirty Central Time. Even though Mr. Solinski is not jumping through hoops to give us access to his story, he has agreed to speak with you tonight. We'll have to see if he keeps his word. It may be a quick trip."

Emily was somewhat confused as to Mr. Solinski's perceived demeanor, so she asked Callaghan, "What makes you think he may back out of giving a statement?"

"I can't say that I have a definite reason other than the fact that he hasn't even given us so much as a screw you in response to our prior requests to speak with him. He just has his nurse tell us no. Before you meet him, I need to give you some background on this guy. Based on our intel, Mr. Solinski has been associated with the Genivicci Crime Family for the better part of his time in New Orleans. They are primarily Italian but have known to associate with some Irish groups. My office has had them under surveillance before I even started at the Bureau."

Emily was intrigued and asked, "Do you have them on racketeering?"

"They do a pretty good job of staying under the radar. We've dragged in a few enforcers in connection with a drug operation gone bad. Let's just say that the deal ended with four people missing, including a local politician. No bodies were ever found, but cameras from a local gas station clearly showed at least one of the missing men in the car with a known Genivicci hit man. No one ever talks. These guys would just as soon die in prison of old age as opposed to being outed for talking with us. We can't figure out how Mr. Solinski fits into the family. He is not a towering, imposing man, and he's not even Italian. We think he's Polish. Regardless, he has seemed to stay in the good graces of the Genivicci group. We have him on video conducting some minor cash transactions for the family. Probably some minor money laundering."

"Why would a group of mobsters even care about some guy with no known prior mob ties?"

"That's the million-dollar question."

Agent Callaghan pulled out his entire file on Jackson Jones and opened a file folder labeled *Witness Statements.*

"Here is what we have from Mr. Solinski."

He opened the blue folder that had two metal tabs at the top to hold the paper, which had been hole punched at the top to keep the papers intact.

"Right after the disappearance, Mr. Solinski was interviewed by an agent from the Office of Strategic Services, and this is what was transcribed."

Mr. Fintel: Mr. Solinski, my name is Frederick Fintel. I am with the Office of Strategic Services. Have we ever met before today?

Mr. Solinski:No, sir, not to my knowledge.

Mr. Fintel:Do you know why I am taking your statement here today?

Mr. Solinski:Yes, sir. I think I do.

Mr. Fintel:Why?

Mr. Solinski:Because a gentleman went missing on the island a couple of days ago.

Mr. Fintel:Yes. That's correct. Did you know that gentleman who disappeared?

Mr. Solinski:No, sir. I did not.

Mr. Fintel:Were you on duty when he disappeared?

Mr. Solinski:I would presume so. I don't know exactly when he disappeared, but I have been on the island for the last twenty days straight.

Mr. Fintel:Fair enough. Do you possess any facts that you would like to share with us here today, which you believe may help us with this investigation?

Mr. Solinski:No sir. Nothing that I am permitted to share. I have some top-secret information, but I cannot divulge that information without a direct order from my superior officer.

Mr. Fintel:Well, Mr. Solinski, obviously he is not here right now, and I am asking you for a direct response.

Mr. Solinski:I cannot give you an answer.

Mr. Fintel:On the record, are you refusing? I am asking under the authority of the president.

Mr. Solinski:With all due respect, sir, you should know what happened if you have that type of clearance.

Mr. Fintel:Are you aware that I can have you subpoenaed and possibly court martialed if you fail to divulge information?

Mr. Solinski:Yes, sir. I will give my responses once directed by my superior officer.

Mr. Fintel:Sir, I am going to take your responses as being evasive and non – responsive. I am going to conclude today's interview but believe me when I say, sir, that you will be hearing from me in the near future.

Agent Callaghan leaned over to Emily and said, "That's where the interview was abruptly ended. What are your thoughts?"

"Honestly, it seems like this Private First Class Solinski was scared of something and was not trying to be evasive, as much as he was just trying to keep out of something that went deeper than his pay grade or giving up any confidential information."

"I agree," Agent Callaghan responded. "There's another piece of this interview, however, that has always bothered me. You're a prosecutor, right? Close your eyes and imagine this interview. Don't just look at these words. Put yourself in that room."

Emily nodded her head to affirm that she was a prosecutor. Then, she closed her eyes, and put herself in the interview room, just as if she were there live.

Agent Callaghan looked at Emily, and when she opened her eyes he said, "What is there about this interview that just doesn't seem correct? Do you know?"

Emily stared at the interview transcript again, and then it finally struck her like a Mack truck hitting her head-on.

"Mr. Fintel just gave up. He didn't even try to follow up on any of the answers."

"Bingo. But why would he do that?"

Emily rubbed the scar under her chin. "He never wanted the truth. He was just testing Mr. Solinski to see if he would keep his mouth shut. This guy did not care whether Mr. Solinski knew anything. Mr. Fintel already knew what Mr. Solinski knew, and probably more, in all actuality. He was just sent there to be sure that Mr. Solinski did not talk to anyone. Damage control. Nothing more."

"That's precisely what I was thinking as well," Agent Callaghan responded like a proud teacher. "It's the one fact that's haunted me in this case."

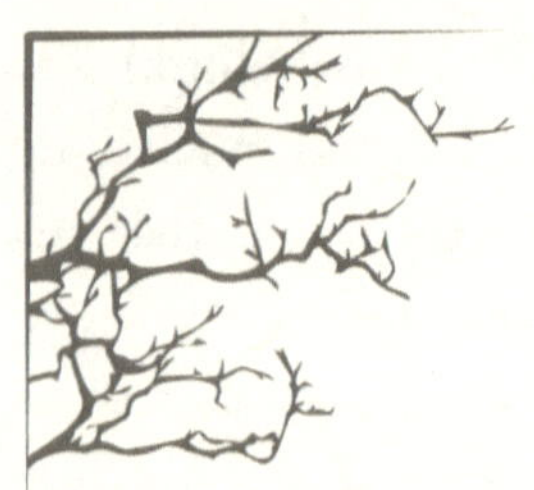

Chapter 28

Emily and Agent Callaghan continued strategizing until they had finished the pot of coffee. They split the last splash from the bottom of the pot. Occasionally, one of the other agents would stop over to the table to ask a question of Callaghan or give him an update on some issue with an active case. However, they knew that Callaghan was focused on getting Emily prepared for her virgin interrogation.

Agent Callaghan gave Emily a few more random transcripts. She read one that was conducted by the FBI in 1993 by a person who was very familiar to her.

Agent Callaghan:Mr. Solinski, you are here today under a direct subpoena by the FBI. Do you agree, and will you agree to provide me with truthful answers to my questions?

Mr. Solinski:Sure. I agree that I was forced to show up here by you guys, and I'm not in the business of lying to people.

Agent Callaghan:Sir, I am trying to solve a cold case involving the disappearance of one Jackson Jones. You know who he is, don't you?

Mr. Solinski:You know damn well that I know who he is. I've been through this process before, and I know that you must have all of that information in one of those nicely stacked folders over there. [Witness points to Interrogator's project files.]

Agent Callaghan:Then why won't you tell anyone what you really know. You can appreciate the fact that you are climbing up on my list of suspects, can't you? I mean you show up here and clearly have no regard for this process, or anything else for that matter. Sir, you reek of alcohol.

Mr. Solinski:You want to know what I know. Not a fucking thing. Got it? Even if I did, I wouldn't tell anyone from Washington. I'm surprised that no one has killed me yet.

Agent Callaghan:Why in the world would anyone want you dead?

Mr. Solinski:I guess you're right, since I don't know anything. [Witness smiles at agent.]

Agent Callaghan:You know. This can go easy, or we can make this much harder. Sir, you are a witness in a potential murder, but you already knew that, didn't you?

Mr. Solinski:Fuck you! Where's the body? Show me. You have nothing, or I would not be here.

Agent Callaghan:You are very observant, Mr. Solinski. But you're hiding something. Look, I don't think you had anything to do with the disappearance, but I know that you do know something about it. Here's how this is going to play out. You either tell me everything here today, or I will follow you to the end of your miserable days on this earth. I'll simply be everywhere you are. I'll be the fucking fly on your soup for the rest of your life. Is that what you want? Try me, you pompous little prick.

[Agent stands up in front of witness.]

Mr. Solinski:I can't say anything, and I really don't know much.

Agent Callaghan:What do you know? Tell me! You know something.

Mr. Solinski:[Witness drinks water and wipes forehead.] I only know that something did happen to that poor bastard. And I know that you need to be directing your questions to Washington. This is way above my level, and your boss should know what happened.

Agent Callaghan:Why do you keep referring to Washington? Who knows what?

Mr. Solinski:Look, Agent. You seem like a straight shooter, and I would love to tell you everything that I know. I really would. But you have to understand. Something happened that night that was so calculated that it can't just be the subject of a tell-all. Think about it.

Who would have such a fear of this man and the means to resolve the basis of that fear without even blinking twice?

Agent Callaghan:Who? Tell me.

Mr. Solinski:In your heart you already know. That's all that I'm going to say. My good friend Lucas was murdered over this whole damn thing.

Agent Callaghan:Are you referring to Lucas Mitchem, the Lieutenant in charge on Cumberland?

Mr. Solinski:That's the one. LT was a good man. He knew what happened, given his status as the officer in charge on the island.

Agent Callaghan:I read in the file where Mr. Mitchem was murdered in a mugging in D.C.. I'm sorry for your loss.

Mr. Solinski:That was a long time ago. He wasn't murdered by some random person. You need to use your intelligent mind, Agent Callaghan. Look at what's right in front of you in the case files.

Emily kept reading, and that's about all that Agent Callaghan was able to muster out of Solinski. The interview got more heated, and Callaghan did everything but beat the truth out of Solinski. After that interview, Del Solinski refused to speak with anyone about that night on the island.

"Agent Callaghan how many times have you spoken with Mr. Solinski?" Emily asked.

"Only a few. This was the only formal interview that he allowed. After this one, he conveniently had some lawyer show up for him to put a stop to all questioning. No doubt a counselor provided by his underworld friends from New Orleans. This guy knows something that we can use to bridge the gap that plagues this case. I know it."

"I'll see what I can get from him, but you know he may just be playing games with all of us. This could just be his final F-U to the FBI. I might show up, and he might already be dead with a note that says, *Good luck* or *I'll tell you all on the other side.*"

Agent Callaghan acknowledged that this was a possibility. "I agree, but we need to take that risk just to try. This guy is going to pass to the other side any day, and with him he's taking any chance we have to solve this thing."

"Copy that," Emily replied. She had been waiting the whole trip to use those words.

Agent Callaghan laughed. He knew that this young girl had all of the makings of an FBI agent if she ever wanted to pursue it as a career. Even if she didn't, he was pleased that she was helping with this assignment. He didn't exactly know she happened to come into his life at this point, but someone or something had certainly put her in this case for a reason, and that reason was to solve it, or at least get another key piece of the puzzle.

Emily looked down at her watch and twisted it around her wrist. She always kept it loose, so she could almost swing it around by just flicking her wrist. She saw that it was nearly six o'clock New Orleans time. Just then, the pilot came over the intercom and advised everyone to buckle their seat belts for final approach to the Louis Armstrong New Orleans International Airport. These planes were tough workhorses, but they were not known for their smooth landings.

Emily's plane landed in New Orleans at six thirty, sharp. The sun was still about shoulder level in the persimmon-colored, Cajun sky. She exited the aircraft and gave a big stretch of her arms. Special Agent Callaghan escorted her to yet another black Suburban with tinted windows. This one had a thicker exterior than the other one that took her to the St. Marys Airport. She measured the width of the door with her thumb as she got inside. This one was bulletproof.

Agent Callaghan astutely caught onto what Emily was observing.

"Your instincts are correct. This one is bulletproof."

Emily laughed as if she had been caught doing something that she wasn't supposed to be doing.

"Why?" she asked.

"We generally get more serious crimes and investigations in this part of the state, so we ride out with the most protection that we have at our disposal."

"Like what?"

"Mob, gangs, human trafficking rings, you name it. We seem to find them from here to Baton Rouge. It's probably because New Orleans has been here so long, and there are so many dumping spots in the bayou. This place has survived pirates, prostitutes, gamblers, and politicians. Don't get me wrong, though, I would never trade this assignment for any in the world. You can't beat the taste of a freshly made Cajun crawfish boil on Decatur Street while drinking some ice-cold, locally brewed beer. If the tastes don't entice you like a sexy voodoo temptress, the creole sun setting over the Mississippi River will do the trick."

It did not take Emily long to understand. She had never been to Louisiana, let alone New Orleans, before today. However, she could feel the majestic presence of this Cajun Queen with all of its ornate, historical architecture and even the slum areas that they passed. This place possessed every passion and facet of human existence, and that made it a one-of-a-kind location. The trip from the airport took about twenty minutes. It didn't hurt that they were essentially in a motorcade that no one would dare break up.

"So where exactly are we heading?" Emily asked with excitement in her eyes. She truly felt like she was a special agent on some secret, dangerous assignment to disarm a bomb or infiltrate a mob boss's hideout. She played out a scene in her head where the SUVs stopped and all of the agents jumped out, guns blasting at some abandoned warehouse filled with drug dealers who were scrambling like roaches.

She would obviously have to get out to provide some suppression fire to help out.

Emily's daydream was abruptly over when Agent Callaghan responded by telling her that they were heading to the French Quarter.

"Our ETA is five minutes," Callaghan said. "This is where everything that you see on television happens. If you think of New Orleans, you are thinking of the French Quarter."

All that Emily knew of New Orleans and the French Quarter was Mardi Gras. The sun was beginning to slide down in the sky as the Suburban reached the heart of the French Quarter. It made a quick left turn on Decatur just past the old U.S. Customs House.

"Is it always this warm in November?"

Callaghan gave a sly, half-smile, and said, "No, ma'am. This is quite unusual, to say the least. The quick temperamental changes of this city have some tourist flare, however."

"How so?"

"When the sun sets, it creates the perfect atmosphere for a rolling mist that hovers just above the ground. The ghost tours eat it up."

"Do you believe in ghosts?" Emily asked.

Agent Callaghan responded, "Nope. I am as pure of a scientific-minded person as they come. If I can't touch it and don't see it with my own eyes, it ain't so to me."

Emily kept her mouth shut and just smiled. After her experience on Cumberland, she was surely a believer. She felt as though she was in the final stages of an on-the-job interview and did not want to come across as being a crazy lunatic. Before she knew it, the motorcade was pulling right in front of Jackson Square. It was magnificent with its statute of Andrew Jackson sitting atop his horse. There were art dealers and street performers everywhere. It was capitalism in its most raw of forms.

To the left, Emily could see a magnificent white cathedral with triple steeples.

Callaghan was just beginning to open his mouth to give Emily some historical facts about the church. Before he could get one word from the tip of his tongue, she interrupted.

"I know this one," she shouted with a proud excitement. "This is the St. Louis Cathedral, the oldest Catholic cathedral in continual use in the U.S."

"Very good, young grasshopper."

"That's one thing that forms my nerd core—history. I love all sorts of history."

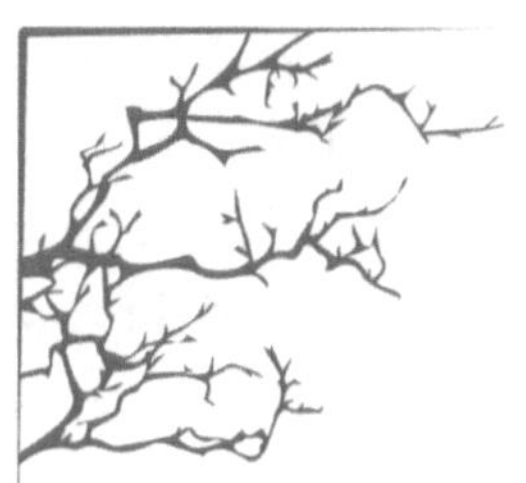

Chapter 29

The Suburban ahead of Emily's SUV pulled to the side of the street. She looked back and noticed that the trailing SUV had likewise pulled to the side and stopped. Only one agent from each SUV left the vehicles to keep a perimeter. Callaghan gave Emily a firm pat on the shoulder.

"Are you ready?"

"Yes," Emily stated with some hesitation in her voice. She tried to sound as confident as she could. She tried to calm herself by reminding her brain that she was not walking into a gunfight. She was just trying to get information from a ninety-three-year-old man. Callaghan gave Emily one last condensed debriefing as to what protocol she needed to follow. After all, if any of the information was to be of any use, it had to be collected properly to avoid any spoliation of evidence.

"Are you sure that you don't want me to come with you? I can just tell Mr. Solinski that the only way this is going to happen is if an agent is present with you."

"No. I appreciate it, but he has some reason to only want to talk to me. You all went to this much trouble to fly me out here on my honeymoon, so I better do my best and get the job done."

Callaghan laughed. Even in the most intense of situations, Emily seemed to keep her humor by her side like an old friend and confidant. Emily looked up at the street signs as she made her way around a corner to the residence. The residence was at the corner of Chartres and Madison Street. As she rounded the corner, the agents were out of sight. She slowly walked to the door. This was a true

French Quarter dwelling set in the creole townhouse architectural style. It had a black iron gate with two cherubs facing the lock.

Emily pushed in the gate, and it made an awful sounding screech that made her arm hairs stand up like a ghost had just passed through her. The door was just as ornate as the gate. It appeared by her novice historical eye to be original late 1700s with its thick cypress. She took just a second to admire the hand etchings in the wood as well as the flakes of faded blue paint that was flaking from the door.

There was no doorbell. Emily reached up and grabbed the old round door knocker. She rapped it three times as hard as she could. The sound reverberated throughout the house. She could hear it like a hammer being hit on hollow wood. She waited for a minute. Just when she was preparing to knock again, the door opened. A hospice nurse answered the door.

"You must be Ms. Decker."

"Yes, ma'am. I am."

"Mr. Solinski has been expecting you. He is upstairs on the balcony. Follow me, please."

Emily followed the young, brunette nurse up a set of narrow stairs. With each step the wood creaked as if it was going to collapse. The living room had several old pieces that most likely held some form of personal value to this elderly gentleman. Beyond that, though, there was not much that caught Emily's eye except the faded, floral wallpaper. It was a basic living arrangement. In her anticipation, she had all but expected this person to have some communist flags, or at least some pictures of himself with infamous people.

As they reached the top, the nurse politely moved to the side to let Emily pass and enter the balcony. There was one round table on the balcony with a set of cheap-looking wooden chairs. There was a sweet smell of cherry emanating from a tobacco pipe.

"My doctor has been telling me for thirty years that I need to give up smoking this thing."

"Hello, sir. My name is Em—."

Before she could finish, Mr. Solinski interrupted her.

"Emily Decker, formerly Duval. I know who you are, Mrs. Decker. Congratulations on the recent wedding."

Emily was taken aback. How could he know that she just got married?

"If you don't mind me asking, how do you know about me?"

"You don't last as long as I have without keeping one step ahead of everyone who is looking for you. I've had ninety-three years on this earth to perfect my preservation skills."

Emily took a look around the balcony to comfort herself. She noticed the cast-iron rails on the balcony with the bluest flowers that she had ever seen hanging from the edge. She also looked up and admired the gas lamps that were flickering above her head. By now, the night was setting in. The yellow light of the lamps jumped and flickered in the early night sky. It was reminiscent of a quaint, post-colonial town with a pub on a nearby corner.

"This is beautiful up here."

"Thank you, my dear. These are all original. Those three gas lamps are from 1798 and have never been changed out. This house was once owned by a famous French doctor, Dr. Bonheur. I can't say that I have done much of anything to make it my own. I prefer to honor it the way it was intended."

The historian in Emily truly appreciated his passion for honoring the basic foundation of this majestic place. He pointed to the wall to show Emily the original brick façade with its three-beam structural support.

"If you look closely you can see the fragment of a cannonball that struck just between the wood beams. Had it been a foot off either way, it would have likely taken down this whole place."

Emily had to ask, "What was the cannon scar from?"

"Battle of New Orleans as part of the War of 1812. A British ship was sitting out in the river bombarding the Quarter."

By this time, Emily was more comfortable and began to look directly at her unsub, suspect, or whatever he was supposed to be. Mr. Solinski was not ominous at all. He looked like a tired grandfather. He was wearing an old fedora hat and was dressed in a white button-up shirt and checkered, salmon bow tie. Emily could tell that this was a special occasion for this man. He wore old, slightly bent wire-framed glasses. Emily could sense a faint creole accent, which he had no doubt picked up from living in New Orleans for so long. Despite his aged appearance, Emily could tell that he was once an attractive young man. She could picture the young private from back on the island.

"Mrs. Decker, please accept my apologies for not being more hospitable. I would have gotten up to kiss your hand and properly greet you, but my dear, my legs are not so good these days."

"No apologies necessary, Mr. Solinski."

"Please call me Del."

Emily smiled and responded, "Thank you, but only if you will call me Emily."

"It's a deal, Emily." Mr. Solinski smiled and tipped his hat.

Del tapped his pipe on the table to get rid of some old tobacco. He reached into a worn tobacco box and used his thumb to push a fresh batch of tobacco into the pipe.

"Emily, do you mind if I smoke? It helps me when I'm nervous."

"Not at all. I wish I smoked those things right now." They both laughed. The scent of the cherry from the pipe filled the air again. Emily was not a smoker and found cigarette smoke hard to be around. This pipe had a different smell. It reminded her of her grandfather's mountain cabin as a child, and the scent was almost like the burning of incense. It actually began to calm her nerves too.

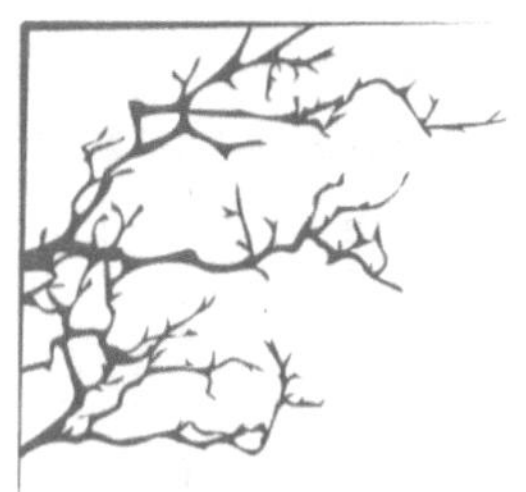

Chapter 30

Del took the pipe from his lips. He took a paused breath. "Okay, Emily, so I suspect that you want to know what happened on Cumberland Island back in 1944, don't you?"

"Yes, sir."

Del winked and said, "You must be pretty powerful if the FBI has enlisted you to pry my secrets from me."

"I don't know about powerful. Maybe just innocent enough to listen."

"Perfect response, young lady. I have never told anyone about that night. It's not that I am some sinister person who thrives on this knowledge. To the contrary, that island made me realize just how powerful and dangerous the powers of government paranoia could be. The secrets that I have held all of these years have devastated lives, mine included. I have married twice, each time for no more than a year. Despite all of my intentions, my emotional scars always show through and kill any chance of absolute happiness."

"That's horrible," Emily softly said.

"It's my penitence for having knowledge of the evil that befell Mr. Jackson on that island. Do you want to know how a simple ex-soldier can afford this luxurious peace of heaven here in New Orleans? It's simple. This is my hell."

Emily was now hanging on every word like a student.

"What do you mean, Mr. Solinski?"

This townhouse is three thousand square feet and is less than a quarter mile from Jackson Square. The problem is that no one but me wanted it. I purchased it in foreclosure back in 1956. There have been ten owners of this place since it was built back in 1719. None have stayed for more than three years. Dr. Bonheur and his wife were the longest residents. During the third year that they lived here, there was a massive fire.

It was during the Battle of New Orleans so there was speculation that a few British soldiers, who had managed to evade the American defenders, had deliberately set fire to houses on Madison Street. No one could prove what the cause was, but either way, the fire took down most houses on this street. For whatever reason, this house managed to escape with only minor structural burns. However, Dr. and Mrs. Bonheur had their windows open. The smoke killed them in their sleep. I am the only one who has lasted here longer than the Bonheurs. The ironic thing is that the name Bonheur translates to mean *good luck*.

"Is it haunted?" Emily asked.

"'Tis, my dear. I have no doubt. See that road below us? That's Madison Street. It goes from here straight to the Mississippi River, exactly one mile that way in the direction of that horn from the steam paddle boat you hear in the distance. This is the very same street where the slave ships would dump the fresh batch of slaves for auction. These poor souls were stuck on ships for months in the unforgiving Atlantic. By the time they made it off of the ship, they were shells of flesh, broken mentally and physically. They were shackled and marched up this street to an auction block where my front door stands. Over two thousand slaves have been brought up this street, and when I say that this is the same street, I mean this is the exact same street. It has never been repaved. This is the original street from 1791. That road has the blood, urine, and tears of human suffering. The years can try to fade it, but those scars never disappear."

"Anything else?" Emily asked on the edge of her seat.

"There have also been nights where you can hear screams of a female coming from the master bedroom. It seems to be the same each time, as if it were repeating on an old, scratched LP record. There are four sharp screams, and then they just disappear. I have heard them while sleeping, but I can never make out where they are coming from in the room. My supposition is that it is Mrs. Bonheur, awaking in the blindness of the smoke, finding her husband dead, and then quickly succumbing to her own death."

"Aren't you afraid? Why stay here?" Emily questioned.

"I have made peace with my sins and with the ghosts that haunt my soul. I would be lying if I said that I don't sometimes get scared or that I don't feel the chill of a person passing through me on certain nights or a tug at the back of my neck hairs. It's always the same feelings. I have a theory that most of the ghosts in this place don't even know I'm here. We're all in different dimensions of time simply passing in the same space."

Del went on to explain to Emily how he hypothesized that even the spirits themselves that inhabited his house seemed to be in different states of passing over to the other side. Some of the sounds, eerie moods, and feelings made it seem as though there were ghosts looking for other ghosts, each trapped in a different reality. As he told Emily his supposition on all things supernatural, he began to wheeze. His voice was crackling from dryness, and Emily could see the exhaustion in his face. Life was catching up to Del.

Emily asked Del, "What do you mean that the ghosts don't even know about the other ghosts?"

Del took at second to take a sip of water from a glass sitting in front of him. There were a couple of mostly-melted ice cubes still hanging on to the bottom of the glass. He wiped the condensation from the rim of the glass with his left hand and enjoyed the cool sensation of the water on his throat.

"Well, my dear child, I doubt that some of the spirits even know that other souls are passing by them. It's a jigsaw puzzle of sorrow, emotion, and confusion comingled here. It wouldn't surprise me in the least if the Mrs. Bonheur were searching each hour of each day for her husband, who had passed violently before she passed into the other side. It's like there's an invisible wall that keeps them from seeing each other, even though they may only be feet apart from each other in the house at any one time. Until there is some resolution to their sorrow, they just keep looking. Regardless, it's just an old man's theory. I have made this my home, and it has provided protection from those who could hurt me. Ghosts aren't going to be my end. I am more afraid of the human factor."

"The government?"

"Yes."

The mood quickly changed, and Emily could see that Del's face was becoming more somber.

"Well, my dear Emily, let's get to that job that you're here to do."

Emily smiled and responded with admiration for this old soul. "Do you mind if I turn on the tape recorder that I brought here with me? The agency is requiring me to take down what is said."

"Be my guest, my dear. I want the world to hear this story.

"Thanks. Before we get started, may I ask why you have held your secrets for so long?"

"That night on Cumberland Island took away my innocence. I was only a young man who believed in serving my country, and I had dreams beyond that—a family of my own, a Ford, a house with a white picket fence. Things have happened that cannot be explained as anything less than gruesome and evil. The very government that I swore my allegiance to returned the favor by forcing me to see the death of innocence and then forever making me a silent keeper of the sins. My life has had an unwritten bounty on it for most of my adulthood by the government. This story demands the respect of innocence, which is why I want someone who still possesses an innocent soul to take it down. Anyone affiliated with the government has had that pure innocence stripped through training. I want all of this on the record, so let's get that fancy recorder started."

Emily began and tried to follow the instructions that she had received from Callaghan. She started with the sterile, basic introduction by speaking her name, stating the date, and then asking Del to say his name on the record.

She then explained the purpose of the meeting and said into the recorder:

"This recording has been sanctioned by the Federal Bureau of Investigation under the direction and authority of Special Agent Aiden Callaghan. The Bureau is investigating a cold case involving the death of Jackson Mitchell Jones. Mr. Jones disappeared on August 21, 1944, and his body has recently been discovered. The Bureau is investigating any government involvement in the death. There is probable cause to believe that Mr. Jones was murdered. This is the interview with Delford Solinski. Mr. Solinski was the Private First Class stationed on Cumberland Island. He is the last-known witness who may have knowledge as to the death of Mr. Jones."

Del took a deep breath, and then slowly exhaled as if he had been holding his breath since 1944. He took another puff from his pipe since it gave him a sense of home and comfort.

"My name is Delford Solinski. I was stationed on Cumberland Island in 1944 as a Private First Class in the United States Army. I have first-hand knowledge as to what happened to Jackson Jones on August 21, 1944. On August 22, 1944, I reluctantly signed a document swearing my allegiance to a top-secret operation that was being conducted by the Office of Strategic Services. I swore under penalty of death under espionage that I would not disseminate any information about the operation during my lifetime. I have never told this story before today, and I am only agreeing to disclose the information to the FBI under the terms that Mrs. Emily Decker take my story."

Del's face became flush as he held back tears.

"Please go on, Mr. Solinski," Emily asked.

Del took a handkerchief from his front left pocket and wiped his forehead.

"I was stationed at Cumberland Island under the command of Lieutenant Lucas Mitchem. We had been working together for about six months. He was a great leader and friend. LT, as I called him, taught me how to be soldier. Our primary mission on the island was to monitor for German U-boats. During the year 1944, the U-boat activity had increased in the Atlantic from the South Georgia coast down past Daytona Beach, Florida. We had reported more than twenty confirmed sightings, and there were two small Navy ships that had mysteriously disappeared in the dead of night. Later investigations revealed evidence of torpedo attacks. There were no survivors on any of the vessels, and the government wanted to keep it from the public to avoid any backlash on the war efforts. On August 20, 1944, LT received a transition from Washington, D.C. informing him that there were going to be two officers from the Office of Strategic Services visiting. There was no other information as to names or even the reason why these OSS guys were coming by. LT kept me in the loop since it was just the two of us at this station."

Del sat back in his chair. He looked faint.

"Are you okay?" Emily inquired.

"I'll be fine." Del smiled. "Do you hear the zydeco music in the background coming from Decatur Street?"

Emily listened and took a moment to enjoy her surroundings again. She pulled her chair closer to Del and patted him on his shoulder. The chair made a scraping sound as she slid it across the old wood-plank balcony floor. Del graciously put his frail hand over her hand like a grandfather would to a child.

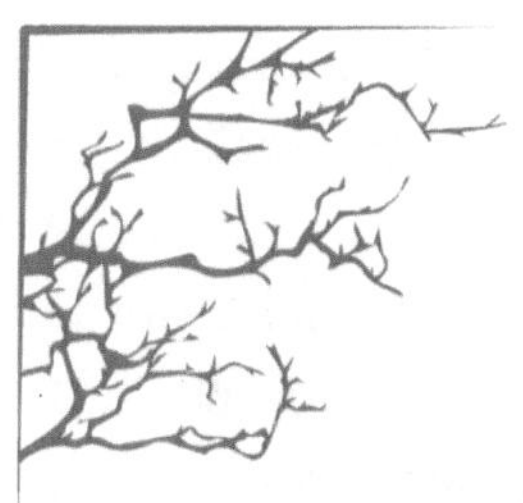

Chapter 31

Del was now ready to finish his story. "We left off with the OSS officers. So, on August 21, 1944, LT met with me in the early afternoon. He instructed me that we were under top-secret status under an operation called *Quiet Night.* I made one final entry in my logbook, and from that point on, all communications were verbal. LT explained that the OSS guys were under the direction of the White House. He never told me that their orders came directly from the President of the United States, but I knew that it was someone associated with the White House. This was a high-level operation. About seven o'clock that evening, the two OSS officers arrived. They were exactly like you would have imaged—black suits and no personalities. These gentlemen were both in their late forties, and they were all business. They met with LT in the back room for two hours and then left. I was tasked with setting them up with a small flatboat that we kept at our station. No one would tell me anything except to just place the boat by the southernmost dock of the island. I remember that because it took me about two hours to carry and drag that boat to the dock by myself. Had I known at that time what they were planning, I probably would have used it myself to get off that island."

Del was visibly upset at this point. His face was flush, and he began to cry. Emily comforted him. Del placed his head on Emily's shoulder like a child. Emily turned off the recorder and called out to Del's nurse. The nurse, who was just inside the door, came rushing out. Emily asked her to get Del something to drink. The nurse soon returned with a pitcher of sweet raspberry tea. Emily and Del took some time to enjoy the sugary taste of the tea. After about fifteen minutes, Del motioned to Emily that he was ready again. Emily clicked the recorder to start again.

"After I returned from placing the boat at the dock, LT stopped me at the door. He was a white as a ghost, and I could tell that he had been sick. I had never seen him that way. He was always such a strong man. Even though he was probably not supposed to tell me, he filled me in on what the OSS's mission was that fateful night. We sat on the front porch of the station, and he told me that these OSS officers were carrying out an assassination of a suspected spy. Neither of us could believe that this was possible. No trial, no witnesses, no appeals, just a shot to the head. It was about that time that we heard a single shot in the distance. The blood rushed from my head at the thought of anyone being shot in the head. It bothered me so much that I reached over to the rail and became ill. LT was in the same condition. However, he had more fire in his soul and was not just sad, he was furious. This was not how the system was supposed to work."

Emily stopped Del for a minute, as if they were in conversation. "Do you know why? What happened next?"

"It was the next day when I realized who Mr. Jones was and why he was killed. The OSS had learned of Mr. Jones's invention. He had created a magnetic device that could essentially jam a ship's electronic-tracking system, thereby making it blind to submarine attacks. When digging into his German descent, some government desk jockey in D.C., probably trying to make a name for himself, made the self-righteous determination that Mr. Jones could only have one purpose for the invention—to sabotage the U.S. Navy. LT never bought into that story and actually dug deeper to learn about the invention. He was convinced that it was simply a young man's dream for a brighter future and not some evil intent. I agreed with LT. We silently sat by as the investigation of Mr. Jones's disappearance took place. Twice, I lied to local authorities and denied any knowledge. I even had the unfortunate experience of running into his distraught fiancée Addison Smith. It had to be about four months after the disappearance, and she was broken. You could see it in her face, as if Mr. Jones had just disappeared. She was a lost soul hoping for a miracle but knowing that the devil had won this battle."

Emily chimed in, "Did you stay in touch with Lieutenant Mitchem?"

"I did for several years. One day I received a call from a mutual friend who advised me that LT was murdered in D.C. in 1946. The official story was that he was mugged near Georgetown."

"You don't seem to believe that?"

"I know what happened. About three weeks before he was killed, LT told me that we could not hold that dark secret inside anymore. He was consumed with fear and hate and washed away each day with a half-bottle of Scotch and cigarettes. Back on the island, he never smoked and would only occasionally indulge in a beer or shot of whiskey. This whole experience destroyed him. He lost his family and became a slave to alcohol. He told me that he was planning to go to Congress to tell an oversight committee what had happened. The committee gave him a hearing date. The one thing that thy overlooked was protection. LT was killed the night before he was supposed to testify before the committee. This was no coincidence. The remnants of the OSS, which by that time had become the newly formed CIA, took LT out.

"LT even went so far as to inquire into the patent on Jackson's invention. He told me on one occasion that he learned that the invention that Jackson created had disappeared from all public existence. It was as if it never existed. No applications, no rejection letters, no assignments of a patent after his death. It died with him. It was from that time on that I knew that I needed to find a place where no one would seek me out, and that I needed to keep my mouth shut to stay alive. I found my solace here in the French Quarter by befriending some local union reps with questionable mob ties. I did some low-level trading work for them on the docks. They kept me protected because they knew that I was a man who was bound to a code of honor and brotherhood to keep certain secrets locked away forever. For the record, I am not willing to discuss any specifics as to names or dealings on this issue on the record and will take the names of my contacts here to the grave."

"That's fine. We'll stick to the Jackson Jones case. Did anyone ever come looking for you?" Emily queried.

"They did. At least on two occasions. Early on when I moved here, I saw a black car parked at the corner. I also had a gentleman follow me home one night. I managed to get inside before he could reach me. My less-than-legal contacts were true to their word and kept me protected. The gentleman who was following me disappeared, and one of my local friends told me with a Machiavellian smile that the guy would not be back. I never asked what happened. I did not want to know the truth of whether the unknown man was threatened by my friends or whether he ended up chained to a cinder block at the bottom of the bayou as alligator bait. From then on, I lived my life without interference as best I could. It was not until Agent Callaghan made contact with me a few days ago that this came back into my life. I figured that it would come back one day."

"Is there anything else that you can tell us for the record?"

"I do have a box of some items that LT's sister sent to me after his death. Apparently, LT knew that he might not make it through the D.C. congressional hearing and gave a shoe box to his sister to send to me at any point after he passed in life. One day, I get it in the mail. It was filled with news clippings and had a picture of Addison in it. It was LT's clandestine investigation. He was consumed with knowing who ordered this hit on Mr. Jones. His obsession invited his death on that fateful night in D.C.. He was shot in the forehead and stabbed in the carotid artery. Whoever killed him had training and wanted to be sure that he was not going to escape from the attack."

Emily placed her hand on her cheek and asked "May I see the box?"

Del looked at Emily as if she were asking for a cursed item. "Are you sure you want this burden upon your life, my dear child?"

"Yes." Emily emphatically responded.

"Okay. You can take it with you. It has brought me nothing but remembrances of a life that I could have had if I had never been on that godforsaken island that night."

This made Emily ask a follow up question that she had overlooked.

She asked, "Have you ever been married at all, or have you had any children?"

"No to both. I have had a few quick flings, but I have never been able to get close to anyone over the fear that I could lose them to a government hit. I have lived my life sentenced to walk alone with no true loves. My love is the occasional cool breeze over this balcony and the sound of carefree people in the distance listening to jazz. Beyond that, I have nothing."

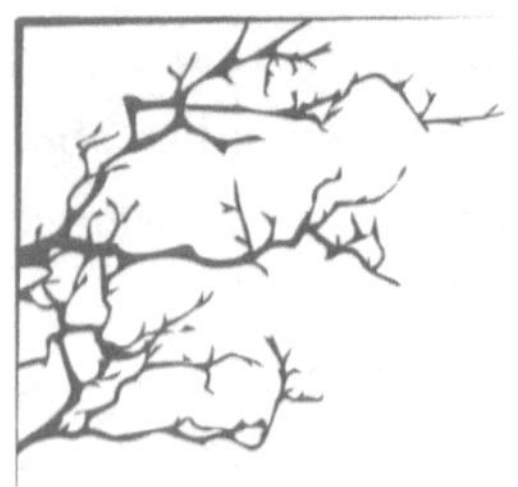

Chapter 32

Del called out for the nurse and asked her to retrieve the box of items that were in his closet. She left for a few minutes and then returned with an old, plain shoe box. It was dusty and was torn at the corners. There was a piece of black electrical tape holding one corner together. Del held the box for one last time in his hands, as if he were saying goodbye to an old friend.

Emily good tell that this was not just a box of clippings and photographs. This was LT. It was the last link that Del had with LT. As he handed it over to Emily, Del began to tear up again. He was saying goodbye to his mentor and friend. Del protectively handed the shoebox over to Emily. Emily put her hand on Del's shoulder as she took the box from him. She truly understood that this was not simply a man giving away a box. It was him closing a chapter in his life after a lifetime of fear, hatred, and secrets. She went back on the record.

"Thank you, Mr. Solinski. You have handed me a box of documents from Mr. Mitchem. I will take care of these items. Do I have permission to turn these over to the FBI?"

"You do."

"Thank you, sir. I appreciate your time. I am going to close out this recording at this time, and I will turn it over to the FBI."

"Thank you, Mrs. Decker. It has been a pleasure having you take my story. It is a shame that you do not work for the Bureau. You have a natural knack for this stuff."

Emily and Del were now off of the record. They had some idle conversation, and she accepted another cup tea. The nurse took a few vitals from him as she prepared to put him down for the night. Emily placed her recorder in her purse. Before she stood up, she opened the shoebox since her curiosity was killing her. She pulled open the top of the box and started looking through a couple of the news clippings. The box was as worn and old as Del himself. One particular article caught Emily's attention. It was about Addison Smith. As she began to read the article, she dropped the box. All of the contents fell to the ground.

Emily clenched the article in disbelief. It was a story about the fiancée of Jackson Jones. Her eyes had to be playing a New Orleans voodoo trick on her brain. She judiciously examined the old, time-weathered article and saw where the story was about a woman named *Liz Smith* who had lost her fiancée in a mysterious disappearance. The article spoke to the fact that she was the prime suspect, even though she professed her innocence to everyone. The article explained how Addison Elizabeth Smith went by her middle name her whole life, typically responding to the nickname *Liz*, which her mother had called her from childhood.

By this time, Del had graciously excused himself to rest for the night. Emily started picking up the items from the floor. Her hands were shaking uncontrollably at this point. She noticed a picture and picked it up. It was a black and white photograph of a young woman. She knew exactly who the woman in the picture was, and she immediately recognized the South Carolina necklace she had seen only days before. She turned the picture over and saw the year 1944 on it. Under the year, she saw a handwritten note that said *Addison "Liz" Smith.*

By this time, an evening storm had begun to pour rain over the picture and clippings on the balcony floor as if to finally cleanse the blood and sins of 1944. As she picked up what she could salvage, she realized that this was only the first piece of this puzzle, and that the answer laid somewhere one thousand miles to the east in

Washington, D.C. Emily had solved the mystery of what happened to Jackson and who the girl from the journal was, but there was something more to this. She wanted to know who had ordered Jackson's death. Emily grabbed at her necklace, which was still hanging around her neck, and cradled it in her right palm. She knew that the remaining mystery would have to wait for the moment. It was time for her to return to her soul mate. Trent was waiting for Emily, just as Liz had waited with devotion for Jackson—the love she lost on Cumberland Island.

Emily stepped inside the doorway of Del's patio. The nurse was done getting Del down for the night, so she met Emily at the doorway.

"Are you okay, ma'am?"

"Yes. Thank you. I just had one of those moments where you think you saw a ghost," Emily replied, still shaken from her revelation.

"With all due respect, you did see a ghost."

"What?"

"Ma'am, I've lived in New Orleans my whole life, and I've worked in this godforsaken house long enough to know that when you think you've seen or felt the presence of a ghost, you have even if only in a snapshot picture from another day or realm."

Emily shook her head as if to agree without saying a word more about it. Emily then asked if she could stay on the balcony patio for a few more minutes. She needed to call Trent, and she was not yet ready to engage in what would be several hours of debriefings regarding the details that Del had provided to her. The nurse agreed and patted Emily gently on the shoulder as she exited back downstairs. Emily made her way back to the table where she and Del had chatted only moments ago.

She pulled out her cell phone and tried to dial Trent. Every time she went to hit the number on her phone she kept messing up a least one of the numbers. She was still feeling the effects of finding out that Liz was, in fact, the ghost of the woman who had so brutally lost her only love. After about five tries, she finally dialed the correct number. The phone seemed to ring for what felt like ten minutes. It was actually only a few seconds.

"Hello?" a tired Trent responded on the other end of the line.

"Hey, babe! Is it good to hear your voice," Emily said with some relief.

"Are you okay? You sound horrible? No offense," Trent asked. He was tucked in under his thin, hospital-white covers watching a public broadcasting special on stars and black holes. The one positive side of being laid up was the fact that he could watch the nerdy, scientific shows that Emily despised out of sheer boredom. His leg was still propped up on a sling contraption that kept his leg suspended above the bed.

"Yeah, but do I have a story to tell you. I doubt that you'll believe it since I don't even believe it myself. I feel like I'm going crazy."

"Okay. But first, how did the interview go? Did you get the dirt from the scoundrel that had Jackson whacked?"

"Oh yeah. However, that wasn't the strangest part. The piece of the puzzle that you won't believe is what I found out about Liz."

"Liz? How does she fit into it? That's actually quite funny since she was just here with her fiancé. He was a nice guy. The perfect southern gentleman. He introduced himself, but I have to confess that I was pretty much out of it since I was doped up on my max-strength pain meds. It was all really hazy. I didn't catch his name. It might have been Jonathon or something like that."

"What? Are you positive it was Liz?" At this point, Emily was sweating from a mixture of confusion and adrenaline on the other side of the phone. In the background, the sounds of the New Orleans night was still as loud as if the night had just begun. Liz, however, was so focused that she barely heard any of the zydeco music mixed with the lively sounds of drunk debauchery. And she surely was paying no attention to the federal agents who were below somewhere waiting anxiously for her debriefing.

"That's a weird question, don't ya think? Of course, I'm sure it was Liz. I know that she was there to make sure that I was okay, but ya know what, I was actually more relieved that she faired the storm without a scratch. I was more worried about her than me. By the way, did you know that she had a fiancé? I didn't remember her mentioning that to us."

Emily was still in shock and was asking questions as if her subconscious was on autopilot. She managed to get a few words out, and asked Trent, "What did she say?"

By this time, Trent had turned off of the television since this conversation was much more intellectually stimulating than any drawn-out story line about the unveiling of the universe. "She told me that she ran up the trail and guided the park ranger to our location. I asked her where she went, and that's when her fiancé managed to say a few words. He said that he was looking for her and just happened to hear her voice near where the ranger was at on the trail. Liz interrupted Jonathon at that point and told me that by the time that they got back to our location, the helicopter had already taken off and carried me away to the hospital. The whole conversation was not that long."

Emily sat on the other end of the phone more stunned than she was just minutes before the call. *How could this be*? she thought to herself. *Trent must have been hallucinating. There is no way that he could have seen Liz and Jackson*. How was any of this possible? She drank the rest of her tea, which by this time was lukewarm from the cool evening temperature.

"Are you still there, babe?" Trent asked.

Emily paused for a minute.

"Yep. I'm so confused."

"About what?"

"Are you one hundred percent certain that you saw Liz?"

"Absolutely. Like I just said, I carried on a conversation with her."

Emily explained the whole story to Trent. This caused Trent to go pale. Trent sought out a rational explanation for Emily's findings. However, even Trent could not dismiss the necklace, together with the fact that Emily swore that the girl in the picture was the spitting image of Liz. Without knowing it, his finger, which had the monitor clip on it, was shaking. Trent's vitals actually dipped a bit, causing a nurse to come into the room to check on him. He explained that he was okay, and the nurse left after running a few tests just to be safe. The nurse gave Trent a cold drink to keep him cold. Trent knew that he was somewhat out of it due to the medications, but he also knew without any doubt in his mind what was real and what was not. He would testify to the end of his life that he saw and spoke to Liz and who he now knew to be Jackson. Trent and Emily spent what had to be two hours working through the whole experience to try to explain it. Neither could dismiss this experience.

When Trent hung up the phone with Emily, he called for the nurse. He asked for the sign-in chart. The nurse retrieved the chart and brought a copy to Trent.

"No one has checked in to see you since your wife came by to see you the other day."

"Are you sure?"

"Yes, sir. If anyone wanted to get back here, they would be on this sign-in chart."

Trent was dumbfounded and still tried to explain it away as some med-induced vision or creation from his mind.

"I thought that I saw someone, but it must have been the painkillers," Trent explained to the nurse.

"Nope," the nurse replied.

"What do you mean?" Trent asked.

"The doctor took you off of the pain meds after the initial round. He said that your vitals were good, and he didn't want your body to get used to them. We've had too many people get hooked on those things post-op. You are only taking some good old-fashioned, over-the-counter aspirin."

Trent said nothing since he knew for sure now that what he saw in his room was a ghost of two souls who finally found their way back to each other. Back in New Orleans, Emily was making her way down the dark staircase of Del's home. With each step, she thought about how it could be that Liz and Jackson could be wandering on the same island without so much as brushing by each other as two strangers passing in the night. Then she remembered what Del had told her about his theory. Emily placed her hand on the scar on her chin, and she thought of how two souls who were separated by a violent death could be caught in two different realms of life, death, or whatever it was that made up this mystical ambit.

Although she still could not explain what had transpired over the course of the past couple of weeks she at least now understood how to explain why Liz and Jackson were lost souls on the same island. When she, Liz, and Trent opened the tomb that held Jackson's body, it brought closure and released his soul, allowing Liz's soul to connect again with Jackson's. This was surely the reason why Liz was searching on the island. She was desperately searching to find Jackson's body so that the pair could be together through the afterlife. Unbeknownst to Emily and Trent, Liz was enlisting them to help her. This was no coincidence. Emily was meant to come across Liz's journal, as if Liz had guided Emily to it. Emily thought this entire time that she was the one making the plans and leading everyone where they needed to go to find Jackson. In fact, however, it was Liz who had orchestrated this entire series of events that started all the way back in St. Augustine, Florida. As she opened the front door and began to walk out of Del's house, she laughed to herself.

"Well played, Liz. Well played," Emily said. Several FBI agents began to walk in her direction from an unmarked, black Suburban that was sitting around the corner. Emily was ready to give Agent Callaghan the full scoop of what Del had told her. There were some things that Emily knew she had to keep to herself. Clearly no one would believe her story. But more importantly, she shared a kindred connection with Liz and Jackson. Emily knew that this bound all of them to a secret that she and Trent would take to the grave until they met up with the ghostly pair again after having lived their full lives.

By this time, the rain was nothing more than a light drizzle, which brought Emily a peaceful feeling as it hit her skin in the cool night air. She could now hear the sounds of the trumpets and horns playing at local bar off Decatur Street. It was as if she had awoken from a passionate trance. There was a smell of lavender all around her in the air. It was Liz.

Author Biography

BRYAN RENDZIO SPENT most of his early years on Florida's Gulf Coast in Tampa, Florida. After graduating from college with a Bachelor of Arts degree in English Literature and from law school with a Juris Doctor degree, he settled down in Ponte Vedra Beach, Florida. This is where he still resides with his wife, two children, and three dogs. When he is not working on his next novel, Bryan spends as much of his time as he can enjoying the simple moments on the beaches of the Atlantic Ocean with his family. It is from this unalloyed connection with nature where inspiration transcends into a living work. At 48 years old, Bryan feels blessed to be surrounded by such good friends and family. Bryan's philosophy of life is straightforward. He believes that everything in life happens for a reason, and that there is no such thing as a chance meeting or event. Every moment in life shapes who we are and who we become as individuals.

www.ingramcontent.com/pod-product-compliance
Lightning Source LLC
LaVergne TN
LVHW041200150826
845673LV00001B/237

* 9 7 9 8 2 3 0 9 5 1 5 1 3 *